Reign of the Dead Outbreak

www.severedpress.com

ISBN: 978-0-9874765-1-7

ACHNOWLEDGEMENTS

I would like to thank my life-long friend Rick for his input. Rick gave me some great ideas when I was writing this book. He spent many hours reading through what I had written and improving upon it. In a world where it is so rare to have even one friend who you trust completely, I count my blessings. I have a few, including my wife, Carol. It is friends like that who make life complete.

Len Barnhart

Website: http://www.reignofthedead.com

Email: lenbarnhart@aol.com

Facebook: http://www.facebook.com/len.barnhart

Twitter: http://twitter.com/LenBarnhart

PART 1
Zero Hour

They're loiterers, cannibalistic vagabonds for the familiar.
—Jim Workman

1
New York City

The blue and white ambulance came to a stop in front of the emergency room entrance and two men hurried from the front of the vehicle. The gurney holding Rebecca Longley slid back and they gripped the handles at each side of her lifeless body, heedless of the haggard man who stumbled out behind her.

Michael Longley's hands shook as he held a white cloth to his head. The cloth was warm and wet, his vision blurred by the mix of sweat and blood building over his brow and he fought for clarity as he neared the doors.

Where was he and why was he there? He couldn't remember, and where was his wife, Becca? His head was pounding and it was all he could do to stay focused and on his feet.

The doors in front of him began to swing shut and for a moment it seemed as if his mind were clearing. Rebecca was behind those doors and all he had to do was walk through them to find her, click his heels three times and all would be as it had been this morning. He was still processing that nonsensical thought when out of nowhere a pretty nurse with dark hair stopped and tried to steady him.

She was speaking, but her words were faint. The confusion was clouding his thoughts again. "I need you to come with me, sir. You're injured...Please, come with me." Michael struggled to understand. Was she speaking English? Yes, she was, but she was jumbling the words. "Omecay auth see."

"What?"

Then, as if suddenly recovering from a mind-altering drug, her words were clear. "Come with me please."

She was trying to help. Dorothy Gale to the rescue, pretty as a picture and decked out in a blue pinafore. All he needed was a one-way ticket to Kansas, via those Ruby slippers. And where was his wife? I need to find my wife and go home is what he wanted to say, but his lips only moved silently.

What was it Becca had said about Clarissa? He remembered her lilting tone as she leaned in to tell him as though she were sharing a vital confidence. She'd said, today would be a new beginning. Today the world would be made new. They were halfway across Pennsylvania, just passing Harrisburg, and her urgency had startled him. Becca's references to Clarissa always startled him a little, even after all this time, but he knew enough to keep his mouth shut whenever Rebecca started in about her. Just let her speak. Get it out of her system. At least that's the way he had come to rationalize it.

In the past, Clarissa's psychic intrusions had never been ill-omened, but she certainly had an uncanny way of always being exactly right whenever she had anything to share with Becca. Was the accident what she meant? It didn't feel like a beginning to Michael. He felt that foreboding dread deepen now as he stood in front of a closed door, a door that was potentially closing on any future he hoped to have with his wife, and his hand trembled as he reached out to push the cold, metal bar latch. He could see his thoughts whirling like thought bubbles in a comic book. "On this side of the door is what I am now. This side is what I was. Don't go through that door, Michael," the bubble whirred past. "You don't want to know what is on the other side of that door." Another bubble blinked by.

Michael shook his head, squeezed his eyes shut and concentrated, trying to clear the images as he pushed through the door.

Suddenly the voice in his head wasn't his. It was Rebecca's. He heard her, saw her, nervous and worried. Her voice was soft as she quoted her friend, "A different world, Michael."

Michael was going down for the count and he knew it. His head was spinning and it was hard to draw breath.

As his knees bent, and he began to slump toward the floor, a tall, middle-aged black man loomed up in his field of vision and grabbed his elbow to help steady his wobbling stance.

The man wore a blue uniform. There was a patch on his right shoulder. Through blurred vision Michael could see the bright yellow proclamation: Security.

With sudden clarity, Michael came full circle, and like getting a jolt of good Java on a bad Saturday morning, he was suddenly awake.

"I have to go in there." He snarled at both of them as he pushed past the nurse. The guard however was not obliging as he placed a firm hand on Michael's chest and stopped him cold in his tracks.

"I'm sorry sir, but I can't let you do that,"

"Please, it's my wife in there," Michael implored, his demeanor changed from brusque to pleading. "I have to know."

Dorothy Gale eased the bloodied cloth away from his head and inspected the gash. She was several inches shorter than Michael, but still tall for a woman, probably five-eight, or nine. "I'm nurse Beatty. That's going to need a few stitches. They will do all they can for her," she assured him as she brushed his blond hair away from the wound. "But first things first. We need to look after that wound."

Michael calmed himself, and nodded in submission. They were after all doing what they perceived to be best. Best for Becca. He would only be in the way. "Will you check on her for me?" He asked the guard. "Please?"

The guard nodded solemnly before his expression suddenly hardened. Looking over Michael's left shoulder; he shoved him to the side and stepped around, pushing the double doors open wide.

Michael's lean frame hugged the wall tightly as four gurneys were rushed through. "There are more on the way," one of the medics called out as he rushed through behind the others.

The nurse pulled Michael over to the admissions desk and made him sit. "I have to go now. They are going to need my help in there," she said, pointing to the double doors. "You sit here and keep holding this cloth to your head. Put pressure on it like this." She held it firmly over the gash as she leaned toward the girl behind the desk. "Get their information," She whispered, and nodded toward Michael. "We won't be able to see him immediately. We're going to have to take care of the more critical patients first."

"Yes ma'am," the girl responded.

Michael nervously bounced his left leg, waiting for her inquisition to begin. He tried to replay the accident in his head.

Rebecca's side of the car had been hit by a swerving eighteen-wheeler. There was a sudden jolt. A whoosh of air popped his ears. It seemed as though the vehicle were coming apart as shards of metal and glass filled the inner compartment. The world spun and he flashed in and out of consciousness. Then the dashboard zoomed up to meet his face.

Suddenly, everything was still, and dark.

Rebecca had not regained consciousness and he feared for her life. She had been so still, quiet and lifeless. Her breathing had been so shallow that at first he couldn't tell if she were breathing at all. Certainly, only a thimble of life remained in her.

He had been more fortunate. Only the bleeding gash over his left eye needed attention. He would gladly give his strength to Rebecca in exchange for her injuries. He would die for her.

"Were you in that pileup out on Route 78?"

The girl's question brought him out of his temporary fog and he stared at her.

"Were you in that pileup out on Route 78?" A man's voice echoed her question so exactly in cadence and timber, he thought for a moment he was hearing things. He turned to his right to see a New York State trooper looking down at him, waiting expectantly for his reply. Before he could process the question and reply, the radio hanging from the trooper's belt blared to life. "Look Mister, this night has turned into a three ring circus, complete with freak shows. Just don't leave until someone can get your statement."

With that, he turned on his heel, and barking orders into his radio, disappeared through the glass lobby doors so quickly that Michael wondered if he had been an apparition.

The receptionist stared absently, first at the lobby doors and then back at Michael; her brows were raised in a quizzical expression, the unanswered question still hanging in the air between them. Michael tried to answer, but he couldn't tell if he was actually speaking, or only mouthing the words.

The girl behind the desk had a sweet, girl-next-door look about her, except for the mole on the tip of her nose. Dark in color, and raised, it seemed to dominate her face, this silly little black spot on an otherwise pretty face. Michael noticed the imperfection and it drew his attention in such a way that he was unable to focus on her words.

"Yes, we were," he finally said, trying not to look at her nose.

"It's a bad one isn't it?" she asked, snapping her gum.

Michael nodded, "Yes." Jesus God she cracks her gum too, he groaned inwardly.

The mole seemed to grow bigger as he struggled to remember the accident. Michael closed his eyes and focused on that memory.

They were passing a big truck when a deer crossed the road in front of it and the driver lost control. The animal exploded like red rain across the trucker's windshield. The rig swerved to the left and into them. The impact sent the car spinning. Then a great roar filled the night as other vehicles piled into the spinning wreckage and the jackknifed truck, which lay crossways in the road. The deer's severed head whizzed past as it bounced across the car hood. Then his door was torn loose as if pulled away into the darkness by an unseen force.

The whooshing sound and then the dashboard.

Fade to black.

Then in the silence, the cries for help. First only whispers, but then they increased in frequency and strength until the night clearly resonated the pain around them.

All that seemed distant and surreal to him as he pulled Rebecca from the wreckage, their cries, mere echoes in the night, detached from his immediate situation. His full attention was focused on her, his love, the only thing that mattered. The rest was just background noise.

He laid her in his lap with her head cradled in his arms and brushed her matted hair away from her face.

There was a shard of metal lodged deeply in her chest. He wanted to pull it out and toss it away, but he was a cop and he had seen enough mortal wounds to know what this meant. He dared not touch it.

"Clarissa," Rebecca sighed.

Michael cried quietly as he held her. The night was dark and the air smelled of gasoline and dampness. He wanted to lay the blame for the night's tragedy squarely at Clarissa's feet. She was supposed to have all the answers. She held the control over Rebecca, control he could never command himself, and for that he hated Clarissa. Fortune-tellers, astrologers, mystics…They carried weight with Rebecca, and through her, him too. And Clarissa was the best. The best at her game, and even if Rebecca was fooled, he was not. He was fully aware that it was only an illusion, a practiced parlor trick. No, she had no real answers, only deception. Then with what seemed like the last wheezing breath of her lungs, Rebecca softly said, "A new beginning, Michael."

A bleak and stifling darkness surrounded him. It threatened suffocation as he drifted in and out of consciousness. He felt alone as he stared down at his one true love. All of the good things that had ever happened in their life came rushing into his thoughts like the first brutal wave of a flash flood. He remembered Becca telling him about the horrors she had endured as a child, and how he had changed her life. These were going to be their good times. These were going to be their happy years.

"Name?"

"What?" Michael said.

"Sir, I need your name."

"Michael Longley," he told the receptionist.

"Address?"

"1135 Oakridge Drive, Chicago, Illinois—Listen, my wife and I were on vacation…" His words faded to silence, not knowing if he were speaking or only mouthing the words again, Michael put his head in his hands. Rubbing his eyes, he brought his head back up, and looking at the girl with the mole on her nose, said. "Some vacation, huh?"

"I'm sorry. No it isn't. What is your wife's name?"

"Rebecca May Longley. We've been married for six years. Is it six? Maybe it's seven."

His mind was drifting. He had to remain focused. All of his police training was failing to bear fruit. He had to keep his wits, keep his head straight. Rebecca needed him.

***

Doctor Adam Riker gently massaged the woman's heart. It had stopped more than two minutes before and he knew precious little time remained. "Come on now. Beat for me. Beat for me," he coaxed as his gloved hands moved inside her open chest cavity.

Nurse Beatty watched as the doctor massaged the smashed organ. The damage to the heart was extensive. She knew Adam Riker was a good doctor. She also knew his attempts were futile.

"She's gone Doctor," she said in a soft, yet sternly professional manner. "We have others who need tending."

Riker stopped, stripped off his bloody gloves, and glanced up at the clock on the wall.

He heard the urgency in nurse Beatty's voice. "Please Doctor Riker; we need you to call it."

Adam Riker did not like losing patients. This one was a heartbreaker for him. "Time of death, 1:05 a.m." he said finally and motioned for Ron Whiteman, the anesthesiologist, to remove the tube from her arm.

"So what do we have next?" Riker turned away from the dead woman on the table.

Denial was his way of dealing with the death of a patient. Once he was out of the room, the woman would be forgotten completely, out of sight, out of mind. This was his mantra on death days. And any day that he lost a patient was a death day. Any day that he lost a patient, with his hands in her chest, that was a triple death day. And to Doctor Riker this was starting to feel like it was going to be a quadruple death day.

"Cover her," he snapped to Nurse Beatty as he moved to the next patient.

***

Michael rose unsteadily and moved from the chair to pace the crowded waiting room. His head ached from a pulsating swell of pressure over the wound above his eye. What he needed was fresh air to clear his thoughts. An exit sign hung above a door on the far side of the waiting room. Just the beacon of light he was looking for. Just under the light and through the door was fresh air. Just under the light and through the door was clarity, and clarity was what he needed to help Becca.

Michael sought the quickest path to the door through the crowd. A motley cast of characters had filled the room since his arrival. One man, balding and pudgy and dressed in a cheap, brown polyester suit, held his wrapped hand and rocked in his seat, moaning in pain. The makeshift wrapping was red with blood. A middle-aged man in a rumpled gray suit held onto a pale and crazed teenaged boy, no older than sixteen. The boy's mouth was covered with duct tape, and his hands were tied. Michael thought that very strange. Why would that kid's mouth be taped shut like that? And before he could catch himself, he was pointing at the makeshift gag and blurting out, "The kid can't breathe like that."

He recoiled instinctively as the boy lurched up and thrust his face onto his captor as if trying to bite him through the tape.

The sight of the spastic kid, duct taped and trussed up like a Thanksgiving turkey was too much for Michael. He had to change the subject. His auto-defense mechanism was kicking in. Change the subject. My wife is hurt, this kid is fucked up. Good thoughts, good thoughts. Change the subject…

And there it was. Michael retreated into thoughts of Rebecca.

Their marriage had been rocky the first three years, but that had changed. Things were good now. Those bad years were a fading memory. But this night had up-ended their lives and threatened to take Rebecca away from him forever. To make things worse, they were a long way from home, and alone, separated from other family members who might give comfort.

"What's going on in there?" He turned and shouted at the receptionist. "It's been over a half hour. I want to know how my wife is doing?" Again he moved toward the double doors and again the guard stopped him.

"Sit," he barked at Michael. The stress of the night showed in the guard's demeanor. "Someone will let you know what's going on when there's time, now sit." He shoved Michael unceremoniously back down into a chair and then moved to break up another scuffle in the rapidly filling waiting area.

***

"Close for me." Doctor Riker told Nurse Beatty as he tossed another pair of rubber gloves into the trashcan.

"This one is going to make it, I think," she said.

"That's two out of five," Riker said. "While I have a minute I should go break the news to the people waiting outside."

Nurse Janice Beatty wiped her forehead. "Do you want me to

do that tonight?"

The doctor furrowed his brow, "What?"

"I'll break the bad news to the families tonight if you want. It will give you a break. You look like you could really use one."

Doctor Riker hesitated, rubbing the bridge of his nose. "No, I'll do it. It is my job. I should be the one to do it." Shaking his head, he sighed, "They expect the doctor to be the one. I don't mean anything by that. It's just that…" His words trailed off as he stared across the room.

The white sheet still covered Rebecca Longley's face as she sat upright on the table and the room fell silent.

Rebecca sat motionless like a covered statue. She had been dead for ten minutes and the fact that she was sitting upright now sent chills up Janice's spine. And even though she was sure it was nothing more than a muscle spasm, the unflappable Nurse Janice Beatty, was visibly shaken.

The nurse moved hesitantly toward Rebecca Longley as though she were moving through a dream. Something was more than unusual. Something was more than wrong. Janice's throat closed in a spasm as an indescribable sensation threatened to overwhelm her.

"Don't touch her!" she screamed. Had she said that aloud? No, she was certain of it. It had been an internal warning alarm.

Nurse Beatty pulled the sheet away from the dead woman's face.

The patient's eyes were closed as she sat unmoving. It was as if an internal spring had forced her dead body to bend upward at the waist.

"Doctor, I believe it was just a—"

Rebecca's eyes opened and her body stiffened.

"She's alive." Janice gasped.

The white sheet fell away from her injured body as she slipped off the gurney and stood. Nurse Beatty tried to steady her and return her to the gurney.

"Please, you must lie down for me," Janice sputtered into Rebecca's face. "Please—you are hurt," Her years of work as a trauma nurse pushed through the dreamlike haze of the situation.

Rebecca reached out and scratched her face. Her other hand knocked the white cap from the nurse's head and latched onto a handful of hair.

"A little help here would be nice!" she yelled, and Adam Riker was jolted into action.

The doctor thrust his right arm between Nurse Beatty and the struggling patient in an attempt to separate them. Rebecca's eyes focused on the nurse's throat and with a faint whimper, she curled back her lips, and clamped down.

The doctor's reaction was swift. He slammed Rebecca in her neck with a force he normally reserved for the biggest, meanest, PCP psychos that came into the trauma unit.

Nurse Beatty shrieked out in pain.

The skin ripped away from beneath her left ear as Rebecca was forced back by the Doctor's well-placed blow.

"God Almighty!" Ron Whiteman screamed. He had been watching the scene play out for what seemed like minutes, but could only have been a matter of seconds. His first impulse was to run from the room, but this was part of the big pile up on Route 78, and he could not move. Like a deer stopped cold by the glaring, blue-white beacon of oncoming headlights, Ron Whiteman could only stand and wait for the impact.

The woman who had been dead for ten minutes moved with ungainly steps toward him. The scissor-like retractor instrument still held the skin and breastbone away from the wound and it rattled as she approached.

Whiteman stepped back and tripped over a box of supplies behind him and hit the floor in an unceremonious sprawl. Rebecca was on him before he could process what was happening.

He screamed in agony as she bit into his left arm. In one potent twist, the flesh tore away and blood gushed out in red jets that splattered the wall behind him in rhythm with his beating heart.

Rebecca sat down cross-legged on the floor and pushed the flopping chunk of flesh into her mouth. As she feasted on her prize, her dead heart dangled loosely from the open cavity. And as Ron Whiteman watched in horror, it appeared as if her heart might snap free and bounce away, but it only wiggled and dangled, held in place by the aorta and vena cavas.

Doctor Whiteman stumbled to his feet and fell into the corner where he removed his belt and used it to create a makeshift tourniquet. Rebecca was on her feet again and lunged for Adam Riker. He met her attack with a powerful thrust and then threw her back onto the operating table.

"Help me tie her down for Christ's sake," Riker screamed to

no one in particular as Rebecca snapped at him.

***

Upon hearing the commotion, the guard charged through the double doors. Michael Longley had taken notice as well and followed him, catching the doors on his way through.

Michael followed the guard down the hospital hallway terrified of what he might find; his wife was in there somewhere. The commotion was coming from the room just ahead and to his left. He'd heard a woman's fear-filled cry and the bellow of a man screaming as though he were being slowly tortured.

Michael stopped cold, and watched the scene unfolding through the open doorway.

The guard was helping a nurse sit down. She was injured and bleeding profusely from her neck. "She needs help now!" the guard shouted to anyone who might be able to help, or coherent enough to respond. Another doctor stood visibly trembling in the corner wrapping a wound on his right arm. Then he saw Rebecca.

Rebecca's upper body was held firmly to an operating table by wide, canvas straps with aluminum buckles. Her legs were free, and she pushed and thrashed against the straps in an attempt to break loose. A hideous squawk erupted from her throat as Michael ran toward her. "She needs help."

Doctor Riker turned quickly, "STAY AWAY FROM HER!"

Michael froze mid-stride, trying to mentally compute the reason for the doctor's distress. As he inched forward, the horror of the situation became clear. His head began to spin as he stared at the gaping wound in his wife's chest. He slowly moved his fingers to his lips. They were dry, as was his throat. Rebecca turned her head toward him and moaned an unintelligible, feeble plea.

Michael's breathing became uneven and he felt himself become weightless. "Becca…Oh my Go—"

Adam Riker reached out and grabbed him as he spun toward the rising tile floor, pulling him upright and propelling him from the middle of the room.

"Someone, for the love of God…tell me what's happening," Michael was unaccustomed to the rising panic he felt in his chest.

No one answered his plea, caught up in their own chaotic emotions at the bizarre scene playing out around them. Ron

Whiteman still cowered in the corner where he had pulled himself, blathering hysterically.

Nurse Beatty had collapsed to the floor in a pool of blood. The guard knelt beside her. Her eyes stared blankly into space.

"I—I think she's dead."

Doctor Riker moved to the nurse's side and took her wrist, feeling for her pulse. "This can't be," he whispered. The nurse's arm slowly slipped from his grasp.

Riker stood and stared incredulously as Rebecca strained to break free of her bonds. What he was witnessing was just not possible. This woman could not be alive. Yet she somehow was.

"Dear God." The guard gasped, and Riker turned.

Against the far wall lay two patients who had been declared dead on arrival, and were covered with white sheets. The sheets fell from their faces as they too sat upright on their gurneys and stood. They wailed mournfully with their arms outstretched as if to feel their way around a dark room.

Adam Riker grabbed Ron Whiteman by the shoulder and they both backed away.

"What in Hell is happening?" Whiteman strangled on the words as he uttered them.

Rebecca slipped free from the straps that held her.

Nurse Beatty opened her eyes.

2

"I don't give a damn what you have to do, just get here!"
Captain Roy Burns slammed down the telephone with enough force to grab the attention of every policeman in the room, squinting narrowly at the stunned assemblage. They avoided his withering glare and quickly went back to their duties. No one wanted to be the next one singled out to draw his wrath.

It was early in the shift, but the night was already wearing on his frazzled nerves. Roy Burns was a career cop. It was in his blood, as it had been in his father's blood before him. His job as a cop in Manhattan was his life's passion. He was certain at this rate it would also be the death of him.

Roy looked into the eyes of Darren Holsinger who was standing in front of him nervously twisting his Class ring. The crazy events of the night were bearing down hard on the young cop. In Roy's opinion, the kid was not ready to handle the rough streets of New York City, despite Holsinger's assurances to the contrary. Just two weeks ago he had been gung-ho and ready to single-handedly fight crime and clean up the city. That was always the way with the new ones until the first real crisis. Then you found out what they were really made of. Darrin Holsinger was a perfect example.

"Sir, we've got more on the way." Holsinger said. His voice was unsteady.

"How did we ever get along before you got here?" Roy wondered aloud and shaking his head.

Normally he would have found the kid's sudden lack of bravado funny, but at the moment, it was only serving to further try his patience with its underlying, whining presence.

"Damn it man, why can't you bring me some good news? After all that's happened tonight, I'm ready for some good news," Burns snapped.

"Sorry sir. Bad news is all I have. They're bringing in another one now."

The Captain shook his head, "What the hell? Is it a full moon tonight? Why does everyone have to lose their fucking mind when it's a full moon? Goddamned freaks. That's all I get to deal with. It's this city, you know?" Rubbing his temples, Burns could feel the beginning of a migraine. "It attracts them."

Two officers entered the revolving doors facing Broadway dragging a man behind them. They stopped in front of the Captain with the handcuffed man squirming on the floor.

"Let me guess," Burns asked when he saw that the man was bound and gagged. "We've got another biter?"

One of the officers held up his left hand. Blood dripped from his index finger. "Yeah, the son of a bitch bit me. How'd you know?" he asked, with a crooked grin.

Burns grimaced, "Get your ass over to the hospital and get that looked at. There's no telling what kind of disease this prick might have. Hepatitis or something worse, the filthy fuck." Burns glanced at the other officer. "Are you hurt too?"

"No, Sir," he responded quickly, as if an injury would only serve to further irritate the Captain.

"Good, then get this bum down to the holding cell with the others and out of the middle of my floor." To add emphasis to his frustration, Burns shoved the biter's backside with his department-issued, size-thirteen boot.

The officer nodded and started to drag the man away.

"Hold up!" Burns paused, furrowing his dark, bushy eyebrows as he reached down and forced the vile smelling, street bum over on his side to get a better look at his face. "He doesn't look right."

"What?"

"There's something wrong with him," Burns said.

"Yeah, he's a bum,"

Roy said, "No, I mean he looks sick or something. Look at his eyes."

The man's pupils were glazed over and his skin was ashen gray.

Captain Burns bent down and placed the back of his hand against the man's forehead. It felt cold and damp under his touch. He pulled away and motioned with a distracted wave of his large hand. "Just be careful. Make sure no one is careless with any of the inmates tonight. We have a growing number of uncooperative, unresponsive nut jobs down there already. Treat each one as a hostile prisoner. I don't know what these people are on, but it's like nothing I've ever seen before."

"Yes, Sir," The officer said, and the two men started to drag the man away.

"Not you, Givens. I want you to get to the hospital and have that finger looked at."

"I will, just as soon as we get this man squared away."

"Make sure you do," the Captain said, "and make sure you get back here as soon as you can. We're short-handed as it is. I need every man I can get tonight." Then he turned away from the two officers and bound man lying on the floor.

Precinct 34 was on Broadway. Any night was a busy night, but this one was different. A normal night in the precinct brought in the everyday, garden-variety prostitutes and petty thieves, nothing too radical. After all, it was the best neighborhood in all of New York City. Unlike the tough boroughs where he'd gotten his start, these were the upscale criminals who kept him in business. On a normal summer evening they could come out in droves. Preying on the tourists and chic Manhattanites, the local crazies could make a twelve-hour shift go by in no time at all. But tonight there seemed to be a pattern emerging. Hospitals were hotspots of violence, and accident scenes were becoming war zones. Victims were turning and attacking their rescuers.

Roy turned and watched from the water cooler as the two young officers dragged the crazed bum from the lobby.

He was letting the night get to him. He had just kicked a prisoner for no good reason. How would he explain that to his superiors should the man file a complaint? Unknowingly, he was rubbing his temples again, the pounding in his head, growing.

Likely, there would be no complaint. The homeless man would just be happy to spend a few days in jail, get the free meals, and go on his merry way again. He was reassuring himself of that likelihood when his longtime friend and fellow New York cop, Daniel Flanagan, lumbered in from the street. For the first time that night, a slight smile creased Roy Burns' face.

At fifty, Daniel's fiery red hair was now mostly gray. He had been with the department for thirty years and was not about to retire anytime soon. Daniel could only be described as a gritty and honest Irishman. Gritty and honest were increasingly rare traits these days and ones that Roy Burns found appealing in a fellow officer. All too often in his career, Burns had run across dirty cops, the kind who would steal dope from a collar and sell it, or just as bad, use it. Cops who would have sex with some poor kid forced to prostitute herself just to survive, then take her cash and leave her to deal with an angry pimp. New York could be a heartless and unforgiving city of broken dreams, a brutal place full of brutal people. Burns had seen it all, and it had left him jaded. He'd seen a lot of guys move through the ranks because of dirty deals and be rewarded for their efforts with promotions and accolades, deals that only other cops knew about.

Cops did not, as a rule, inform on other cops. Theirs was a brotherhood built on trust and loyalty. Even when trusting your brother was, in Roy's mind, akin to getting a blood test for your cholesterol, an unpleasant, but necessary evil. Their dirty little secrets were safe. Even with honest guys like Roy and Daniel.

Roy's smile widened and tugged at the corners of his stern mouth as Daniel approached. It soon diminished though. Something was wrong. Danny's face said it all. His expression was hard and determined as he moved stiffly and with a slight limp. Roy placed a firm hand on his shoulder. "You okay Danny-boy?"

Daniel nodded, "Aye, I'll be fine. Just a bit of a tussle with one of the town folk. There'll be a lot of strange ones out there tonight," Daniel observed in his still thick Irish brogue. It was a charming trait he had never lost despite the fact that his family had immigrated to the states when he was just a tot.

Roy said, "You don't have to tell me. The pokey's filling up with them. It seems that everyone's coming unglued."

"They are indeed." Daniel said gruffly, and limped to his desk.

Roy Burns watched his friend fall into the chair with a heavy sigh. "You sure you're okay?

"I'm a beat cop, not a kindergarten teacher, Roy. Bumps and

bruises come with the territory on this job."

Daniel raised his pant leg to expose a swollen ankle. "I twisted it tonight fightin' off a nut on 42nd. Saints preserve us, somethin's outta sorts on the streets tonight," he said with a raised eyebrow.

Roy had to smile. The incredulous look on Daniel's face when he raised that brow made him look like a cross between Mister Spock and Jim Carrey. He was sure that Daniel was blissfully unaware of the exaggerated elasticity of his face. He spent so much time trying to hide his emotions from everyone. When he did something like raising his eyebrow, or smiling too widely, it gave him away. You could see his true humanity in a single smile. In truth, he was as transparent as glass if you knew how to read him. It was Danny's heart, not on his sleeve, but in that raised eyebrow. That is where he wore his heart and that was why he was Roy's best friend.

"It's more than the streets, Danny. It's the whole city. I swear I believe the lunatics are running the asylum tonight. Whoever opened the gate, I wish they'd close the damned thing."

Daniel laughed at his comment and dropped the pant leg down over his pure argyle sock onto his shiny, black oxford and covered the swollen ankle. "Well, I'm done for this night. My twelve hours are in and I'm goin' home."

Roy grunted his displeasure. "I could use you a bit longer tonight… Overtime—gravy my man—gravy."

Daniel took a flask of whiskey from the top drawer of his desk and took a long pull from it. He looked up at the smoldering captain with a muted grin as the last drop of fiery liquid trickled down his throat. "Gravy? I think not on this night. Besides, I can't be doin' that now can I? It's against procedures to be on duty—under the influence that is."

"I don't give a damn if you're falling down drunk. I need—"

Suddenly a scream that could have shattered glass erupted from outside the precinct doors.

The Broadway side of the police station allowed a good view of the street with its floor to ceiling windows and revolving glass doors. The façade would be considered stunning in a less intimidating setting. It did afford one the chance to see from the edge of the sidewalk to the other side of the thoroughfare. Unlike a newer building with smaller windows, the street traffic was visible to anyone standing in the main entrance. Precinct 34 was built in nineteen thirty-six and was straight out of a Dick Tracy movie. Its rich oak trim, high ceilings, and marble tiled floors would never be incorporated into a modern police precinct. It was too rich, too extravagant.

Roy Burns ran for the door, and Daniel Flanagan hobbled along right behind him. He still moved quickly when needed, in spite of the ankle. Outside, two men pulled a middle-aged woman to the ground like a couple of hyenas taking down a lithe gazelle. One of them, a tall fellow with a long beard, dragged his mangled left leg. The other man had frizzy-gray hair. His cheeks were abnormally sunken and his face gave off a waxy gleam under the streetlights.

The woman screamed as the older of the two men loomed over her prostrate body, mouth opened wide as though a lover who might hungrily cover her in an open-mouth kiss. But instead, he clamped his visibly crooked teeth over her pert, little nose. The other man moved in and fell on her body and began groping her midriff. She flailed and kicked at her attackers, determined that she was not going down without a fight. Burns and Flanagan, who had been momentarily stunned by the struggle, snapped out of their trance and sprang into action.

Roy reached the heap of writhing humanity first and yanked the closest man away from her. He pushed him face down on the concrete walkway and held him there. The woman emitted a strangled, wet scream as blood gushed like a fountain from the place where her nose had been just a minute ago. Daniel moved in on the second man and pulled him away from her by jerking hard on the hood of his blood-soaked sweatshirt. The action rolled the man up onto his knees. At first, he fell forward on his hands, then he staggered unsteadily to his feet again. To Daniel's horror the man was chewing on the gristle and flesh that had been the woman's nose and before he could mentally process what he was witnessing, the man lunged for him.

Daniel laid into him with a roundhouse punch to the jaw and reached for his sidearm with a single, fluid motion. The man went down, but only long enough to regain his footing. He bounced back to his feet like a child's punching bag with a sand-weighted bottom, impossible to keep down. Daniel had knocked more than a few men into oblivion with a punch like that, but this man was coming for him again.

Daniel raised his service revolver, pointing the muzzle at the attacker. "Stop. Get down now. I mean what I say when I tell you I'll put ya down for good."

The man staggered forward and reached for Daniel who promptly squeezed two rounds into his chest at point-blank range. The force of the impact spun him away and he fell forward, off the curb and onto the pavement between two parked police cruisers.

Before Daniel could move to check him, the woman, whose face was a gruesome mask of the macabre, grabbed him by the cuff of his trousers. Her eyes had rolled back in their sockets and she seemed to be in the throes of some kind of seizure as she emitted the most mournful wail he had ever heard. Like the legendary Banshee her scream rose again to a glass-shattering pitch. "Holy Jesus, Mary and Joseph," Daniel swore, staring in disbelief at the apparition.

In that moment, he caught movement in his peripheral vision as he felt the impact. With a grunting rush of air from his lungs Daniel sidestepped and turned.

The man had somehow managed to regain his footing and charge the big cop. Daniel only had a split second to process what was happening, but it was enough time for him to react.

With a sweeping motion, he took the legs out from under the fiend and fell on him, pinning him face down on the concrete.

Daniel pulled the man's thrashing arms behind his back. It was a practiced motion that he had used to restrain literally thousands of other criminals in his thirty years on the job. He quickly managed the task and clicked on the cuffs. He was virtually standing on his prisoner, pinning him to the ground by placing his big foot from the man's shoulder to the small of his back. "Can't get me there can you, you fucking asshole?" Daniel was screaming now, and hot flashes of adrenaline were coursing through his veins, causing him to breathe heavy and fast.

The scene that had just played out had momentarily distracted Roy Burns, allowing the gray-toothed attacker he was holding onto to grab at him. He spun his prisoner around as two officers came barreling through the station entrance. They quickly lent their combined strength and subdued the man, slamming him hard against the brick wall of the precinct house.

"Jesus Christ—what the hell is going on?" Burns said as the man continued to reach for him from where the two officers had pinned him. And Daniel, where was Daniel? Roy scanned the crowd that had gathered around the ruckus. Daniel was standing over the other man, flexing his hand.

"You okay, Danny?"

Daniel took his foot off the man's back as he jerked him roughly to his feet and handed him off to the young rookie who had just appeared to lend assistance.

"Be careful Laddie, he's a biter, and possessed by Satan himself. Shot him twice, I did, and he acts as though I've given him heartburn." Turning to Roy, Daniel said. "Aye. I'm okay, but she's a goner for sure." He looked toward the woman who had stumbled back against the wall of the building, continuing to jerk and seize. She suddenly heaved violently and slid down the brick wall to a heap on the walkway.

Roy knelt down and made an attempt to stop the bleeding that had formed a deep, red pool around her. He applied pressure to the wound just as he had been taught. "Someone get me a towel or something and call an ambulance." Roy said, and Holsinger dashed inside, dragging his prisoner along with him.

"I can't stop the blood—Jesus, I'm going to lose her."

The blood was flowing between Roy's fingers and dripping to the sidewalk. The Captain placed one hand over the other and pushed harder. "Hold on, Miss…help's on the way," he said soothingly.

Just as the words left his lips, the woman became still and the blood stopped flowing from the bites on her face and neck.

"Miss?—Can you hear me?—Ma'am"

She didn't respond to his pleas and she had stopped breathing in mid-breath. Roy released the pressure he had been applying to the bite wounds and sat down on his rump beside her lifeless body.

"This doesn't make any sense," Roy said. "This is crazy. Has everyone gone insane?"

Daniel rubbed his busted and bloody knuckles. "Aye, I'll not be disagreeing with that."

Roy watched Daniel as he wiped the blood from his knuckles onto his shirt. "What happened?"

"I scraped them on the bastard's teeth when I hit him. I think I knocked a few of them out when I did. I hope I hurt the bastard."

"Is she going to be okay?" A stunned bystander asked.

"She's dead," Roy told him. "But the man who did this was

shot twice and unfortunately, he's still quite alive."

Roy laid the woman's head down gently on the cold sidewalk and rose, giving Danny a knowing look. "I've got half a mind to go in there and beat that son of a bitch to death myself."

"You'd better go wash your hands first, my friend."

Roy glanced down and his hands. They were covered in the woman's blood. As if on cue, Holsinger emerged from the building holding a white towel. When he only stood there with his mouth hung open in shock, and staring at the dead woman, Daniel took the towel from him and handed it to Roy.

Minutes later, the woman was loaded onto a gurney by an ambulance crew. The prisoner had already been restrained and removed to the hospital under armed guard. Roy, who rarely lost his composure, was visibly shaken by the bizarre incident and Daniel knew he needed to shore up his friend. He laid a big, freckled paw on his buddy's shoulder as the paramedics loaded the body of the woman into the ambulance. They declared her dead and zipped closed the black bag that had become her death cocoon. The stretcher was rolled up to the back of the vehicle and its legs collapsed as she was shoved into the bay. The attendant strapped down the bagged body and pulled the restraints tight. "This will hold her until we can get her to the morgue," he told Roy, and slammed the door shut.

"Wait a minute," Roy said, and motioned to open the door again. "She's not dead. I just saw that bag move. You were shutting the door, and I saw it move. And not a little move, either," he stated firmly.

"Believe me Captain, she is dead." He grinned lopsidedly at Roy and furrowed his brow as though he might be speaking to someone who was slightly touched.

"Look, I saw it. I saw it!" Roy's voice pitched under the strain of the night's events. "That damn bag moved. Check it out."

The radio in the front of the ambulance crackled to life and the medic walked toward the open cab door to listen.

Roy rubbed his eyes, beginning now to doubt it himself. "I am telling you, she is not dead. I saw it. She needs to be checked out," he insisted, though less adamantly now.

"We have to go. Just got another call…Stat," the driver said.

"Sorry man, gotta run." The medic gave Roy a skeptical glance.

"What a crazy night. Believe me brother, she is definitely dead," he said as he ran to the door and jumped inside.

The vehicle sped away into the warm, summer night. Roy and Danny stood side by side, still not fully comprehending what had just occurred.

Roy straightened his bloody and disheveled uniform and headed for the safety of the station house. He turned at the entrance to look down the unusually busy thoroughfare.

"It has to get better from here, Danny. It can't possibly get worse."

3

The street was dark and the car was just beyond their line of sight. Chuck Longfellow slipped back into the alley next to his friend Duane and disappeared into the shadows.

Chuck's hands shook, betraying his anxiety over the task at hand as he lit another cigarette to soothe his jangling nerves. He inhaled and waited for the smoke to hit his lungs. He needed a moment to collect himself, to mask the fear he was feeling. Not from himself, but from Duane, who was always ready to pounce on him for every little mistake. Something that might be easier to tolerate if Duane actually had an idea of his own other than to give up and go home.

Duane watched as the front of Chuck's bald head glowed with each drag. His dome was only visible for a second before disappearing again as the oxygen left the tip of the cigarette. Duane coughed and irritably swatted at the foul smelling smoke.

"If you'd quit those nasty things we'd still have enough money for food," and pointing down the street for emphasis, he added, "and that guy down there could keep his stereo."

"Nobody twisted your arm and made you come to New York, Duane. You can go back to Virginia anytime you want," he added with a hint of venom, like a schoolyard bully taunting a weaker kid. It seemed to be the only way to keep Duane's accusing insults at bay…intimidation. Counter his attacks with some of his own. Only then would he back down and shut his mouth, at least for a while.

Of course Duane had to know that if it were that easy to go back to Virginia, they would have been there by now. But it was easier for him to blame others rather than accept responsibility himself, like using the last of their funds on a common street hooker, or pissing away what little they could come by on a three-day drinking binge. That was always the case with Duane. Blame others to shift attention away from his own slothful, reckless behavior.

"We need to go, Chuck."

"Be quiet," Chuck said, glancing back over his shoulder. "I have a plan and I can't think if you're making all that noise."

Chuck had focused all of his attention on a beautiful red muscle car parked on the dimly lit street. With a nervous sigh he slipped out of the shadows and crossed the street, crouching as he slid between the parked vehicles so he could break in from the passenger's side. The tall buildings offered more cover in their strangely shifting shadows.

Chuck adeptly slid the Slim Jim through the top of the window and fished for the locking mechanism. He hooked it and pulled up. The door unlocked and Chuck grinned like the proverbial Cheshire cat as he reached for the door.

A glimpse of movement made him freeze in place, his hand inches from the chrome handle. Suddenly, his wiry frame was slammed onto the pavement before he had time to react.

Duane slunk unnoticed into the dark cover of an unlit door stoop and watched silently as the blackest man he had ever seen slammed the butt of his pistol against the side of Chuck's head. "Tryin' to jack my car you redneck motherfucker?" he said, and then spat on Chuck's Rebel Flag T-shirt which proudly proclaimed, 'Fighting Terrorism since 1861'. "How about I take my fuckin' reparations right here and now," he growled as he drove the sharp toe of his expensive leather boot into Chuck's side.

"Dude, wait," Duane stepped forward from his shadowy hiding place with his hands raised in submission as soon as he registered the familiar, black face. It was Jamal Owens. He recognized him from the many tabloid newspapers that his grandmother kept in the large reading basket in her bathroom, not to mention the endless procession of half hour tabloid entertainment shows that she kept her old RCA television tuned to.

Jamal Owens was the New York gang member, turned rapper, turned underwear model, turned daytime soap-opera star. He had most recently been in the news for a wild night partying with that blonde pop star bimbo who was always getting caught without her panties. In the case in question, Owens' underwear had not been evident either as a paparazzi had managed to get a shot of Blondie giving him a private oral performance of a different nature, which sold more magazines than her last two CDs combined.

"Dude don't," Duane pleaded. "We didn't know it was your car man—we were just tryin' to…"

Jamal Owens turned his gaze toward Duane. Chuck scuttled away toward the shadowed stoop on all fours like a cockroach caught foraging in the kitchen when the fluorescent light is switched on.

Suddenly a loud wolf-whistle cut the air.

"Woooo-whoo... Well, if it ain't our old friend Jamal. Come to take a look at how the other half lives Jam-Man?"

The taunt had come from a gaunt, wiry man, judging by his accent, a Latino. He wore a black and yellow bandanna tied around his long, unruly hair. Four other young Latinos followed in his wake, each wearing the same adornment on their heads and clearly looking to him for their cues as to how this might play out. The wiry man tapped a miniature ball bat against his palm as he strolled nonchalantly toward Jamal.

Duane slunk deeper into the shadowed doorway and Chuck flattened himself against the wall, eyes darting back and forth between Owens and his antagonist.

"Best back the fuck up Pablo." Jamal narrowed his eyes at the ringleader. "I'm in no mood for your shit tonight. Consider yourself warned." Jamal flipped the revolver around in his grasp and wiped away the blood left by Chuck's head.

"Looks like that rich white pussy has caused more than your little dick to go soft." The ringleader laughed, and glanced back at his buddies who laughed on cue. Before he could finish laughing at his own joke, he saw the blur of Jamal's big foot as it drove his knee backward with a well-placed kick. The kick was followed by the sickening snap of bone. Pablo went down in a screaming heap on the pavement. His friends reacted by moving out of range of his long, well-muscled legs.

"Oh Man…that was fucked up," cried a little nervous, mousy looking follower. "Fuck. Man. That was unnecessary."

Duane could see something in Jamal's countenance that clearly said this guy was not stable. He was a man on the edge and like a cornered animal it made him dangerous. If what he had heard in the tabloids was correct, Jamal Owens was dangerous on a good day. Tonight he looked deadly.

As if taking an acting cue, and making sure to hit his mark, Jamal drew down on one of the gang members who had pulled a pistol from behind his back where it had been snugly tucked into his belt. In the split second it took for all this to unfold, the gun in Jamal's hand went off. With a sound like a clap of thunder the weapon blew a hole in his attacker's chest. As the guy spun away, Duane could see that the exit wound was larger. He fell dead in the street as Jamal turned the gun on the others.

"*Chingada madre!*" another one swore at Jamal, hysteria edging his voice as he clicked off an empty chamber "*Carajo!*"

Jamal squeezed off a round into the gang member's crotch, sending his bloody form tumbling onto the broken, dirty, asphalt pavement. "Press ONE for English, Motherfucker!" Jamal screamed down at the writhing gang-banger who spewed another string of Spanish expletives.

Jamal was in a rage, and he failed to notice that one of Pablo's cohorts had slipped around behind him, close enough to get off a wild shot that had it hit its target, would surely have ended all of Jamal's aspirations of further stardom.

The shot rang out and missed its mark as the bullet whizzed past his long braids of hair causing the glass beads that were woven into them to rattle together. It slid with a quiet *thu-wauk* into the the throat of the cursing gang member who was up again and dancing around in front of Jamal.

Jamal spun like an Old West gunfighter and with catlike reflexes, fired off a shot at his would-be assassin. The shot hit its target with the precision of a professional marksman as Jamal crouched low, poised to dispense more attackers.

"Shit the bed Fred," Duane whispered to Chuck "We'd better stay down and out of this one. This ain't our fight. What the hell have you gotten us in the middle of?"

"Yeah," Chuck whispered, slinking further back into the shadows and well out of sight as three more black men stolled onto the scene.

One of them fired a shot into the back of the last fleeing Latino gang member. The shooter stalked up to Jamal and stood face to face with him, staring unblinking, as his two accomplices rummaged through the pockets of the dead and dying Latinos. They hastily removed items of value, including a large wad of cash, a plastic baggie full of coarse, brownish, crystaline powder and a baggie containing three prescription bottles.

As the two black men continued to size each other up, Duane tugged silently on Chuck's shirttail urging him wordlessly to make a hasty retreat before the whole thing could erupt again. In that moment a huge, gleaming smile spread from ear to ear on Jamal's face, neutralizing the dangerous animal that had been there only a moment before. The two men bumped chests and embraced, seperating with an exchange of complicated handshakes and gestures that Duane could not see well in the shifting shadows of the dim streetlights.

"What'chu doin' out here my Nigga?" the unnamed shooter asked Owens. "Tryin' to get yourself killed? What would we do without my brother here to represent?"

The two men laughed like old partners in crime who had lost touch with one another. It was as if they were completely oblivious to the bloody carnage on the street around them. The other two men continued to comb the area for guns, drugs and any other loot they might have missed at first perusal.

"Jerome, you've got perfect timing as always." Jamal took a step back to look at the man in front of him. "These fuckin' Greaser-Bangers think they know somethin'. They know Jesus now."

Jamal motioned to the Latino kid with a bullet hole in his back. "They fucked with the wrong nigga this time."

Jamal's eyes grew wide with shock as the kid began to struggle up from the pavement and move toward Jerome. Jerome's back was turned and he could not see the approaching apparition, only the shocked look on his friend's face alerted him as Jamal uttered, "What the fuck?"

The pock-faced kid Jamal had shot in the crotch was now pulling himself up the side of Jamal's Mustang. Two others staggered to their feet simultaneously from the black pavement. The two looters were now facing their bloody, shambling, upright corpses.

Pock-face fell on the nearest looter with his maw opened wide. Saliva rolled from the gaping orifice as he chomped down on his nemesis like he were taking a bite out of a human burrito. As he struggled to get away from the determined grip of his attacker, a huge blade appeared in his hand seemingly out of thin air. He buried it up to the hilt in the throat of the crotch-less Mexican.

Pock-face fell back against Jamal's car chewing on the piece of flesh that he had torn out of the human burrito's bare back. He seemed temporarily contented to just enjoy his little snack, oblivious of the fact that his genitals had been effectively blown off, or that there was a knife handle protruding from his throat just beneath his chin. It bobbed up and down rhythmically as he chewed the chunk of ragged flesh from the looter's back.

"Fuck man. Fuck," Jamal exclaimed to his friend, "I can't be in this shit, Jerome. I've got too much to lose." Jamal tucked the pistol into the waistband of his baggy jeans, shaking his head emphatically at his former partner in crime and like a track star at the sound of a starting pistol, Jamal took off, sprinting up the alley toward Fifth Avenue. "Jerome, man, I can't be in this, Dog. I can't." He glanced back at Jerome over his shoulder as he retreated. "You deal with this, you know what to do. You know who to call," he shouted, as the macabre dance of black and brown mutilated gang members began to tear at each other behind him. "Man—shit has done gone bad."

Jamal stopped then, reached in his pocket, and threw the keys of the vintage Mustang to Jerome who promptly reached out in the semi-darkness and miraculously plucked the flying keys from the air in front of him.

"Jamal?" Jerome stood stunned, watching the back of his retreating friend.

"Take it man. It's a borrowed ride. Know what I mean? Get the fuck outta here. You ain't seen me, understand? You ain't seen me. You keep it clean now. No tracks back to me."

Jerome stared at the keys and then to his friend as he hurried away. "What, you want me to take care of your hot shit and this mess in the alley? Fuck that, and fuck you!"

Jamal did not stop again as he hurried away, trying to grasp what he had seen unfold and process what it meant for him. It meant trouble; big, career ending, life in prison kind of trouble. Jamal didn't know much, but he did know that he was not going back to living that kind of life again. "This shit has done gone bad, bad, bad. Believe it," he repeated, as he disappeared around the corner with not so much as a wave to his friend and rescuer. His parting words echoed back to Jerome, bouncing off the buildings, fire escapes and dumpsters in the alley. "I owe you brother,"

It was a debt that Jerome would never collect. It was the last thing he heard before the crotch-less Mexican spun him around and promptly ripped out his throat with the prettiest, whitest, straightest teeth Jerome had ever seen.

Deep in the shadows of the door stoop behind a blue dumpster, Chuck Longfellow held his friend Duane in a headlock. His hand firmly covered his endlessly moving mouth. Chuck pointed to the retreating form of Jamal Owens. With his lips pressed against Duane's ear, he whispered, "There—stay out of sight or we're both as good as dead. Follow him outta here."

The two country mice slipped past the fray of blood and carnage and moved silently up the alley in the wake of the black antagonist, unnoticed by the other actors in the macabre play.

4

Nurse Beatty lunged for Doctor Adam Riker.

He met her attack with extended arms, holding her at bay as she clawed at his face. Her eyes were wide and wild; a crazed look replaced her usually calm veneer. In spite of her feral thrashing, it required only minimal effort to control her. It was the mental effort that took most of Adam Riker's strength. He had known her for most of his professional career. To see her like this now made it difficult to stay focused. He called out to her and she lunged in close, her throat releasing a raspy whine.

Doctor Whiteman leaped from the corner to help the guard as he struggled to keep the other two reanimates at bay. With his uninjured arm, he grabbed a middle aged, potbellied man with a fat face. The injuries to his internal organs seemed to have little effect on his ability to be aggressive and move offensively. He bulled forward, pinning the doctor against the wall.

Riker slung nurse Beatty away from him and grabbed a metal stand that held two IV bags and hit her in the face with the bottom of it. The nurse fell against the wall and slid to the floor, landing firmly on her rump.

"Everyone, out of the room!" Riker screamed, and tossed away the IV stand in favor of a push broom. He used the broom to push the other two reanimates away as he backed out of the room and swung the double doors closed.

"We need something to keep these doors shut."

The guard pushed him aside and wrapped an extension cord through the two handles several times, then tied it into a triple knot before joining Doctor Riker and the others who were watching from several feet away.

Two dead faces screamed at them from the other side of the door's small windows. Then a crash, as Janice joined them.

"They'll get out of there eventually," the Guard said.

Riker nodded, "There's something wrong with them. They aren't rational. They don't seem to be thinking clearly—like rabid animals. Has anyone called the police?"

A special report on the waiting room television grabbed their attention and in spite of the cacophony beyond the emergency room doors, they turned to watch as the reporter reluctantly gave them the news.

Michael collapsed into a chair by the window. He was trying to make sense of what had happened as he listened to the man on the television. A nightmare, he thought. But that was wishful thinking. This was really happening.

"This is a special report from the WVNY television studios," the talking head announced from behind a shiny, blue desk.

"Now from the field, here's Peter Johnson."

The operating room door thundered with the relentless pounding of fists and furniture as the reanimated bodies continued their assault on it.

"Reports are beginning to cross the wires of numerous acts of violence in Atlanta, Washington D.C, Philadelphia, and New York. Perpetrators of these crimes are said to be strange in appearance and often injured in some way. In many cases they seem to be in a trance-like state and unresponsive. Communication or reason with these violent individuals has so far been unsuccessful."

Riker turned and watched the crazies on the other side of the door with growing interest as the reporter spoke.

"It is the recommendation of the President of the United States that all citizens in affected areas remain indoors until this emergency has passed."

The screen changed to a field reporter in Atlanta, Georgia. The man was obviously only minutes from being in bed asleep, his hair and clothes disheveled. In the background a hellish mob pushed and shoved its way through a street sealed off with concrete barricades and policemen.

"A state of emergency exists in Atlanta." The reporter shouted above the clamor. Once past the barriers, the mob crashed into the line of policemen. The ones that reacted quickly enough withdrew and ran past the reporter. Others fell under the sudden swarm and were lost beneath them.

"We have to go now," the reporter said nervously, and dropped his microphone. The camera became shaky and fell to the ground beside it where the scene unfolding was seen at an angle as the crowd lurched forward. There was a scream, and the picture went blank.

Riker sent a lamp crashing from the top of a table and then shoved the table in front of the ER doors. The guard followed suit and in a few minutes the doors were covered with the furniture from the emergency room waiting area. Michael stared into the room. "My wife is in there with them," he said, softly.

"Your wife is one of them." Riker said, a bit harshly. He regretted his tone as soon as he had said it. "Don't try to open those doors," he continued more evenly, trying his best to put forth his professional bedside manner and at the same time sound calm.

Michael wanted to ignore the Doctor's warning and pull Rebecca from inside the room with the others. If he could isolate her from them, maybe she would calm down. But he knew that he was trying to rationalize an irrational situation. That was not his Becca. It was something else.

"What has she become? What are they?" Michael asked.

Riker walked close and stared into the room with him. "I'm not sure, but I think—they are dead."

***

Jeffrey Brown listened as the morgue became an echoing chamber of howls and moans. The walls pulsed with whatever was on the other side, thrashing about inside the shelved drawers.

At first he thought he was surely going mad. Certainly the sounds were his imagination and not from within the walls where the dead were kept in cold storage.

From time to time, Jeffrey Brown would pull them from their cool slumber for a peek, especially the more attractive females. He liked to touch them, and caress their cool skin. Even into death he appreciated their beauty and their quiet compliance. The unmoving dead were clean virgins, unstained by life's problems, sinful lusts, and greedy ambitions. In his mind, they were perfection in its truest sense. But now he wondered if his fetish for the deceased had gotten him into trouble with the keepers of afterlife and he grabbed his hair and pulled from both sides until he screamed.

For a moment, the racket stopped, the room was silent, and he was once again alone with his thoughts. It had been his imagination after all. Something he had eaten maybe. What would the dead want with the living? Certainly they were dead, and dead meant dead. The dead were unmoving…silent…perfect.

Jeffrey sat in his chair, both hands over his heart, breathing deeply. With each breath his temporary madness faded until he was again calm. Yes, something he had eaten. Or maybe he had fallen asleep in his chair. That was it, a nightmare, just a bad dream.

Jeffrey blew a long sigh of relief and swallowed the lump that had formed in his throat.

Then, two recent cases for study on the tables to his left fluttered beneath the sheets. Jeffrey's heart began to pound again as he watched, breathless.

The sheets slid from their faces as they sat up revealing pale, vacant stares. The first one to rise was a young brunette that he'd fancied right away. Earlier that night he had leaned down over her face. He hovered there briefly, staring at her perfect features. How beautiful she was with her waist-length, chocolate mane and slender form. For a moment he contemplated a kiss. Her full lips beckoned him to do so. But he covered her again, unable to find the courage to do such a thing.

She stood there now, at least six-feet tall with her right arm extended. Her hand closed as if grabbing an imaginary object from the empty air. A raspy sigh escaped her full, dark lips as they parted.

Jeffrey stood, unable to take his eyes from her now that she was alive and standing in front of him.

"No, you're dead to me now." He could hear himself saying it, but somehow he still wanted her, even in her imperfect state.

"Do you HEAR? Leave me alone…you're dead. Go back to sleep. I wish you had never been brought in here. You're not real. You're just a bad dream." He felt a warm tear slide down his cheek and realized that he was crying and that he was also very awake.

One of the wall doors popped open and the corpse stored there fought to free itself from the confined space; an old woman with many wrinkles stuck her face out and screamed loudly at him.

She was not one of his desirables. She was nothing like the thirty-something brunette with the full lips. "No…I don't want you. Get back in the wall. I don't want ANY OF YOU!" he cried.

The two corpses from the tables moved toward him in ungraceful steps. The other, a man with his left arm severed in a car crash, groaned hellishly as he lumbered across the hard floor in baby steps as though learning to walk for the very first time. The woman, no longer attractive to Jeffrey, bugged her glazed eyes. Both were nearly on top of him before he reacted and ran for the door.

***

Riker moved to the main desk and dialed nine for an outside line. He was met by a busy signal. Not the normal kind of busy signal but a fast, irritating one. The kind that usually meant 'out of order.'

Two police cars raced past the hospital with their lights on and sirens blaring. Doctor Riker watched them through the window as they raced by. Their piercing wails were followed by the hospital's fire alarm. This provoked even more panic, and the waiting room emptied. Only the doctors, a few staff members, and Michael remained. Riker was staring at the red alarm bell on the ceiling as it rang when Jeffrey Brown exited the elevator and fell into the waiting room.

Jeffrey placed his back to the wall and tip toed as if walking the ledge of a tall building to the other side of the room. Once there, he cocked his head and squinted his eyes in interest, fascinated by the reanimates that were slamming their bodies against the double doors of the Emergency room.

Jeffrey pointed back toward the elevator. "There are more of them downstairs," he said barely above a whisper to Doctor Riker. "The dead, they got up. The morgue is full of them. I didn't touch them. It's not my fault." He spoke slowly, and without emotion in an effort to retain his composure.

It seemed the absence of a response from Riker led Jeffrey to believe he had not heard him. "Did you hear me?" he said. "They're coming up."

Riker said, "How many are down there?"

"Eight or ten, I think. I'm not sure. I didn't stick around to count them." Jeffrey pointed to the hall. "They'll come up the elevator, or the stairs. They came after me. It isn't my fault. I didn't touch them. Understand? You believe me, don't you?"

"We need to try to keep them down there." Riker told him. "We can block off the stairs. Maybe they won't know how to use the elevator."

Suddenly, the door to the stairs flew open and Riker spun on his heels.

The morgue's occupants staggered into the hallway, first one, then two, until the hall was filled. Jeffrey Brown whimpered, bolted for the exit door, and disappeared into the early morning darkness.

Adam Riker slammed the door shut between the waiting room and hall and then backed away as that door too became a rhythmic pulse of beating hands.

"They'll figure out how to open the door," Riker explained. "I'm going upstairs with the other patients. They'll need my help. You should all follow me."

Michael Longley could take no more. "No! If we go to the upper floors we could get trapped. In case you weren't paying attention to the man on TV, this is not a phenomenon limited to this hospital. This is something worse, much worse. Besides, that goddamned fire alarm probably means there's a fire in the building somewhere. It's best we leave, and leave now."

"It might be even more dangerous outside." Riker cautioned. "What if we go out there and there's more of them?"

"It will be light soon. The police will be on top of this—whatever it is. And quickly, I hope."

Adam said, "Thc patients upstairs...I should be up there with them."

"Fine, you do what you want Doc," Michael said, "But I'm leaving. I won't allow myself to be backed into a corner with no escape."

"Neither will I," the big hospital guard said. "Upstairs is a bad idea."

Riker's instinct for self-preservation took momentary precedence over his Hippocratic Oath and he reluctantly followed the others outside. Indeed he did smell smoke. And he was sure there was nothing in the rule book that said he was duty-bound to lay down his life in an impossible situation. And with that thought, Adam Riker did feel better for the moment.

Last to leave, Michael stopped and turned at the door.

He had seen the dead on more than one occasion. His job as a policeman in Chicago had given him a front row seat to all sorts of atrocities. He watched his wife as she continued to bang her hands against the blood-stained window. The hospital alarm only slightly registered in his ears as if it were far away. The sound of her fingernails clawing at the door with shrill scrapes as they dug into the wood rang louder in his mind than the alarm. He continued to watch as she moaned pathetically. She did not know him. He could see it in her deadened eyes. And yet, she seemed to hold a kind of passion for him there. And though there was vacancy of life in her eyes, there was also that strange, unfamiliar passion and longing. For what, he could not grasp. What could the dead desire? The back of Michael's throat tightened and he forced himself to turn away. He would never see her again. And this is how he would remember her.

5

Chuck stopped before leaving the alley to sneak a peek into Wall Street.

"I don't know man," he whispered. "I don't like it."

The night always carried ghostly sounds down the wide Manhattan avenues, but tonight it was lonely moans echoing from the shadows that caught Chuck's attention. The movers and shakers were all quiet on Wall Street. In the distance, sirens pierced the city night with rhythmic, chaotic wails. Fires burned to the west, filling the Manhattan skyline with an orange glow.

An instant later, a police car roared up behind them. Its siren blared loudly as it passed. It raced down Wall Street and turned left with screaming wheels. Jamal turned to watch it, and for the first time spotted Duane and Chuck trailing him.

"What the fuck is this shit? You followin' me?" Jamal said, and took a defensive posture by reaching for his weapon.

"No…It's just that…something's really fucked up." Chuck said, and nervously fumbled to light a cigarette. He leaned against the red brick wall behind him, trying his best to act casual and in control. The last thing he wanted to do around someone like Jamal Owens was show weakness. He had been weak in the alley. It was time for damage control. "Those son of a bitches down the alley…they weren't just fucked up man, they were something else.

Your guys killed them. You know it to be true. But they came back and tore into your boys like a pack of hyenas."

Jamal moved his hand from the pistol and quietly regarded the wiry looking character that had just tried to steal a car that he, himself had stolen. "Do you have another one of those?" He asked, and patted his jacket pocket as if looking for a smoke of his own.

Chuck flicked a cigarette from his pack and silently offered it to Jamal. His hands shook slightly as he reached forward to light it for him. He was sure his anxiety did not escape Jamal's notice. Once the cigarette was lit, Chuck pocketed the silver lighter with an eagle on the front and waited for the black man's next move.

"Minor setback man. Those guys won't be fucking us over again," Jamal told Chuck, peering at him with thoughtful reserve.

"Have you heard a word I just said?" Chuck shook his head ruefully and glanced back into the dark alley. "We'd better put some space between us and whatever those things were in the alley. I'm bettin' they'll come out of there—sooner or later."

Chuck stepped off the curb to cross the street and Duane and Jamal both followed him. Jamal had decided to do what he always did when no better alternative occurred to him. Just go with it. Go with it and see what happens. Deal with it later if he needed to, after he'd had time to think it through.

On the other side, the streetlights showered the sidewalk in an icy fluorescent glow. The night was warm, but the street appeared cold and desolate as the three walked toward the bluish light.

They were halfway across the street when Chuck placed his arm in front of Duane and brought them all to an abrupt stop.

There was movement in the shadows of a tall, granite and glass building.

It was a man.

He leaned slightly forward as he shuffled his way toward them with as much speed as it seemed he could muster. His shirt was ripped from his chest and hung raggedly at his side. His right arm was missing from the elbow down and he growled an unintelligible call to them. A commotion erupted behind him as a crowd materialized from the shadows and followed. Some lumbered along slowly, too mutilated to remain very mobile. Others moved more quickly and they were pulling ahead of the pack. The approaching figures resembled the mob they had left behind in the alley. Not the same ones, but like them, and mortally injured.

Duane and Jamal turned quickly and ran back toward the alley.

"NO!" Chuck screamed, as Jamal's friends appeared from the darkness along with the mangled walking-corpses of the Hispanic gang members. They came pouring out, crawling and staggering from the black void. Duane reeled backward, crashing into Chuck, who caught him and jerked him upright before he could hit the ground. Jamal turned and fled north, running into another alley between two buildings with Chuck and Duane on his heels.

Chuck jumped from a full run into a chain link fence at an intersection with another street. Duane and Jamal scrambled up the wire behind him and tumbled over the top, dropping down to the asphalt on the other side.

Behind the fence, the alley was becoming filled. A ghoulish man with a broken neck fell into the fence ahead of the others. His head hung to the left, but his eyes stared straight ahead, watching them intently. Duane stumbled away from the fence just as the throng crashed into it.

"Jesus!" Duane shouted. The horde drowned out his cry in a crescendo of moans, screams, and howls. Some of them were on their knees attempting to dig under the fence, heedless of the fact that they were on asphalt and their labors would gain nothing. Others tried to climb up, only to lose their grip and fall back again. The rest of them were pawing at the wire, pushing and pulling in hopes of reaching the fleeing trio.

Chuck searched his mind for a rational explanation for what he was witnessing, and as he watched them claw at the fence, it was painfully clear what they were. These people were dead, and they were not the nice, quiet kind of dead. They were wicked-dead, possessed, and full of ill intent.

And so they ran, putting distance between themselves and the mob, traveling north until they saw the light of Pine Street. They stopped there on the corner beneath a street lamp to catch their breath. Duane was the first to speak.

"What's happening, Chuck? Whats wrong with those people? Why are they after us?"

Chuck could see the fear pasted on Duane's face as he spoke and the descent into all out panic that was soon to follow. If he didn't do something to get him under control it could cost his friend his life, and probably his own as well.

Chuck grabbed Duane by the front of his flowered shirt and stared into his almond-shaped eyes, still wide with fear. "Listen to me. We're in some bad shit here. Do you understand what I'm saying to you?"

Duane didn't answer.

Chuck tightened his grip. He was not getting through to him. He shook him roughly, hoping to drive his point home. "Wake up and listen to me."

Duane straightened his posture and appeared to be more focused.

"If we're not on our toes tonight we could end up like those things back there." Chuck pointed toward the alley. "We've got to be alert. Are you alert?"

Duane nodded, and pulled away from Chuck's grip. "I got it, okay? I got it. I'll be fine," he told him, struggling to conceal his embarrassment at crumbling under pressure. Don't worry about me, but since you seem to have all the answers, what do we do now?"

"I don't know. It'll be light soon. Maybe things will be better then. Maybe the cops will figure this shit out and take care of it," Chuck said.

Jamal laughed, "Yeah right, are you shittin' me? And if frogs had wings they wouldn't bump their asses on lily pads either. Those fools can't fix this shit. It ain't fixable." Jamal kicked a liquor bottle laying by the curb down the street and it crashed and broke on the other side. "How in the hell do you fix this shit?" he shrieked, casting his eyes heavenward.

"We have to keep it down." Chuck warned. You want more of those things showing up? I'll bet it's safe to say there are more of them hanging around in the shadows somewhere."

Duane said, "What are you talking about?—More? Why must there be more? And more what?…crazies?"

The words had just left Duane's lips when they heard it.

It was the roaring hum of a combined effort and it was growing louder and more intense. Duane stepped away from the curb and into the street for a better look. Chuck was right. They had made too much noise and drawn attention to themselves. But this was a different mob, different people, and with different injuries.

Holy shit, there's more coming," Duane said. "A lot more. Jesus, there's so many."

"We have to move." Chuck told Jamal. "I've got friends across town. That's where we're going. What are you gonna do? Are you coming with us?"

Jamal didn't answer at first. He was watching the approaching mob and listening to the sounds they were making. Some of them were being quite vocal and this seemed to excite the others who in turn upped the volume.

"I'm can't go back to my streets. There's too many of those fucked up people in between. It doesn't look like I've got a choice, does it? Looks like I'm with you, huh homeboys?" The way in which Jamal said it was an obvious stab at their lack of New York City behavior and genuine gang savvy. When they spoke, the South was heard in every word.

"Then I guess you're coming with us," Chuck said, and the three men moved north.

6

Blue lights flashed against the auburn walls of the buildings lining Broadway. The sky was aglow in the east as the sun kept its reliable date with morning.

Captain Roy Burns gazed toward the eastern sky. It was his hope that the arrival of the new day would bring some relief to the strange events that had unfolded during the night.

A state of emergency had been declared in the City of New York. Six police cars blocked Broadway at the intersections around the station in an effort to quell the chaos that had ensued in the immediate area.

Burns smoked a cigarette as he watched the sun rise above the apartment buildings in the distance. He had not smoked in ten years. But today he was willing to risk the addiction again. The effect of the nicotine went to work quickly. His head spun and he felt a little queasy, but in a good way. He was suddenly lighter on his feet and his mood improved.

Roy took one last drag and crushed the spent cigarette butt beneath his boot. He was still twisting his shoe on it when Darrin Holsinger came rushing through the doors waving a fax sheet high in the air.

"Sir, you're not going to believe this," he said, and shoved the paper into Roy's hand.

His inexperience was showing again. He was nervous and fidgeted from one foot to the other as he waited for the Captain to read the fax.

Roy finished reading. Shaking his head with an uncharacteristic chuckle, he handed the paper back to the young cop. "Where'd you get this? This is a joke."

"It's right off the fax machine, Captain. It's from the Associated Press."

Roy said, "It's a joke. It's gotta be."

"No sir, I don't think so." Holsinger shot back with a serious look.

"You're telling me you believe this garbage?"

Holsinger said, "Captain, word is starting to come in more frequently now. This isn't confined to New York anymore."

Burns started to walk to the southern end of the barricaded street as Holsinger shuffled along behind. "What are you telling me?" The Captain asked.

"The entire nation is affected. Almost all the way to California now," Holsinger replied.

Burns placed his right hand on the young cop's chest and the two men came to a stop.

"So that means we're dealing with walking dead men? Is that what you're telling me? Because that's what this paper says. If you ask me, it sounds like utter horse shit. What nut-job came up with that?" Roy Burns took off his hat and ran his hand from his forehead to the back of his neck. He could not believe the report. He certainly did not want to listen to some rookie. Walking dead men my ass, he thought, as he looked at Holsinger and stated gruffly. "That's ridiculous. That report is wrong."

"No sir, it's what the newswire is saying, and that's not the worst of it, Captain."

"Let me guess, aliens are causing it, Plan 9 from outer space, right?" Burns grinned sardonically.

Holsinger frowned at the implied jib, "No sir." He replied, and fell silent.

"Well, spit it out. What's worse than walking dead men? I mean, come on now, what could be more far-fetched than that?" He shook his head at the absurdity of words he heard himself speaking.

Holsinger said, "They're eating their victims, Captain. The dead are not just attacking the living…they are eating them." He spit the words out slowly and his voice shook.

Burns' brow furrowed deeply, processing this latest bit of impossible information. He wasn't laughing at the boy's ramblings now. Overnight, three of his men had been bitten by crazies from the street. Two of them had become ill, and were sent home. The other man, nursing the small bite to his finger, was holding out so far.

Daniel Flanagan approached from the southern roadblock. Roy watched him as he hobbled his way closer. His left hand was wrapped in white gauze and he rubbed at it. Concern for his friend showed in Roy's face.

"Go back inside and tell me if anything new comes over the wire," Burns ordered the young officer, who nodded grimly and walked away.

"You doing okay, Danny?" Roy called out to his friend as he approached.

"Aye, I'll be fine," he said, "My hand's just a wee bit sore."

Danny held out his hand, shaking it as if it would in some way make it feel better. Burns studied the bandage and saw that blood had seeped through, staining the gauze with spots of dark red.

"Let me take a look at that." Roy said.

"I told you, it'll be just fine. Besides, I'm a lefty. You know that. I won't be needin' the right one too much. It's a minor thing. Nothing to worry yourself over."

Burns bristled, "And I also told you to let me see it. Now that's an order. You let me worry about what I'll worry about."

Daniel Flanagan removed the cloth wrapping. He cursed to himself as he did so. Burns ignored his rants.

The scrapes on his knuckles had been mere scratches earlier. They were now swollen and oozed with infection. Red streaks moved up his arm, an indication that the infection was in full swing of invading his body. The wound looked painful and Danny winced as Roy lightly touched his hand.

"You need to go have that looked at. There's no tellin' what kind of infection you've got there. Didn't you say you busted your knuckles on one of those freaks last night?"

"Aye, and I'll have it looked at later. Right now you need my help, remember? Besides, I doubt they'd have time to look at me and this little injury with everything that's going on."

Roy looked him sternly in the eyes. "Well, if you will promise me that you will see a doctor when you get off shift. No bullshit Danny. Promise me."

Flannigan looked him in the eyes, smiled, and shook his head yes.

"You are right, I do need your help right now," Roy said. "I don't think I could handle what's happening without you, my old friend."

Danny wrapped the cloth tightly around the wound.

"Have you heard anything about what's happening Danny? I mean…anything strange?"

"Me? I've not had the time to hear a thing, well, other than that drivel coming over the tellies."

Burns nodded, "Follow me. I want to check something out."

"Where are we going?"

"Down to the cells. I just need to look at this more closely."

***

The jail cells were on the basement level, one floor below the street. It was a dank place with brick walls and concrete floors. A constant smell of mildew and urine permeated the walls of the subterranean cellblock. There were ten holding cages, five to the left, and five to the right. Most were full as they tended to be on any given morning, though the occupants of the precinct were more than a little unusual on this particular morning.

In the first cell to the right, a man cowered in the far corner. In the opposite corner, another man lie crumpled, his face hidden from view. The cowering man appeared to be on the verge of insanity. He shivered and shook with his fingers over his mouth, chewing at their tips. When he noticed them, he leaped from the floor and fell against the bars screaming wildly.

"You've got to get me outta here!" He shrieked, "And don't put anyone else in here with me."

Burns stopped. "What do you mean? And what's wrong with the guy in the cell with you? He's not moving."

"He wouldn't stop trying to bite me."

"What did you do?"

"I banged his head into the bars a few times. He stopped trying to bite me then. Look around. Can't you see?" The man began to whisper and pointed to the other cells. "The others…they're just like him. It's us against them. We are in a war. It's the dead against the living. Haven't you been watching the TV? It all started last night. I tried to tell your officers when they were arresting me at the bar. It's all over the news."

Burns moved in closer so he could hear what the prisoner was saying more clearly; close enough to smell the man's breath, and it reeked of alcohol.

"There must be something in Hell that's not quite right." The man said. "The devil's sending all the bad ones back to us. He's shipping their good for nothin' souls right back up to good ole planet Earth. They're getting returned to sender. Get it?" And then, at the top of his lungs, he started to sing—

"And the Devil wrote upon it,
Return to sender.
That address unknown.
No such person.
No such zone.
Return to sender.
That address unknown.
No such person.
And no fucking soul."

Then he started to cough and fell into the corner where he curled himself into a ball and wept. The cellblock erupted with the cries and moans of its other occupants. They extended their arms through the bars, their bodies pressed tightly there for maximum reach. Pale and emotionless faces as though their heads were simply propped onto animated bodies stared out at them, arms thrashing.

"Stay away from them." Burns whispered to his friend.

"Don't let them touch you. Stay to the middle of the aisle."

In the next line of cells there were two and sometimes three and four prisoners housed together. They all lashed out through the bars if they got close. Burns tugged at Daniel and the two men silently backed away.

A man in a gray sports jacket held his right arm through the bars and moaned. His fingers twitched as he extended them as far as he could. The prisoners in the other cells followed suit. They cried out, a peculiar mix of shrill squeals and animalistic cries. Some bounced and thrashed against the bars. Others held out their hands like hungry refugees begging for sustenance. Burns studied them, watching their actions and their eyes. Daniel moved to his side.

"Are you seeing what I'm seeing, laddy?" Daniel said. "I'm thinkin' there's something awfully wrong with these folks."

"How could I have missed this?" Burns whispered, "There's no mistaking it. I've seen the faces of the dead enough to know."

"As have I, Cap'n. There is no life left in these people. Somethin's far amiss and the old drunkard might be more right than we know."

Burns turned to the man again. "You!" He yelled. The man raised his head. "What are you in here for? You didn't kill anyone, did you?"

"I only had two beers, I swear. I could've driven home just fine. I told one of your boys that last night, but he would hear nothing of it—wouldn't listen to anything I tried to tell him. It was all over the news. With all that going on and he felt the need to bring in little ole me at two in the morning, and then put me in here with one of them. I swear, if this ain't the end of the world, you'll be hearing from my lawyer."

Burns pulled a set of keys out of the pocket of his blue pants and unlocked the cell door. "There was nothing about walking dead men coming over the wire last night. Not at this station. This is all news to me."

"Two beers…two goddamned beers. He didn't even give me a breath test. He threw my ass in here and forgot about me. If it's the end of the world, you get a pass. Otherwise, you ain't heard the last of this."

"Somehow I doubt it was only two beers since as far as I can tell, you're still drunk. I am going to let you out now, mainly because I just don't know what else to do with you, so just shut up and follow me."

Daniel followed Roy and the prisoner through the hallway, up the stairs, and through the precinct into the morning sun outside.

"Now, go before I change my mind. Go home, do you hear me? It's crazy out here on the streets, and if all this they are saying is true, it's not just crazy, but very dangerous. Go home and lock your doors. You're in no shape to take chances. And for God's sake, sober up."

Roy and Daniel watched the man as he walked away unsteadily to the south. To the North, a line of green military vehicles appeared at the barricade. Three soldiers jumped out of the back of one of the trucks and ordered his men to move the police cars so they could pass. They did so and the convoy rolled to a stop in front of the station. A small green Jeep pulled up to the curb in front of Roy and Daniel. A man in uniform stepped out of the passenger seat. The driver moved the vehicle forward another few feet where he waited with the engine running.

***

Colonel John Westinghouse of the National Guard surveyed his surroundings as if he were about to lay claim to his kingdom. His silvery hair was high and tight, barely visible under his combat helmet. His eyes were a steely blue that seemed to take in every minor detail as he scanned the area.

Speaking to no one in particular, and to anyone within earshot, he proclaimed. "By order of the President of the United States, all local law enforcement agencies are to surrender authority of command to the National Guard. My unit has been ordered to this section of the city. I am Colonel John Westinghouse."

Turning to Roy Burns and Daniel Flanigan he asked, "Who's in charge here?"

7

Michael Longley and the hospital guard remained with Doctor Riker. The rest had opted for the safety of their homes and to protect their families.

Adam Riker worried for his own family, his wife Meena in particular. He had tried several times to call her. The message repeated...

All circuits are busy. Please try again later.

Cell phones, landlines, everything was bogging down in the escalating chaos.

Riker watched the sun in the East as it crept above the horizon. In the distance sirens blared, wailing forlornly. In the street ahead, two cars had crashed into each other. A crowd of people were beating their fists against the crumpled, blue metal of a late, 70's Ford Pinto. The man who had been driving the other car was running to the north and away from the accident scene.

Unable to open the jammed door, one of them, a black man with much of his left side ripped open and hanging in shreds of torn flesh, picked up a large chunk of broken concrete and smashed the windshield. An unconscious teenager was dragged from the driver's seat and ripped apart on the street. He regained consciousness just in time to meet his fate, screaming as he died.

The small crowd feasted on his warm, young flesh as the three men watched, horrified.

It's not just in the hospital, it's out here too," Doctor Riker said. "It's in the streets—other cities. It's everywhere."

"How do they know?" The guard asked, his dark, powerful eyes narrowed as he watched.

"What?" Riker asked, turning his attention away from the carnage.

"They're not attacking each other. How did they know that guy in the car was still alive? Why aren't they hurting each other?"

Riker watched as more walking corpses slowly spilled from open doorways and into the street. They lurched forward as fast as their frail bodies would allow and joined the bloodbath.

Like too many dogs gnawing on a bone, each one fought for its fair share of meat. Some of them fought each other for small morsels of flesh, while others sat on the sidelines, their mangled faces buried in their gory feast.

"They're not just biting." Riker said, with disgust. "They're eating him—dear God."

They watched as the reanimates, one by one, abandoned their attack on the teenage traffic fatality. They got to their feet and shuffled away. Just then, the mangled victim struggled to find his own footing and followed his attackers. Even from their distance they could see the horrendous damage done to the boy. His head bent awkwardly onto his left shoulder. The right side of his neck had been completely devoured. His stomach was a gaping, dark hole. His entire stomach cavity had been eviscerated. Yet, he was standing and moving now and the others were no longer interested in him. He had become one of them.

Riker said, "Whatever is happening, it's escalating. I've got to get home. The roads will soon be impassable."

No one responded as the realization that time was growing short hit home. Michael put his hand on Doctor Riker's forearm to draw his attention. He put his index finger to his lips, "Shhhhhhhh," he exhaled as he slowly backed them away.

The growing crowd had spotted them. An ear-piercing wail echoed between the skyscrapers as the crowd began to move.

They moved slowly at first, as if stalking prey that was not yet aware of their presence. After a few steps forward, some of them increased their pace. A few of the less damaged ones were able to muster more speed than others and pulled ahead. Some jerked and poked along in an absurd and awkward gait, but the group moved as if one mind controlled them.

"Guys, I think we're in trouble." Michael stated the obvious, as if quoting a bad line from a B-movie.

"Shit," was all Adam could muster as Michael grabbed the tail of his coat and pulled him down the street. The guard followed them for a few yards, then abruptly changed direction and ran for a parked car. Michael turned and watched as he locked himself inside the vehicle.

"No!" Michael screamed, "It's not safe. They'll break in."

"Maybe it's his car," the doctor said.

The crowd changed direction and moved toward it.

"I don't think so," Michael said. "He'd have started it by now if he had the keys."

"He saw what happened to that guy up the street." Adam said. "Why would he lock himself in like that?"

The mob slammed into the car. The driver's door crumpled under the weight of their assault. Some of the slower, more damaged creatures lurched forward to join the fray until the car was totally surrounded.

"We've got to do something," Riker said. "They'll tear him apart."

"And what do you expect us to do, Doc? There are two of us and twenty of those—things. There's nothing we can do for him now. He's on his own."

The Doctor ignored Michael's warning and took a few steps toward the car. A middle-aged woman in a red leather mini-skirt jerked her head away from the vehicle. Her hair was long and blond with dark, black roots. Blood matted it, dried in clumps around her neck and chest. She moved away from the car, locking him in her gaze, then drew her lips back in a bloody grimace and screamed out.

Riker stopped.

Three more took notice.

One shrieked, and the other two forced their twisted bodies into awkward, but efficient movement.

There was a crash and the car's side window exploded in a shower of pebbled glass and the dead things lunged inside, covering the guard. His screams were muffled as he thrashed under their groping hands and gnashing teeth. The webbed windshield turned red with a spray of blood and the rocking stopped. Some of the attackers relaxed and feasted on the now motionless, murdered man. The rest turned to face Adam and Michael. Wide-eyed and painted in blood, they screamed out in ravenous anticipation.

Michael did his best to follow the doctor as he sprinted around the hospital and down a ramp into an underground parking garage. A shower of glass rained down on him as he sidestepped to his left. The falling glass splintered on the ground beside him, its shards exploding on impact. Above him, a woman on the fifth floor leaned out of a window and screamed before being pulled back inside.

"And you wanted to stay behind to go up there?" he reminded the doctor as he pointed up.

Without answering, Adam Riker sprinted into the darkness of the garage.

Adam found his black Lincoln Navigator right where he had left it on the third level. He fumbled with the keys as he took them from his pocket, managing to hit the small unlock button in full stride. Pressing the little button once opened the driver's door. Pressing it twice opened them all. Adam Riker pressed it once and slid to a stop in front of the driver's door.

Michael was just behind him. The dead things had not yet entered level three and Adam thought maybe they had lost them as he glanced over Michael's shoulder for their pursuers.

"Do you have a car to drive out of here?"

Michael was stooped over with his hands on his knees. He laughed at the doctor's question. "No, my car's on the interstate somewhere folded in half."

"Oh yeah, that was a stupid question. I'm sorry."

Michael waved off the doctor's blunder. "It's an honest mistake Doc. It's easy to forget the little details right now. Hell I can hardly remember my own name. It's Michael by the way."

"Do you have a place to go, Michael?" The doctor asked.

"Well, I'd like to get back to Oakridge Drive, but seeing as I have no transportation, and those things aren't likely to let me walk there, I'd say no."

"Okay, just tell me how to get to Oakridge Drive and I'll take you there."

Michael ran to the passenger's door. Adam unlocked it, and he jumped inside with a thud. "Get on the interstate traveling west and go halfway across the country."

Riker gave him a hard glare. "What?"

"I live in Chicago," He stated flatly.

Riker sighed.

"Don't worry Doc. I won't cause you any trouble. I'm a cop. Let's just get away from this hospital. I'll figure it out later."

"You can come with me to my place for now. We'll be safe there. Maybe things will be under control by tonight. Then you can figure out how to get back to Chicago. Maybe by then we'll know what caused this to happen and if there's a cure for those people."

"A cure? How can there be a cure? How do you cure someone who's had their guts ripped out and devoured? Can you cure my wife, Doctor? She's been dead for almost an hour, you said it yourself. They're dead. They just don't know it yet."

Doctor Riker nodded in agreement and put the vehicle in reverse.

Both men were looking over their shoulders when they felt a jolt from the first onslaught of undead pursuers. The horde moved from the front, then down the sides of the vehicle until they were completely surrounded. Their torn and tortured faces pressed against the windows as they pounded bloody fists to gain entrance. Adam Riker hit the lock button and the beautiful sound of locks dropping into place filled their ears.

Michael pressed tensely into the back of his seat as the windows on his side were smeared red by bloody appendages. One of them forced its way close to the vehicle, its scream piercing loudly through the din as though it were meant for his ears alone. It was Rebecca. His Becca. The metal scissor clamps still hung from her gapping chest cavity. They clanged against the glass as she thrust against it. She was like a wild animal, pawing and gnashing her teeth. Her eyes fixed on him and deadly intent filled her gaze. There was no love in her deadened eyes. He saw no recognition of him there as her husband, or the man she loved in life. For a moment he lost focus in her glazed and uncomprehending eyes. He had unconsciously pressed his own hand against the glass to hers as she groped for him. He wanted to reach through the window and grab her, to tell her he loved her one last time.

Adam stomped on the accelerator and the crowd fell behind. Michael wailed a high-pitched distress call as Adam swerved the vehicle to the left, dragging one of them with him for several yards before it lost its grip and fell away.

The doctor gave his new acquaintance a quick, sideward glance. "You okay?"

Michael nodded curtly. Swallowing the dry knot in his throat, he watched Rebecca fade until she was lost in the enveloping crowd behind them.

8

Colonel Westinghouse placed his maps on a folding table and weighed down the corners with spare ammunition clips. As he spoke, he traced a circle in the center of the map with his fingertip.

"We must move the population to the center of the city. Once we have everyone, we create a barrier, here, here, and at this point for protection." He pointed to several strategic locations in downtown Manhattan.

Roy shook his head in disbelief as he studied the barrier points that the Colonel had just plotted. He knew this particular strategy, while a neat and tidy plan on paper, it was virtually impossible in reality. "No goddamned way is that gonna work. You're creating a deathtrap. The best thing you can do is get everyone *out* of the city."

Westinghouse glared up at him. "Have you been to the outer perimeters of the city, Captain?"

"No, I've not had a chance to get off this goddamned street. But I know one thing Sir, if you corral everyone into the location you just showed me on this map, there will be no place for a retreat."

"Yes that is true," Westinghouse said, "Unfortunately, retreat will not be an option. The outer perimeters have all fallen to the infected. There is no place left to run. We must make a stand here. We simply don't have another choice. If we could have acted sooner…maybe saw this coming."

Roy opened his mouth to speak, but before he could counter with another protest, Colonel Westinghouse continued.

"It seems the bite is the key to this illness. As people slept, this thing spread unchecked. The roads are clogged and those things are everywhere. The traffic jams at the tunnels and bridges are breeding grounds for infection. We've had thousands of fleeing citizens attacked as they sat in their cars with no escape. No sir…This plan is our only option at this point. We set up our lines here in the city at these points and fight them as they come in. We'll blow the bridges and block the tunnels if need be, but we'll hold the lines here in Manhattan."

Roy Burns stared into the endless stretch of Broadway and to what would be the last semblance of relative calm for the street and his men. The glittering Boulevard had no visible end as its marquee lights still sparkled in the early dawn, their gleam extending into infinity. Turning to the Colonel, he asked, "You're telling me that we are going to crowd several million people into the middle of Manhattan Island and wait this thing out?" With more than a hint of sarcasm, he continued. "Well now, that's certainly going to be quite a task."

Westinghouse ignored the stone in Roy's voice, and circled Central Park on the map. "Just to the south of the park we'll set up an area that is four blocks by eight blocks in size. If we need to, we will blow up a few buildings and bulldoze the rubble into the streets to create barricades."

Roy shook his head in disbelief. "You'll never get all those people into an area that size."

The Colonel thought for a moment. He considered sugar coating the situation. Maybe that would make things move more smoothly with a man like Burns. He knew that when dealing with civilians, a light touch, and sometimes bending the truth could go a long way in eliciting cooperation. So the Colonel carefully considered his next move. The Captain was a stern looking fellow, and he was sure the events of the night had shaken him. But there was something there in his eyes; a determination of will that a lifetime of police work had etched into his outer veneer. He was the kind of man who could spot deception, a man who had seen enough of the dark side to know when the light was being dimmed. The truth was his best option with Roy Burns.

"Captain, we just fought our way through the Lincoln Tunnel, not to mention half this city to get here. I know what's out there. We're not going to have to accommodate that many people. We will be doing battle with more souls than we will be protecting."

"How can that be?" Burns asked. But thinking back on the scene he had witnessed in the cellblock he knew it was the truth. As if his protests might have the power to stop the inevitable, he stammered on, "I've been on duty through the night. Whatever this is…it just started."

"It's even worse than that Captain Burns, at least here in New York. Yesterday evening, at approximately twenty-two hundred hours, reports started coming in from western Pennsylvania. Acts of violence committed by unknown assailants. The reports were widespread and grew in frequency as the night progressed. By midnight reports were also coming in from Cleveland, Cincinnati, Washington, D.C, and Atlanta. Shortly thereafter New York City was affected as well. As we speak, the problem has become worldwide. Today at twelve hundred hours, the President will declare Martial Law in most major U.S cities. It is my job to prepare this city for that decision and protect civilians from further infection. I am in command here, Captain, but I will need the help of local law enforcement. I need to count on your cooperation."

Burns nodded, but was unsure if he understood completely. Was it the end of the world? Is that what the Colonel was implying? "What's causing it, do they know?" he asked, as he refocused his thoughts.

"No one knows. There are lots of theories. The television news channels are full of kooks with all kinds of far-fetched stories. Right now we need facts. We have to combat this situation in the best and most efficient way possible. It's spreading and it's spreading fast. Because of the population density, New York has been affected worse than anywhere else. We're in some bad shit here, Captain."

"Colonel, reports have been coming in that the dead are coming back to life and that they're responsible." Burns said. "Of course I know how fantastic that sounds, but my men are starting to come a little unglued when they hear crap like that and I'd like to believe those reports are wrong."

The Colonel said, "Captain, my advice to you is to go on the assumption that those rumors are true. Forget about what you've come to think of as your comfortable little world. The rules have changed. We are in a whole new situation now."

The Colonel locked eyes with Roy Burns to emphasize how serious the situation had become. He glared at him; steely eyed and uttered six words…

"This is a whole new world."

Stepping forward and putting his right hand on Roy's shoulder, he spoke to him in a subdued and gravely serious tone. "It would be a good idea to have all your men outfitted in riot gear. Make sure they understand that the infected mobs are transferring the illness through the saliva of bites. And stay clear of contaminated blood. If you get any on you, wash it off as soon as you can. As of twelve hundred hours, their orders will be to shoot suspected diseased persons in the head on sight. No exceptions"

When Captain Burns only stared at him he said, "Did you hear me, Captain? In the head. Body shots are no good. You can shoot the bastards in the stomach and chest all day and they will keep coming, but one shot in the head…well, that puts them down. They're saying it's something to do with the brain. That's what allows them to get back up again. Oh yeah, they're dead all right. There's no way they are anything but dead. You just make sure your men don't hesitate. If they do, it'll cost them their lives."

"I'll brief my men. They'll be ready." Burns told him, "They're good men."

"Good men hesitate, Captain." Westinghouse said softly, "Good men die. If we're to set up our defenses for the inner part of the city it is imperative that you hold Broadway right here." The General said, and pointed to the intersection at the next block. "Keep them from crossing that barricade."

"We'll do our part," Burns said.

The Colonel pulled a half-smoked cigar from his pocket. Chomping down on the partially chewed end with his murmur barely audible, he said, "As we all will Captain and God help us."

9

The city had come to life only to find itself in the spasms of a death throe. The streets were impossible to navigate by automobile. There were abandoned vehicles and scattered accident scenes. The number of roving corpses was increasing exponentially. They wandered the streets and alleys like gangs of mindless murderers. Anyone with a beating heart was attacked. Car alarms droned over the already panicking and noisy street as people ran this way and that. Some ran unwittingly into the arms of walking corpses where they were wrestled to the ground in a frenzy of blood and gore. A huge explosion echoed against the buildings and the street shook with the blast. Chuck dove to the ground as Duane and Jamal fell in his wake. Black smoke billowed up from behind a building just east of them. Chuck raised his head for a glimpse and realized that he was lying face to face with a dead man on the sidewalk. The corpse wore a shredded white shirt and his blue tie was pulled up around his head. An iron pipe was lying loosely in his open hand and Chuck grabbed it as he scrambled to his feet.

The man stared blankly up at him as if still in shock over what had happened. A pointed and bloody shard of glass protruded from the man's stomach. It had been used to rip open a gapping cavity and spill the intestinal contents. In that same instance, Chuck detected a hunched and furtive figure close by; a bald man, with his full face buried in a handful of trailing, purple intestines, which he greedily ate. He gobbled them down in huge mouthfuls never once choking on his hideous bounty. Duane recoiled at the site and crawled backward, crashing into the brick wall behind him. He flattened himself there as if trying to blend into the brown and sand colored brick. Jamal simply stared in stunned silence, unable to move or say a word.

Chuck felt a tug as his ankle turned and his balance was knocked askew. The man at his feet had awakened and reached out for him. His mouth was opened wide and presented jagged, broken teeth.

Chuck pulled away and brought the pipe down hard on the animated cadaver's back. There was a loud crack as club met bone and it fell back to the concrete walkway. It squirmed in search of solid footing. Three times Chuck swung, and three times the ghoul went down only to rise again. Finally Chuck laid a crushing blow to its left temple. It went down then, dead at last.

Without warning the squatted man rose and lunged. It fell into Chuck and clasped its bloody hands around his throat. Chuck bulled forward and swung, this time with a deliberate shot to the head. The creature's skull exploded in a shower of grey matter and skull fragments. Chuck and Duane were spared the gruesome spray, but Jamal was not so fortunate. His face was covered in the foul spillage and he dropped to his knees where he knelt, vomiting.

"We've gotta go man." Chuck warned, speaking deliberately to Jamal who was choking and gagging out a steady stream. Chuck suddenly seemed unfazed by the confrontation and resulting carnage. It was an illusion, another act to hide his true feelings and fears. It was something he was experienced at doing. Chuck's calm veneer and wise-cracking jokes were often just cover for his own insecurities, weaknesses he would rather not show. Not to anyone, not even Duane, and certainly not to Jamal.

Jamal gagged again and another torrent of vomit splashed onto the concrete between his outstretched arms.

"It's too dangerous here, Jamal. There are too many and they've seen us," Chuck said. "We've got to move—right fucking now!"

Jamal looked up from his position on all fours. People were running. Some ran fast, others slowed by various injuries. It was difficult to tell at first glance which ones were alive and which ones were not. Across the street, an old man held tightly to his leashed dog. The dog was alive enough as he pulled the old man along, but the old man himself was one of the dead things. Blood caked the right side of his face, and even from across the street his glazed eyes were noticeable. He was dead, and the dead man was taking his dog for a morning stroll, or was it the other way around?

"If you don't come now we are going to leave you here. Do you hear me?"

"Why don't they try to eat the dog?" Jamal asked.

"What?"

Jamal pointed to the old man with the dog. "See? He ain't trying to eat the dog. Neither are any of the others."

Chuck couldn't wait any longer and pulled Jamal to his feet, and said. "I know a place over on Thirty-third to hole up. We'll be safe there until we can figure out what to do."

"What to do?" Duane laughed, "We get the hell out of this city, that's what we do. We get out of New York and back to our families in Virginia."

"Talk as we walk." Chuck said, and pulled them along. "We can't just run for the hills. We have to have a plan. Imagine if we try to get out of town by way of the Lincoln Tunnel. What if it's blocked with traffic and those things are down there too? We'd have a real problem getting through."

Duane said. "Do you have a better idea, Chuck? That's the only doable way for us to get home. Any other will be too far and too difficult. It's the fastest way out of the City."

"That may very well be, or maybe it isn't. Too much is happening right now and if we don't get off these streets we won't have to worry about it. I need time to think."

***

Chuck knew Duane was right. The Tunnel *was* their best way out of the city and getting out must be their first priority. New York was falling apart and it wouldn't be long before they were cut off completely. Less populated areas would be much safer than where they were. In a city the size of New York, rationality was breaking down quickly. In the few short blocks they had come, it had become noticeably more dangerous. Maybe it wasn't happening anywhere else, Chuck thought. Maybe the phenomenon was confined to New York; all the more reason to escape.

***

Chuck ducked into an alley and pulled the other two in with him, out of sight of the carnage happening in the streets. They would soon reach the docks and what could only be described as a street gang's crack hole. "You might want to think twice about going where we're going, but you're welcome to come with us if you like," he said to Jamal.

He secretly hoped Jamal would decline the offer and find his own way out of the city. Where they were going, Jamal would not be welcome. "We're entering Skipjack territory. You know what that means."

Jamal's jaw tightened. "I know what it means. It don't matter much. I'll be okay."

Chuck nodded, and without further thought to it, he and Duane darted back into the street.

Jamal waited there for a moment as if weighing his options. That indecision was short-lived. There was a resounding crash, and two trashcans tumbled from the corner where they had been stacked.

From the darkness, a figure lurched forward. Its movement was jerky and unwieldy as it entered the semi-light at the front of the alley.

Jamal recognized the ghoulish man. It was Scar.

Scar was a street bum named for the large scar that creased the entire left side of his face. He was a life-long panhandler and well-known in this part of the city. Word on the street was that he had received the injury to his face in hand-to-hand combat with a Vietnamese soldier. It was 1968 and in the Quảng Trị province of Vietnam. His valor had saved his entire outfit. He was a decorated war hero who had fallen on hard times. But Jamal always figured it to be nothing more than, 'urban legend'.

Scar fell hard into him.

"Help me," Scar cried. "Help me, please." He held out an injured hand as he begged. There was a bite wound between his thumb and forefinger.

Jamal shoved him back and sprinted out of the alley to where Chuck and Duane waited. The three men then continued on their way without further mind to the old man's plight.

Scar slid down the damp, smooth limestone wall and crouched there on the cold concrete, where he cried.

10

Michael didn't realize the vehicle had come to a stop.

Awareness came gradually. He noticed the silence first, as if waking from a dream world, likely still affected by the concussion. He came back to reality as the screams and sirens rose to deafening levels around him and a man on the car's radio telling people to stay in their homes.

To his right stood the familiar façade of The United Nations building. Tall and slender, it stood on some of the most expensive real estate in the city. Armed guards were stationed at its entrance. There were several dead bodies splayed on the sidewalk, blood pooled around their heads.

Again the car began to move forward.

Michael watched as wailing police cars screamed, plowing past them on the sidewalk as the traffic thickened. The red flash of break lights caught Michael's attention as the squeal of tires on asphalt heralded the abrupt halt of their vehicle. "Good God, man." He loudly proclaimed to the universe. "This is crazy. The traffic is too thick, and those things could be anywhere." He expelled a sigh of relief and gazed through his window at a car parked on his right. A homeless man washed its windshield. He marveled at the ignorance of the street bum still pandering for quarters even as the world fell apart. Was he so pre-occupied with his eventless life that he had failed to recognize the destruction around him?

But Michael had judged too quickly. On closer inspection, he realized the man was not a panhandler at all. The man was pounding the vehicle with a staccato jerk of his body, trying to break through the windshield. The driver looked over at Michael, his eyes wide in disbelief, his mouth wrapped around a silent scream. He recognized the look on the driver's face. For Michael, it was like looking into a mirror. The eyes said it all. The fear shone starkly in the dark irises surrounded by the whites of shock, a rational mind not comprehending the madness of the moment.

He wanted to calmly explain to the driver. "It is what it is." That is what he would say to him. "Sir, we have entered a new reality. My good man, we are living not like yesterday, but for all of our new tomorrows. For all of our days now we will need to fight to survive." This is what he would tell the man if he could. But it would make no difference. He could see reflected in the man's eyes, that same message, that same fear, that indeed the worst had happened.

The driver looked up into the windshield of his car and screamed something that was lost behind the windows of the closed up automobile. Then the car lurched forward as the man drove up onto the wide Manhattan sidewalk running over people, dead and undead. The car jerked to a stop for a few seconds, only to lurch forward as one reanimate stepped in front of him. Once he was on the street, he stepped down hard on the gas and weaved through the clogged traffic until he got to the next intersection where he turned the wrong way on a one-way street.

Michael wanted to flee. He had an incredible urge to jump from his ride and run as fast and far as his legs would carry him. It seemed to be what most others were doing. But logic dictated a better course of action. Where would he run? The city was too big and too dense with traffic. To panic would mean certain death, or as certain as death might now be.

The Doctor veered left at a Y in the road and crept along with the rest of the traffic. There was a bronze and glass tower on their left. Above the green awning of its main entrance in large letters, Trump World Tower shone in the morning sun. It was a work of art, architecturally speaking, in the way a building could be a work of art. Ostentatiously built to be impressive and beautiful, this residential skyscraper was one of the most elite and expensive places to live in all of New York. The Doctor inched the vehicle forward and turned left beside the World Tower. A man ran in front of them and came to a stop to their right. He balanced himself on a waist-high wall overlooking a road that ran below normal street level and disappeared into a tunnel. He steadied himself there for rest until another grotesquely injured man crashed into him. Both men went sailing over the edge and out of sight to the pavement below. The presence of evil was stirring in the air. Michael could sense it. It was building to a fever pitch and threatened to consume everyone and everything around them.

Adam pulled into the entrance of the World Tower and came to a stop in front of the parking garage. The gate was open, the attendant's post, abandoned. Adam hesitated for a moment, then slowly inched forward and down into the darkened confines of the underground space.

The garage was exclusive to World Tower residents, and each resident had their own private parking space and marked as such—Apt 101, 102 and so on. But on this day, Adam made no attempt to find his own. Today, he made a beeline for an open area beside the elevator clearly marked, 'Authorized personnel only.'

They sat there for a while, silently. Each unable to move or utter a word. The morning's events raced through Adam's mind in menacing fashion, threatening his now tenuous grip on sanity. He had made it safely home, but he wondered how long it would be before the horror outside followed him there as well? His hands shook as they gripped the steering wheel until his knuckles turned red. First, he would call Meena. He had to know if she was safe. Only then could he fully concentrate on his own well-being.

"Why are we here?" Michael blurted out. "This is parking for the World Tower. Why are we here?"

"It's where I live—on the eighth floor. The radio said we should stay in our homes so that's what we'll do. We can find out more from the television."

"They should have instructed everyone to just stay where they were. The streets are clogged with people trying to get home. They're running right into the danger they are being told to avoid."

Adam pulled his keys from the ignition.

"Security is tight here so just follow me and you'll have no problem getting inside."

Michael followed closely behind Adam as they walked toward the elevator doors. The garage was eerily quiet with only the echoes of the chaos outside drifting in to them as muted background noise. There in the confined, hardened darkness, their steps echoed in repeated pings off the concrete walls as they walked to the elevator, splitting the welcomed calm.

Adam stopped and stooped down to touch the floor at his feet and then examined his fingers. They were red with fresh blood as was the floor all around them. A chill ran down his spine and he could feel himself become rigid. The horror had indeed found them again, even here in their exclusive, high-dollar sanctuary.

"They're in here," he whispered. "Or they were." He showed Michael the blood on his fingertip and on the floor.

"We don't have any weapons. Do you have any guns in your home? Anything we can use to protect ourselves?"

"Are you kidding? This is New York City. Only the criminals have guns here."

"A pipe, a good solid club…anything?"

"There's a tire iron in the back of my car. Will that do?"

"It'll help." Michael said.

Adam pulled the keys from his pocket and pressed the button twice. With two quick chirps the rear door unlatched and he removed a side panel that concealed a tire jack and lug wrench. With a pop, the wrench came loose and he slammed the rear door shut again.

Adam held out the tire iron for Michael to take, who examined it for a moment, then waved it away. "You should keep it. I'm better with my hands."

"As you wish," Adam said, and pressed the button on the elevator.

After a minute the doors slid open and the two men were caught by surprise.

The two elevator passengers lunged forward and both Adam and Michael fell to the floor under the weight of the unexpected onslaught. The tire iron slipped from Adam's grip and skidded across the floor as he fought to hold his attacker at arm's length. It moaned and squirmed to break free, all the while snapping like some kind of vicious animal. It was all he could do to just hold it there and not get bitten. To his left he could hear thrashing as

Michael wrestled with his own fiend. Adam had glanced over just in time to see him get to his feet and grab the tire iron.

With a swooshing swing, the weapon made contact with the monster's head. The brute spun around and fell to the concrete. In that moment, Adam found the strength to kick his own demon away and with a devilish look in his eyes, Michael wasted no time and swung again at the second man.

This time he swung harder, and with more emotion as he screamed out his anguish. The crooked end of the weapon came down hard on the monster's skull. It created the most disturbing sound as metal met bone. Adam Riker was a surgeon and was familiar with the sound of sawing bone, but this was different. It was the violent attack itself that created the nauseating thud that made Adam swallow hard and feel sick to his stomach. The man stepped back and wobbled for a moment before collapsing to the concrete floor of the parking garage. Michael was breathing heavily as Adam stood and brushed off his clothes.

"It's the garage attendant." Adam said, and pointed down to the one killed last. He wore a blue uniform with a black collar. "That one there is Phillip Westbank. He lives in the building too. I never did care too much for him. Arrogant asshole."

"You've got blood on your face, Doctor," Michael said.

Adam wiped the blood from his cheek with the tail of his dirty white coat. It blended in with the blood already there from the surgeries earlier. He had not been bitten. The blood was from the dead man and not himself. He wiped his cheek again to make sure he had gotten it all.

"Were you bitten, Michael?"

"What?"

"Were you bitten? I think it may be important."

"No, I wasn't." Michael told him, "Why important?"

"In the emergency room earlier this morning, one of our nurses was bitten. She died of blood loss, I know, I saw, but she came back as one of these…revived, dead things soon after."

"So you're saying it's linked?"

"Maybe."

"No, that's not right. My wife was not bitten and she turned into one of them too. That can't be right. Anyone that dies must become one of them. That has to be it, if they are indeed dead."

Adam said, "Oh they're dead, as we know the definition of dead to be, anyway. There's no way your wife was alive. Look, until we know for sure, just be careful. Do your best to not let them bite you."

"Doc, I saw what they were doing in the street near the hospital. They're doing more than biting. They're eating the people they attack. Now I don't know what that means exactly, but you can bet your ass I will try my best to avoid getting bitten." Michael held out the tire iron again and Adam took it. "You'd better learn how to use that thing and hold on to it next time. I hit these men in the head and it brought them down. At least we know they can be killed."

Adam nodded, and said, "Who's to say they won't get back up again? They were dead before you hit them with that tire iron. What *is* dead? I don't know anymore."

Michael said, "Maybe you better gimme that thing back—at least for now."

Adam handed him the weapon and pressed the elevator button again. The door had closed while they were wrestling with the two dead men. This time, the doors swished open right away to reveal an empty elevator and the two stepped inside.

"We'll go straight to my apartment. There's no reason to endanger ourselves in the lobby just yet."

"Those two were in the elevator. For all we know the whole damned building could be overrun too. We had better be prepared when that door opens again." Michael said.

***

There was a dead man lying in the middle of the hall when the doors opened to the eighth floor. He had been stabbed in the left eye and stared blankly up at them with the one still in its socket. Adam hesitated, and then stepped over it on his way to Apartment 803. Michael walked around it all the while watching for movement with a suspicious eye. Adam's lack of surprise or shock at the sight did not register right away as he walked to his door. His mind was on other things, mainly Meena. She was out of the country on business. His first priority was to make sure she was safe. It would be later in the day there. He wasn't even sure if England was having the same problem. Maybe she was safe after all. If so, he would tell her to stay put until things were under control.

The Apartment door opened to a large foyer and living room with plush carpet and ceilings that rose to twelve feet in height. Windows that were nearly as tall lined the room, spaced every three feet along two walls. The furniture was ultra modern with sharp angles and corners. Dark blue curtains lined the walls in contrast to the light paint and furnishings. Adam went directly to the phone and address book. He flipped through the pages until he found Meena's number, and dialed.

It rang only once before the recording picked up;

We're sorry, but you cannot reach that number as dialed. Please hang up and call your operator.

The message repeated and Adam hung up in frustration and then tried again. When he got the same message he hung up and just dialed zero. He was rewarded for his efforts with another recording,

All circuits are busy. Please try your call later.

Adam drew back as if to throw the phone against the wall, but then thought better of it and placed it on the table in front of the sofa.

"Phones are down," Adam said.

"I'm sorry. Maybe they'll work later."

Adam nodded, and walked to the window facing West towards the Empire State Building. He stood there silently taking in the scene below before motioning for Michael to join him.

The view from the eighth floor was far from perfect to see all of Manhattan, but what they could see took their breath away. Fires burned and smoke billowed from high-rise windows. Cars were strewn across the streets in barricades of charred frames and burning heaps of twisted metal. Chaos reigned supreme in the streets below them. The same streets only minutes before had been chaotic, but passable. Now they were impenetrable walls of death. The revived dead were everywhere.

Michael leaned forward into the window until his head rested against his own forearm. "As I see it, we've got two choices. "We can either barricade ourselves here in your building and wait this thing out, or we can make a run for the other side of the river."

Adam sighed, "And what if this doesn't end anytime soon? What then?"

"How much food do you have here?" Michael said.

"I don't know, enough for the two of us for a week or more. We ate out a lot." Adam said.

"We'll have to get as much water as we can before the power fails," Michael added. "Judging by what's going on down there, I'd say it will eventually."

"What about Meena? I have to find out if she's okay."

"I'd say the best place to do that is right here. Have you tried your cell phone?"

Adam threw him a defeated glance.

"You do have one, don't you?" Michael asked.

Yes, of course I have one, but in all the commotion I left it at the hospital. How bout you? Do you have one?"

"It's still in my car somewhere, lost in the accident last night."

"Then I guess my hopes rest in the good ole land lines working again."

"And until then?" Michael asked.

"I guess we take option number one and hole up here for a while."

"Then we've got a lot of work to do," Michael said with authority, "starting with the dead guy in the hall. Did you know him?"

"Never saw him before today, but I don't know most of the people in this building."

"What if it gets up again and starts to walk around? He could still come after us."

"No, I don't think so," Adam said. "He looked dead. I mean really dead. The transformation is fast. It seems like he would have been up by now. But I can't be sure. Who could?"

Michael said, "Maybe we should do as you said and turn on that television. Someone has to know more about what's going on than we do. I mean, how many times do we have to kill what's already dead?"

11

The Skipjacks had been known to call Chuck and Duane foot soldiers. It meant they were on the lowest end of the totem pole or on the bottom rung of the ladder. Some even referred to them as being from *'no where'* which meant they were not part of the outfit at all, but rather outsiders and not privy to most gang activities. Outsiders were not trusted and Chuck knew he was taking a chance to be at the group's hideout uninvited. With so many dying in the streets, it would be easy to come up missing or get a 'bus ticket.' And anyone who hung with gangs knew a bus ticket was really a ticket to hell. To make matters worse, Jamal was surely not welcome. Those from the streets no longer respected him. He too was outside their ring of trust. Chuck had good reason to be nervous, and he was regretting more and more his rash invitation for Jamal to tag along with them.

Chuck turned, "You gotta be cool, Jamal. I'm nobody from nowhere here, know what I mean? I've got no leverage. If someone shows up and you step outta line, even a little, someone's liable to bust a cap in your ass. And they won't stop there. Me and Dewey will end up floating face down in the East River with you."

"Yeah? Well, I'm strapped, so if anyone wants to take that shot, they'll get one back. This little Tray Eight is sure to be my best friend today."

"What the hell is a Tray Eight?"

"Man, you really are a poor boy, aren't you?

Jamal laughed, but Chuck found no humor in the fact that he didn't know some of the accepted gang lingo. That meant he was out of the loop, and out of the loop meant weak to gangers. Weak meant of no use. The river was full of those who had no use. That much he did know.

"It's a .38 Special man. It does the trick."

Chuck grumbled at Jamal. The gun could be useful, but it was just as likely that he'd use it on them as it was anyone else. He needed to establish his dominance as the alpha male to ensure Jamal's continued cooperation.

"You just keep that thing tucked away unless it's really needed, understand? I don't care what half ass soap opera star or bullshit rapper wannabe you think you are, or were…or whatever. When you're with me, I'm in charge. This ain't the set of one of your stupid shows. It's the real world and shit's done gone crazy. We need to be on the same page to get through this."

Jamal seemed to puff up for a moment. His angular jaw flexed, sawed back and forth, and for an instant it seemed as though he would make a move. His brown eyes narrowed and Chuck could see the anger there. Then as though nothing were wrong at all, he mellowed and a slight smile eased his expression.

"It's not a big deal," he said, "We'll call this your turf for now. But I do expect a little respect while I'm here."

"Fair enough. Just keep your cool. No flying off the handle. I don't want you accidentally shooting one of us."

Jamal licked his lips and nodded his agreement.

***

The door to the Dock hideout was opened inward. And at first glance, the little shack appeared to be abandoned. The salt air was strong. Not that the East River was all that salty. Rather, it was the wind that blew in from the east on this morning. It brought with it the scent of the sea and freshness not found in the inner part of the city. Downtown Manhattan reeked of exhaust fumes, asphalt and the homeless. It was always a breath of fresh air to come down to the docks. Maybe not as pleasurable as the smells associated with Chuck's real home in the Shenandoah Valley with its honeysuckle and freshly cut grass, but it was still a welcome experience to the senses.

Chuck entered the room first, squinting in the dim light and bumped his knee on a table on his way to turn on the lamp. He stumbled and winced at the pain. Nerves all but shot, his eyes darted from left to right, then back to the left again, half expecting to be pounced on by a walking dead thing, or worse yet, a pissed off Skipjack gangbanger. But the room was empty and he was thus far, unmolested.

Chuck moved silently to the door of the back room. The hideout was a dismal little place and the back room was a damp, dirty, little screw hole. It smelled of sweat and old sex. A mattress lay caddy-corner with a few dingy blankets strewn about, its center stained with urine. Chuck was hesitant to touch anything. He had seen some of the trash brought in, the toothless, skeleton-like heroine addicts with bruised arms, dirty and disheveled. If you stood too close to them you could smell their unwashed femininity.

As Chuck took in the room he couldn't help but think that Duane was right. This wasn't the place for them. They were better than this. He wasn't sure what he had been thinking when he came up with the bright idea to stay in New York. Endless opportunities he had thought. Really what you needed was endless pockets. Their money had run out in a matter of weeks. If not for the Skipjacks they would've gone hungry. Without them, they would've had no choice but to go home. For a while that didn't appeal to Chuck, but now all he could think about was the safety of the mountains and how could he get there in one piece. Surely it was better there than in the mega-metropolis of New York City. Nothing could be worse than this.

"It's clear," Chuck shouted over his shoulder to Duane and Jamal, still crouched by the door outside. "No one's here. From the looks of it, no one's been here all night. We can hole up for a while and get some rest, clear our heads. I've not closed my eyes since the night before last."

Duane entered hesitantly, but Jamal bounded into the room slamming the door shut behind him. He flopped down on a torn, vinyl chair by a window facing the river. All this seemed not to bother him so much. Chuck considered the choices that either Jamal was very brave or very foolish. The latter was more likely.

"Maybe we should lock the door and board up that window," Jamal said, motioning to the cracked and dirty glass. It was a small window, but none-the-less, could be a weakness in their defense. "We don't want those things getting in here."

"No, that's a bad idea," Chuck countered. "If those things come down here we need to see them before they get us cornered in this little shit-hole. We also need an easy way out. Boarding everything up in my opinion is the wrong move. They're slow and weak. We can handle it."

Jamal said, "You might be right. This place will have me bored shitless in short order. Best we don't get stuck here too long, but I'll tell you this…they ain't all so damned slow and weak. Some of 'em put up a fight. Don't forget, some of those things gutted several of my boys last night. They may be slow but they are dangerous."

Chuck walked to the window and leaned against the wall so that he could more easily see the street in the direction of downtown Manhattan. He considered rubbing away some of the grime so he could see better, and did start to do so, but stopped in mid-motion and whispered to Duane. "Lock the door—hurry."

Duane moved quickly to the door and turned the lever on the deadbolt to the upright position just as the thump came. Instinctively, he drew away from it until his back was flat against the far wall as the doorknob giggled.

"Quiet," Chuck whispered, and with a finger in front of his lips, he said, "Don't let them hear you."

Chuck pulled the grimy curtains closed over the window and backed away. "There are two of them out there. Maybe they'll go away if we stay quiet. Maybe they don't know we're in here. Did they see us come inside?"

Jamal leaped from the chair and brandished his weapon about recklessly. "Check it out, I'll blow their fucking brains out. Just let 'em come crashing in here."

"Put that thing away" Chuck told him in the quietest voice he could muster and still get his point across. "Sit down and stay quiet. I'm telling you, they don't know we're in here."

"Then why are they at the door?" Duane asked, "If they don't know we're here, why are they trying to get inside?"

Chuck skulked back to the window and peered between the curtain and the wall. One man groped at the door. He had stopped messing with the knob and was now feeling around the exterior wall with his hands, infantile in his attempt to gain entrance. He was old, but not one of the homeless. He wore a gray, three-piece, pinstriped suit that was covered in blood down the front to his knees. The left sleeve of his jacket and shirt were ripped off and his arm was badly injured. He paid no mind to the wound, nor seemed to be bothered by pain at all. His face was expressionless and without discernable emotion. The other man took baby steps and walked in a small circle staring at the concrete directly in front of him as he moved. He repeated the motion over and over like some mentally retarded dog on Quaaludes chasing his own tail. It was a strange and humorous sight, and it almost made Chuck laugh out loud.

Jamal leaned in and watched with Chuck as the two men did their thing outside. "What are they?" Jamal asked.

"You know what they are…you saw some of them die and come back," Chuck said.

"No," Jamal explained, "I mean why? Why are they coming back to life? Why are they coming after us?"

Chuck let the curtain fall back into place.

"It's the Great Tribulation," Duane interjected from the corner of the room, "All Satan's demons are here on Earth. They know their time is short and they're pretty pissed off."

Chuck let out a deep sigh and gave Duane a sideways glance, "We need to get out of this city."

12

The Colonel and his men had stayed long enough to raise eight-foot plywood walls at the intersection south of the station before leaving again. Minutes later, the call to arms went out and Roy's men scurried to man their positions behind the walls.

The city was alive with sirens and alarms as Roy Burns charged through the station doors into the sunlight with his remaining force trailing in his wake. He turned and watched as Daniel Flanagan hobbled from the precinct house, his long-tailed shirt flapping in the wind. Daniel wrestled to get it on properly as he juggled his rifle from one hand to the other, wincing when it was held in his injured hand.

"Come'on laddy," Daniel said with a sly grin. "You're doin' no good standin' there. Get your arse in gear. There's someone a knockin' at the door."

Roy managed a half-hearted smile, no small task under the circumstances. The barricade was breaking down as an unknown number of dead cannibals beat and pounded at the plywood walls built there to slow them down. Three-foot high concrete barriers stood between his men, the wall, and the hordes of corpses making their way up Broadway.

The wall bowed inward with their combined weight, and some of the supporting struts split apart and separated from the sections they were designed to brace.

Roy watched as the last of his men came streaming from the building in full riot gear and ran toward the barricades. They took up position with the posture any well-trained officer would during a riot with their shields held out in front and their night sticks in hand.

"Put your sticks away," The Captain said, as he walked among his men. "We can't allow this line to fall. We are under orders to kill on sight. Remove your weapon from its holster."

Thirty-one men, that's how many Roy Burns counted. It was all that stood between a growing number of corpses on the opposite side of the wall and the safety zone. A massive march of the dead all the way to Central Park would be the result of a failed defense. It was the area just south of the park that Colonel Westinghouse was preparing as an evacuation zone. They needed time to close off the streets and get people to safety there. Roy's men were ready for the task at hand, but that had little bearing on his confidence of success.

"Listen to me," the Captain told them, "Aim for the head. That's the kill zone." He raised his voice above the racket caused by the increasing effort to break through. "You must shoot them in the head. Nothing, I repeat, nothing else works. Kill the brain. I don't care who you see breaking in from the other side of the wall. I don't care if it's an old woman or your best friend. I can assure you, if you hesitate, you will pay with your life. These things are not the shopkeepers down the street. They are not the newspaper boys, or the hooker on the corner. They may look like them, but if you fall prey to such thinking, you will not only pay with *your* life, but possibly with the lives of the men who stand beside you."

Holsinger ran full-tilt toward them; head forward, pushing a stainless steel cart from inside the station. It had three shelves, all filled with ammunition. He stopped short of the barricade and began arranging its items in a way that would make it easier to hand out reloads in a hurry and without confusion. Burns paused for a moment as he watched the rookie from the corner of his eye.

"If you run out of ammo, go to the cart and reload." The Captain explained, and pointed before checking his own weapon.

Daniel Flanagan leaned in close. "You know, I just took a peek on the other side of that wall."

Burns looked up from his weapon, "And?"

"Once they start to surge forward, that wall's gonna come down pretty fast. There are literally thousands of those things over there."

Burns nodded, "I know. There's nothing else we can do except wait and do our best."

"This is futile. There's no way we can hold off that many of them. We're nothin' more than a stumblin' block for that unholy horde," Daniel explained.

"Then we're a stumbling block," Roy countered, "That's why we're here. We're here to slow those things down until the people up the road can be made safe."

"Then you're sayin' we're expendable?"

Roy smiled. He couldn't help but to smile now as a sort of inner peace settled over him. He had finally realized the truth, that this day…this place, would probably be his last sight and experience in life. He would die in the line of duty. Probably, they all would.

"Haven't we always been?" he said to Daniel, and shrugged.

"It's coming down!" Someone yelled from the front line near the wall. Roy looked up just in time to see an eight-foot section of the wall come down on top of the men standing closest to it. The sudden surge of bodies behind it quickly took down the rest of the wall and the entire south end of Broadway came into full view.

The officers closest to the wall when it fell were knocked off balance and tumbled to the ground. They were quickly overrun and covered by the advancing ghouls. Those who could retreat took positions behind the concrete barricades and opened fire.

Roy Burns was totally unprepared for the sheer numbers about to overrun them. There were thousands spread out before them. They were four or five blocks deep and elbow-to-elbow, like a herd of cattle being driven down the chute of tall buildings that flanked them on both sides. They were Blacks, Whites, Asians, and Latinos, the whole melting pot array for which the city was famous. There were children too. A shambling corpse in full firefighter gear reached out and grabbed one of Roy's men, taking him gracefully to the ground as he moved in for a bite.

One man in his twenties had a knife buried in the right side of his chest. Roy zeroed in on him and fired a shot into the center of his forehead. Just as he had been told, the bullet did its job and the man fell. He took a step back and took aim at the next one and fired. Again, it went down. It was much easier than he had thought it would be. Again he fired, and again, and again. That was five. He had killed five of them now. Why didn't he feel anything? Why no remorse? A bald man with his lower lip dangling precariously by a tab of flesh lunged forward and Roy almost failed to respond in time. He fired, disintegrating the upper part of its skull, and yes, right to the ground it went. He began looking for a good one. What would a good one be? A good one would be one that caught his eye. And indeed there she was. She was a six-foot blonde in a blue power suit. She was attractive, if you like that half-eaten, no left arm look. She came for him and Roy raised his pistol and, "*click.*"

Roy staggered backward.

"No!" he screamed, just as Daniel pulled him away, firing point blank into the skull of the dressed-for-success, walking corpse.

"We've gotta move. There are too many." Daniel said.

Roy jerked away from him and hesitated just a moment. A moment was long enough to see three more of his men taken down. "FALL BACK!" he shouted as loudly as possible. "FALL BACK!"

Roy stumbled as he felt himself being jerked harshly back and to the left. The darkened hand of a corpse to his left had latched on to the collar of his jacket. Roy thrashed as it groped for a good hold. It was a big man with a crooked nose. Like a fighter, Roy thought as he looked into its glazed eyes. He cast his gaze around furtively, wondering why Daniel, his wingman, had not come to his aid for a second time. How had the fiend gotten behind him unseen? Then he saw Daniel, surrounded by fifteen, maybe twenty of them. The sounds were maddening. Screams and wails echoed down the corridor of tall buildings as thousands of undead cried out in a chorus of longing. With a burst of energy, Roy finished reloading, tore away from the corpse's grip, and got off a shot to its brain. It danced sideways as it fell dead, its eyes open, staring at nothing.

Daniel fought and kicked at his assailants. Their arms reached straight out for him, in what looked like a ridiculous slap fighting parody. Two were crouched down and reaching up between the legs of their walking dead brethren. Roy raised his weapon and unloaded his clip into enough of them to give Daniel a chance to escape. Roy grabbed him then and pulled him toward the station.

Once at the door they turned. The street was full now. Not just to the south, but the north as well. There was a semi-circle of unpopulated street just in front of the station and it too was filling with a relentless surge of dead bodies. Some of his men broke ranks and ran north toward what Roy hoped was safety. But most were on the ground now being consumed by the ravenous fiends. If any were still alive, their cries were drowned out by the howls and screams of the ghoulish throng. It seemed to be the more animated ones that screamed out. The slower ones, the mangled ones, were not as loud or ambitious. The slow ones were easier to defeat. A man could use speed to his advantage. But the fresh-looking ones, the ones that moved more quickly, they were also stronger. And even though their numbers were less, they were deadly.

"We've got no place else to go, Laddy." Daniel said calmly, and then lit a cigar that had been half-smoked already.

Roy wondered at his friend's casual acceptance of their fate. As always, Daniel was calm, even now. "No, I guess we don't," Roy sighed, and checked his weapon's load.

The crowd of hellish cannibals closed in. "I'm out of ammo and I'm not about to let those things rip me to shreds. You'll have to do me first." Roy said, as he eyed the silver cart on its side, its ammo scattered beneath the feet of the surging horde. He suddenly wondered where the young rookie, Holsinger, had gone. Had he been able to escape? Or was he in the middle of one of those feeding frenzies?

"Cap'n, I don't intend to do either." Daniel said, and nodded toward the station.

Roy's brow furrowed, "That's no good. The side door is overrun and there are too many windows to keep these things out. It's a dead end."

"Aye, that it might be, but the jail cells are safe. We can lock ourselves in until help comes."

"It might buy us some time." Roy said. "But I wouldn't count on help coming too soon."

Daniel nodded, "Better than a bullet in your brain now, I'll tell ya that."

They moved back to the station's revolving door and pushed their way inside just ahead of the approaching mob. From inside they watched as the growing mass moved in.

"Can we lock this thing?" Roy asked, pointing to the door.

Daniel said, "Hell, we've never had to before. Where's the key?"

Roy scanned the room. "There's no time. Lodge something in there so it won't turn," he said, then grabbed a chair from against the wall.

Roy wedged the chair in between the revolving door and circular glass frame. "We need another one. Cram it in the other side. If we can keep it from turning…"

Hopes of barricading themselves safely inside were soon dashed. The floor to ceiling windows to the right of the revolving doors came crashing in on the beautifully tiled floors. The first ghoul inside was the one that broke the window. As it fell forward, it suddenly reminded Daniel of the nightclub scene from the movie *Scarface*. The ghoul on the floor was at least fifty pounds overweight and looked just like the silly clown dancing across the Miami dance floor. Pacino, stoned drunk, was abruptly thrown into overdrive by the resounding report of automatic weapons. And that silly clown, suddenly dancing a different dance. A dance of bullets and death.

As the dead man staggered into an upright position, more bodies pushed and struggled in through the broken window and Daniel was no longer in a movie. The room was suddenly full of the dancing dead.

Daniel shouted, "MOVE YOUR ARSE!" And he grabbed Roy Burns by the arm. Both men raced down the steps to the basement cellblock.

***

There was a vacant holding cell on the left. Its door was open and the two men raced inside. Roy slammed the door shut behind them, and then gave it a tug to make sure it was locked.

Several cells still contained the walking dead brought in overnight, but for the most part they kept quiet, choosing to simply reach out from their cells in hopes of reaching their prize.

A sad looking lot, Roy thought. God had sentenced them to an eternity of semi-consciousness, driven by flesh lust and devoid of soul or reason. Yes, it was pity that Roy felt for them. But hate was what he should be feeling. Hate was a more comfortable emotion for him. Hate was easy.

Roy found pleasure in the sudden relative peace and quiet of the basement cellblock. However, he knew it would be short-lived.

Even now he could hear the advancing army as it made its way down the steps to them. Soon the calm would be lost.

"We're done, you know?" Roy said.

"What?" Daniel asked, as he tried to relight his stub of a cigar. He clicked the lighter several times, but it only flickered and flashed.

"We're done. No one will ever come to save us. Do you know how I know?" Roy asked.

"Now how do you know that?" Daniel coughed it out, sliding down the back wall until he was sitting on his haunches.

"Because there's no one left out there to save us. That's how I know. And as long as we are in this cell those things will be just on the other side of those bars. They'll wait us out."

Daniel showed little interest in what Roy was saying. His face was noticeably pale and there were dark circles under his eyes. It was remarkable how Daniel could hold himself together when he needed to. Only now did Roy notice how sick he really was.

"It's your hand isn't it?

Daniel kept quiet, his head dropped downward.

"Shit Danny, it's your hand isn't it? It's where you busted your knuckles on one of them." Suddenly the pity he was feeling for them vanished, replaced by good ole reliable and comfortable hate. Roy was no longer confused.

"Aye, it is indeed. And it's on fire too. It burns clear up to my brain and down to my feet." Daniel looked up to meet Roy's gaze. "Damned near hurts all over now," he said with a crooked grin. "You'll be needin' this more than I will," Daniel said, and pushed his pistol across the floor to Roy's feet.

Roy stared down at it. "What do I need that for? Those things can't get in here." He could hear them coming still, louder now. They were almost in the room with them.

"Not for them my old friend, for me." Daniel said, hoarsely.

Roy seemed perplexed and made a funny face. "What the hell are you talking about?"

"The bite, it's deadly. You know it, and I know it. I'll soon be dyin.' And you'll need that gun to do me in when I come back at'cha with a rage."

Roy reached down and picked it up. He held it out in his hand and rubbed its sleekness. Danny sure did keep a clean weapon.

"I can't do it." Roy said, nearly stuttering.

"And, you'll not do it until I'm gone." Daniel said. "Cause maybe I won't come back. Maybe it's just the weak-willed democrat-liberals that come back and grind on the bones of the living."

Roy held the weapon. "I'm a democrat, you know?"

"I know Laddy, and I luv ya anyway."

Roy smiled.

The advancing crowd of reanimates crashed into the bars of the holding cell. The force of the dead jolting the bars caused the whole cage to reverberate and sing a song of defiance. Roy, thinking the bars might collapse, dove for the floor. Daniel grabbed for him, and pulled him away from the reaching arms and close to the back wall. Putting his face squarely in front of his friend's, Daniel said, "Don't move. Be perfectly still."

Every inch of the outer perimeter of the cell was occupied. A thunderous rhythm of cries and motion rocked the outer cell walls as a sea of bodies filled the basement cellblock. Roy froze, and watched from his position close to Daniel.

Outstretched hands reaching through the bars were mere inches from grabbing him and pulling him back into their eager embrace.

Roy's gaze fell to the pistol in his hand. It was almost preferable to end it right now, rather than listen to them, rather than look at them.

Roy closed his eyes. It was all just a dream anyway. Once awake, he'd be home in bed where he belonged. He wished for it, thought it over and over. Just a few more minutes and he'd be awake. The alarm would go off; he'd hit the snooze and lie in bed for five extra minutes.

Then Roy opened his eyes.

Daniel was slumped forward and completely still.

"Danny, are you ok?"

Daniel didn't answer.

Roy sputtered, unable to verbalize his despair, his eyes welled up for the loss of his dear friend.

"Danny?"

Part 2
An Apocalypse Trumps Luxury

Hey…Do you want fries with that?
—Duane

13

Stay in your homes. Do not attempt to reach loved ones or friends. Martial Law is in effect in the City of New York and all residents are hereby ordered to stay indoors.

The man on the television was not one Adam had seen before. He had gray hair and a noticeable Boston accent, not the slick, young New York talking head that usually filled the screen every weekday afternoon.

In the background, co-workers raced around like headless chickens with no real destination or purpose. The announcer's voice was barely audible over the commotion.

If you are not already in the city do not attempt to come to New York. You will not be allowed entrance. The National Guard has been mobilized and units are patrolling the streets in an attempt to restore order.

Michael faced the window as the man spoke. In only a few minutes, there had been three car accidents, and dozens dragged to their deaths by the roving maniacs. A high-rise one street over was on fire. "Restore order?" Michael laughed. "That's bullshit."

Until Noon today there had been no explanation for the sudden worldwide outbreak of violence. But according to reports released from Atlanta, the recently dead are returning to life and attacking the living. We have no details as to how or why this extraordinary event is happening, but as soon as we have that information we will pass it along to you. I know this is hard to believe, but these are the facts given us.

Michael said, "We've got to find a way outta here, Doc. Have you tried the phone recently?"

"Yes, still nothing," Adam said.

Adam peered over Michael's shoulder to the carnage below and his heart sank. "It doesn't look like we're leaving anytime soon anyway. It will take them some time to get *this* under control."

Michael moved from the window and stopped in the middle of the room with his head lowered, his fingers caressing the bridge of his nose as another headache began to darken the edge of his vision. "Life as we've known it is over," Michael said.

"Yes, I think so," Adam said.

"My wife is gone and I'll never see Chicago again."

Adam shook his head slowly, "Probably not."

"And you've got no fucking guns?" Michael turned, and allowed what sounded to Adam like a small giggle.

"I'm sorry. I'm a doctor, not a militiaman," Adam told him.

"Then we'd better get to work on securing this building. We can lock all the exterior doors first. Those things are not too interested in getting in here right now. But once they run out of people to kill outside, I think it's a safe bet that they'll begin looking for other victims. We'll start in the garage. Does it have a door we can close?"

"It has a gate," Adam said.

"A gate?" Michael asked, seemingly puzzled. "Can people get through the gate?"

"Look, it's a gate. It's about six feet high. If you're asking if those things can get through—yes, if they really want to get through it, or over it, they can,"

"I thought you said this place was secure?"

"It is when the streets aren't filled with cannibalistic corpses," Adam explained, his irritation was evident in his tone now. "There are usually guards on duty."

"It'll have to do," Michael said. "We'll start there. Then we'll lock all the ground-floor doors. Where's your tire iron?"

Adam glanced to the couch where he had tossed it earlier. It was still there. He reached out and picked it up. A small red stain now soiled the cushion.

***

Adam was about to push the button for the elevator when Michael stopped him.

"Wait, no more surprises. That elevator is full of surprises. Do the stairs go all the way down to the parking garage?"

"I don't know. I've never taken the stairs, but I would think so," Adam told him.

"Take me to them."

"They're at the end of the hall," Adam said, and motioned for Michael to follow.

The plush carpet made their steps silent. Michael counted six apartments as they walked to the stairs, all spacious, and spacious meant expensive. He wondered how an emergency room doctor could afford such luxury in the heart of New York's finest real estate. Certainly an apartment in this building would cost millions. It was much more extravagant than his small, brick Cape Cod in the suburbs outside Chicago.

"Here they are," Adam said, stopping in front of a metal door with a small square window at face level.

Michael opened the door and listened. He was greeted with silence. As a Chicago cop, he knew unwelcome events happen when you least expect them and he dwelled on that as they descended the stairwell.

At each floor they stopped long enough for Michael to peer through the door's small window. Thus far, the halls had been peaceful and unpopulated. But the next floor in their halting descent was the lobby. If there was going to be trouble he fully expected it to be there, and as they turned the corner to that door, Michael held his finger up in front of his mouth to caution Adam. Hopefully they could pass unnoticed. The world was falling apart outside and Michael felt helpless to do anything about it, just as he had been helpless to save Rebecca. She died, and now the world was dying with her. For all intents and purposes, he might as well be dead as well. What really was left for him, destiny? Men like him did not have a destiny, only the poor man's version of it, which was simply fate. There was no grand scheme in fate, only the relentless passage of time and eventual predetermined outcome.

Michael eased up to the window in the door from the side. He had been hoping to get a good look into the lobby, but instead, he saw only another wall. The door opened into a corner. He would need to actually enter the hall to investigate further and that would have to wait.

The next door was to the parking garage. From what he could remember, it had two levels. They had parked on the upper level. Therefore, this door would lead them there and to the gate.

Michael studied the door before opening it. Like the others, it was solid, two inches of steel thickness. It was strong enough to keep out just about anything. The little window was far too small for anyone to climb through. It had two locks. One was a deadbolt. They would need to locate the keys to properly secure it, but first the gate.

Michael pushed open the door and a sudden breeze brushed his face. Warm and smoky, it gave the silent carnage he'd witnessed from the eighth floor life and solidity.

He stood there, frozen for a moment, unable to move forward. After what seemed like an eternity, a nudge from Adam got him moving again. The fear and hesitation had returned...

It was a damp, rainy night when he got the call, a 211 at a nearby liquor store. A 211 meant, 'armed robbery'. In those days the number codes were still used. Now they simply stated over the radio the exact nature of the emergency. It was supposed to make things easier. But somehow to Michael, it made his job seem less professional.

He had brought his cruiser to a halt outside the store as the gunman left on foot and he followed. He gave chase for several blocks through the south side before cornering him in a narrow, dark alley. With nowhere to escape, the man turned and Michael was face to face with his own mortality and the barrel of a gun between his eyes. He was unable to move, frozen in fear, waiting for his fate to be realized. The gun had been fired recently. He could smell the gunpowder residue still left in the barrel. His body trembled.

Then the man pulled the trigger.

But instead of the loud bang to end his life, there was only the soft metallic click of a misfire. That's when he should've made his move. That's when he should've taken control. Instead, he remained paralyzed and the man struck him with the weapon and made his escape.

He had told no one of the incident. Instead, he had let it eat at him until it had become a recurring demon that consumed him when he most needed self-control. Usually he was perfectly fine, but when it did happen, it was uncontrollable and the fear returned. He was not a coward and he assured himself of that, time and time again. It was a small issue and correctable. And one day he would talk himself back to mental health. But today, this moment, he could not afford to fight that demon again.

***

Apart from a few sporadically parked cars, the garage was vacant. Michael figured there to be no more than ten or twelve on that level. He was sure there would be more below, and with that many cars there would certainly be more people in the building. Once they had finished the task at hand they would need to seek them out.

***

The City's turmoil was much more audible by the gate. Security alarms rang out from countless vehicles in the streets outside. There were screams and cries for help. There was glass breaking somewhere, and the wail of distant sirens and gunfire.

Michael and Adam were crouched a few feet from the guard post at the entrance gate. They were unable to see the chaos in the streets, but they were also unseen by those who might wish to do them harm. Michael would need to work fast and he knew it. He was unfamiliar with the workings of the gate and that could hamper his chances for success, but Adam, who lived in the building, knew even less. Indeed, it was Michael's sense of duty that brought him to the realization that he was better suited to close the gate. It was Michael's fear of failure at a key moment that pushed him further, and harder.

"Stay out of sight for God's sake." Adam said. "Don't let any of those things see you or they'll be in here on us."

Michael crouched low to the concrete floor and made his way to the door of the booth. Now he could see outside and understood the importance of staying covert.

A group of walking dead was just on the other side of the opened gate. Three of them were crouched over and devouring some poor unfortunate soul on the sidewalk. Then the half-eaten man began to move and they stopped their feast. No longer interested, they moved away. The partially devoured man could only drag himself along the ground behind them as they lurched into the clogged street.

Michael could make his move now and reached out with his left hand and pushed the booth door open and crawled inside.

It was a small dank room, and between the solid concrete walls moisture hung heavy and stale. Michael figured if he grabbed a cat by the tail and swung it around and around, its skull would surely impact all four of its windowed walls. There was hardly enough room for a chair at the control panel. The damned cat, he thought. It was home alone. If things were as horrific in Chicago as in New York, there would be no one around to feed him or change the litter box. Ralph the cat would first go crazy, and then die of starvation on the living room floor. Michael wondered if the cat would come back to life too. Was the epidemic affecting everything, or only humans? He shook off the question. It was something better left to the doctors and scientists to figure out. The gate…where was the button to close the gate? There were buttons for lights, signs, the ticket dispenser, and of course, there it was, the gate. Michael toggled the switch and pressed the green button beside it. There was a clanging sound and he sat up in the chair to watch.

The red and white metal gate slowly rattled its way across the entrance from the wall to the right. The dead things in the immediate area turned to the new sound.

At first they stared in bewilderment at its movement. They cocked their heads to the side and watched. Then, one of them noticed Michael sitting there in the booth. It bellowed out a raspy howl and lunged toward the closing gate. The dead things close to it moved in just as it found its spot and locked into place. With a crash, the group fell into it. They pressed their bodies forward and reached in through the bars. Michael saw this as his cue and ran back into the shadows with Adam and skidded to a stop just out of sight.

"You did it," Adam said with a grin. He peered around the corner just enough to see the gate. There were still some of the reanimates there, but they no longer pressed their bodies up against it.

Adam said, "They're not trying to get in here anymore. It looks like as soon as you left their field of vision they lost interest. Maybe their attention span isn't so good."

Michael allowed himself a quick glance too. "Why do you suppose that is?"

"The television says that the recently dead are returning to life."

Michael shook his head, "I could've told you that before daybreak."

"From what I saw in the operating room, it takes several minutes for reanimation. After only a few minutes, brain damage can occur if it is deprived of oxygen. I'd say that plays a part in the amount of reasoning power those things have once they get back up."

"Do you think that's what makes them cannibalistic psychos too?" Michael asked.

"I don't know." Adam said. "I doubt it. That's something else entirely if you ask me. They seem to be driven by some kind of primitive urge. It seems that feeding on the living is what keeps them going. It must be. Why else would they do it?"

Michael felt a chill run down his spine. "Why does that have to be the case? Why can't they just eat a damned cheeseburger? No, that's not the reason they're tearing into us. It doesn't make sense. They're going after the living, not each other."

"It's just a guess, but the people they kill come back. If nothing else, it's an efficient way to grow their numbers."

"We'd better get back inside and try to lock this place down before it's too late," Michael said, and made a move to leave.

Adam grabbed his arm. His voice was low and troubled. "If we are what keeps these things going, they are going to put all their energy into getting inside this building once they realize we are in here and there's no one left outside to keep them occupied."

"All the more reason to get this place locked down. The way I see it, we have what we need to ride this out right here. This place needs to be our fortress. We fight our war from inside these walls and fight to the death."

"I'll tell you what this place is, Michael. It's our Alamo. We will never get out of here alive. You've seen what I've seen. Maybe they won't get in here, but we're not going out there either."

14

Melissa stepped away from the stained glass window and hid behind her older sister Mary for comfort. "I want Mommy," she whispered. Mary wearily bent down and lifted the small child, holding her in her arms. She clung to her tightly for a moment, relishing the comfort of the little girl's trust and the illusion of safety offered by their temporary sanctuary. "I know baby, so do I," Mary said.

"Are they going to come in here now?"

"No Melissa. I locked all the doors."

"And the windows too?"

"Yes, the windows too. They can't get inside to hurt us. Don't be afraid. I won't let anything happen to you—I promise."

Melissa lifted her teary face from Mary's shoulder and looked her squarely in the eyes, "No, we're not. They'll get inside and bad things will happen. Terrible things."

"Now don't start with that again," Mary scolded.

She instantly regretted the harshness of her tone and softened. "No, they won't. This is a house of God. I don't think they're allowed in here."

Melissa said, "God isn't here. He never was." She was whispering now.

"Enough, do you hear me?" And again, Mary's tone betrayed her. "Stop saying that." She ended with a whisper of her own as though she might hide the remarks from God, himself. "He is—He is here. Never say that."

Melissa had an uncanny way of making Mary feel uneasy. And even though she would never say it to Melissa, Mary thought, in her heart of hearts, that Melissa was right. God wasn't there. She didn't feel his presence either. It seemed this house of God was an empty house except for the two of them. The world was coming apart, and yet, they were alone in the church. It seemed strange for that to be the case, all things considered. It was why she had chosen it as their best hope for safety. Surely, with things as they were, there would be people in the churches, others to protect them.

A sudden crash at the door sent Mary scurrying to the corner. She pulled Melissa in close as she slid down to a crouched position. She closed her eyes and held tightly again to her sister as crash after crash boomed and echoed through the empty chamber.

***

After a while, things settled and the assault on the doors stopped. The church's double doors faced Forty-Seventh Street. The building was being restored, and like many others in the city, scaffolding was raised against the side of the church all the way to the roof.

Mary watched through a clear portion of a stained glass window as some of the strange people outside ripped portions of the scaffolding's support structure loose. They were using the metal strips to beat against the doors. She could see them from the window where she stood as they moved to continue their assault once again. They swung their weapons slowly, as if the four-foot strips of metal were almost too heavy to lift. But they were methodical in their approach. Slow, but steady. When one of them came close to the window, Mary moved away.

Only two hours earlier, she and Melissa had seen close up the horrors of this bizarre epidemic and the pain and death caused by those who were trying to enter the church. That morning, an unruly mob had forced them from their car, then driven away with it to escape the traffic jam and panicking crowds. That's when she snatched up Melissa and ran from the commotion that was mostly congregated in the streets and around the stopped traffic. When she felt they were at a safe distance, she stopped and turned.

At first she thought she was watching looters or angry protesters, but those thoughts were quickly replaced by confusion and the terrible realization that something else was happening. They were not protesters or looters, or any kind of activist or demonstrator she had ever seen, at least not all of them. There were monsters too, crazed, terrible things with an appetite for human flesh.

A delivery girl riding a bicycle weaved through some of them until she was pulled from her bike by her trailing pigtails. A circle of wild-eyed psychopaths ripped and pulled at her clothing until she was almost naked. Then they started to bite her, tearing strips of flesh from her body as one after the other took its turn. She cried out in agony and for help, screaming and kicking at her attackers. Then she quieted, and became still.

People ran this way and that, vain attempts to escape the carnage. By now, First Avenue's traffic had come to a complete stop and the madness was suddenly everywhere, in every direction and as far as she could see.

Mary had missed something in her haste to get Melissa to her appointment with the child psychologist. They were dressed and gone from their home in Queens in minutes. In that short time, they had merely crossed the river. Yet here in Manhattan it was a different world. Was this same terror in Queens as well? Thinking back, Mary was certain that it was. What she had brushed off to be an inordinate number of homeless must have surely been what she was seeing now, murdering crazies, only to a lesser degree. But there was no returning to Queens, that way blocked by a growing number of people infected with the need to kill. The streets ran red with blood. Body parts littered the walkway as if blown off by bombs or hand grenades, and all the while, more and more were becoming like the others and consumed with murderous desires. Right before their eyes an explosion in numbers was taking place.

Indeed, it seemed little time passed before the victim became the attacker. Some of their injuries seemed life threatening, to the point that Mary wondered how they could yet live. One shirtless man was hollowed out from his chest to his waist. Only bloody ribs remained over the cavity his vital organs once filled. But he was moving, even if he could no longer keep his upper body fully erect and he limped across the road toward them. That was when she scooped Melissa into her arms and ran for the church.

Mary sat down beside Melissa and tried to make a call on her cell phone. A busy signal followed by an *all circuits are busy* message repeated over and over.

"Mary?" Melissa said.

"What is it, sweetheart?"

"We have to go to the roof."

"Why?"

"The voice says we have to go to the roof. We have to go right now before it's too late."

And there it was again, the voice. The constant barrage of third party thought. It was why they were on their way to the doctor. Melissa had issues, deep issues. Things only a skilled practitioner could cure. Mary wondered which voice it was this time. Was it the kindly old woman, or the dark, shadowy figure that stood at the foot of Melissa's bed sometimes late at night? Or possibly it was one of the countless other voices that seemed to invade the child's head with strange thoughts and ideas.

Mary said, "We're not going to the roof. I don't want to hear any more of this. I've told you. The voice is not real. It's only in your head."

"No Mary, it's here." Melissa pointed to her heart. "Some of them are from here."

15

Jamal searched the cabinets in the small, dirty kitchenette for something to eat. He found only an old box of Corn Flakes. It was in the cabinet on its side with the top flap open and he scattered some of its contents across the counter.

The action forced the unseen roaches hidden inside to pour out with the flakes. They scurried in waves across the counter in route to the cracks and crevasses along the wall and backsplash. Jamal flinched, tossing the almost empty box backward, and reeled away from the nasty little creatures. He hated them. The sight reminded him of an old movie he had seen once. A man who had a similar fear of bugs and germs had his life cut short by the revolting little creepy-crawlies.

Jamal shook off the vision of the roaches spewing from the old man's mouth and eye sockets and opened the refrigerator door. He hoped something there would catch his fancy. When he found only a jar of moldy grape jelly, he closed it.

"How about the water?"

Jamal turned to see Chuck standing behind him. He sneered and turned on the faucet. It gurgled for a moment and then spewed a brown, smelly liquid into the filthy, stained sink. He turned it off and wiped his hands. "Nah man, I ain't drinkin' that."

Chuck grunted, "We can't stay here. There's no food and if those things don't get in here and kill us, drinking that water surely will."

Jamal meant to laugh, but it came out as a snort. It was the sound made by the fact that he'd tried to cut off the laugh completely and was only partially successful. "And just where in hell do you think we're gonna go? Do you think we are gonna just waltz right out of here and get ourselves a taxi? Shit man, we won't make it two blocks."

"We made it over here, didn't we?" Chuck said.

"That was different."

"And how was that different?"

"Have you looked outside lately?"

"No," Chuck answered, and swallowed uneasily." He really hadn't. He had fallen asleep shortly after arriving, but the rest had been needed. At least now he could think more clearly.

"Then maybe you'd better have a look out that window." Jamal said.

Chuck moved to the window and pulled the curtain back just far enough to peek through.

The streets were now filled with idle traffic. The doors were open on some of them. Others had driven up onto the sidewalk only to find that way impassable too.

And there were dead things…

They filled the space between the automobiles and grassy areas. And they were moving, but they were moving in the direction of downtown Manhattan. If they were to make a move, now might be the time. The sun would be setting soon. In two hours it would be dark and the thought of spending the night in the little shack by the docks gave Chuck the shivers.

"Shit!" Chuck shook his head in disbelief at the overwhelming number of infected deadies.

"Yeah…shit," Jamal mocked him. "As in deep shit if we don't leave soon."

"I vote we leave the city completely," Duane interjected, looking as though he'd just awakened from a nap of his own. "Let's make a run for the tunnel and get out of this God-forsaken place."

"Yeah, the tunnel. We'll run for the tunnel. We'll have to take the risk," Chuck said. "We can do it now while they're moving away from us. Get your things together. We need to get out of the city before dark."

Chuck went to the kitchen and flipped a large, wooden table over onto its top and kicked off two of its legs. Each one split away easily and skidded across the peeling green and yellow vinyl tiles. He handed one to Duane.

"If any of those things get close, blast 'em in the head, do you hear me?" he said, and made a downward swinging motion with his own weapon, the iron pipe he'd used earlier. "Hit 'em in the head," he repeated, and tapped Duane on his temple with his finger.

"I got it," Duane said, and smacked his hand away.

Jamal pulled his pistol from his pants pocket and held it up beside his face. It looked comfortable there. Even now, in the good times when money was no problem and his face was recognized by so many, even now he felt the need for a weapon. You could take the thug out of the streets, but he would always be a thug. At least that was how Chuck saw it.

Chuck said, "How many bullets do you have in that thing?"

"There's three in it, and a few in my pocket." Jamal said, without moving his gun away from its place by his right temple.

"You had better load that thing full now before we head out. If we get in trouble you might not have time to reload. Just try to use them sparingly. You want that other table leg? It might come in handy if you run out of bullets."

Jamal said, "Nah man. I'll be fine. If it gets that bad I'll save one bullet and use it on myself."

"Suit yourself," Chuck told him.

Jamal lowered the weapon to his side. "I can save some for you guys too if you want."

Chuck ignored the comment, opened the door, and stepped outside.

The first maimed figure turned and reached for him with an injured hand. It was a portly man in a torn and bloodied jogging suit. The top matched the pants, black with white stripes. His face was ashen gray and he dragged his left foot behind him, scraping its side against the concrete walkway with each step. The closer he came to Chuck, the lower his jaw dropped, exposing yellowed teeth. A faint whine emitted from his gullet. The breath forced out with the whine was rotten, like road kill. And there was a bitterness to it, like poison.

Chuck shied away at first, but then swung the iron pipe at its head and thumped it to the ground. It squirmed there, trying to regain its footing. Another one came at him from the street. This one was faster and was on Chuck before he could react. It screamed out when it made contact, and both Chuck and the corpse fell to the ground. It groped and yanked at his clothes in an attempt to rip them from his body. A small, clear plastic tube extended from the side of its neck. It flopped and dangled as the man fought.

Finally, Jamal reached down and pulled the ghoul out of Chuck's grasp and with a heave, threw it to the side. A sickening thud rang out as Chuck, again on his feet, smashed it on the head with the pipe. It fell facedown and motionless beside another one that Duane had managed to dispatch while Chuck was struggling with the fat jogger.

"That kills them for sure. Crack 'em in the head—beat 'em right down to the ground." Chuck was grinning now, and huffing for breath. "I didn't know you had it in you, Duane," Chuck said, noticing the other one.

"I don't," Duane answered. "I got lucky, and that's a fact."

Chuck was rubbing his elbow. It had impacted the sidewalk when he fell. He didn't think it was broken. It sure did hurt though, like electricity running through his arm, it tingled painfully. He checked it to be sure it wasn't a bite. Bites could be bad, even minor ones. To his relief it was clean.

The one with the clear tube in its neck now had a cracked skull and a thin, red liquid pooled beneath it. There was an odd, chemical odor, like seventh grade science lab, an odor Chuck would never forget. His mother seemed to be much smaller lying there in her coffin than she did in life, so active, so alive. It was as if death had taken some part of her physical body with it and left only the shell. It would be the last time he would ever gaze upon her sweet face, the face that had smiled at him so often as a child. She was the only person who would always love him, no matter what. When he bent down and kissed her on the cheek, the odor was the same. The dead monster in front of him had been embalmed. Now was it truly dead and ready for burial. At least they weren't unstoppable. A gun or a good, solid club did the trick nicely.

Chuck flexed his arm, trying to ease the pain that simply refused to go away. "They're pretty spread out. We don't have to run, just do this like it's a video game. Be alert—be smart, and above all…stay calm. Keep your head about you. We can do this. Just stay away from them. Keep your distance and don't fuck around. If they get too close, fuck 'em up. But keep moving—always moving."

Chuck could see in their faces that his point was understood and he began walking west toward the Lincoln Tunnel. The other two fell in line with him.

***

They kept an even pace as they walked up Thirty-Fifth Street. Just ahead, a man in a business suit came sprinting from a small park. At first they were sure he was running from more dead crazies, but it was soon apparent that he was probably one of them. He moved faster than most. Not running, but certainly a sustained, staggering jog. There was no blood on him and even his skin color was better than the others. Maybe he wasn't infected after all, or maybe he was freshly infected and able to get around better. There was just no way for them to know for sure.

The man stopped in the middle of the street and watched the sun as it hung low in the western sky. It was at its most stunning visual point of the evening and he seemed to be simply enjoying the view as he stood there tilting his head from one shoulder to the other.

They stopped fifty feet from where the stargazer stood. It was Chuck that moved first.

He did the logical thing. He tried to communicate. After all, it seemed like the right thing to do. If it were a *living* man, he might need help. If not, they could simply kill it and be on their way.

In his quietest voice, Chuck said, "Hey buddy—do you need some help?"

He had barely been audible and he was genuinely surprised that the man could hear him at all. He was even more surprised when the man turned with a staccato jerk.

His eyes were glazed with the milky film of death, and he screamed at the top of his lungs as if auditioning for the Metropolitan Opera. Then the others chimed in…

A wail rose up all around them, from the buildings, from the next street over, and from behind them. It was a rising storm of howls and cries. Jamal pulled out his pistol and shot the man wearing the business suit in the head. He fell instantly, but the damage had been done, and now that damage had been doubled by the fact that Jamal had fired his weapon. The proverbial cat was out of the bag. They were revealed to every lurching sack of rot within earshot of the man's scream and Jamal's gunshot.

Behind them the crowd thickened, heaping column upon column and shoulder to shoulder the entire width of the wide city street. To the west, the street filled three blocks deep. It seemed the entire city was dead, and every glazed eye was on them. Chuck could only stare into his companions' fearful eyes. Suddenly he felt very helpless and impotent. He should have crept up behind the man in the business suit and clobbered him over the head, end of problem. It was kill or be killed now. It was a simple matter of whose life was more important to you, someone else's or your own. To Chuck, that was an easy choice, especially when the 'someone else' was a stranger. With the streets filling and nowhere else to run, they darted into the park from where the man in the business suit had appeared. They tried to place as much distance between themselves and the advancing hordes as possible, dodging strays along the way. They ran until they were breathless, until their sides ached from the exertion. Finally they paused on a pitcher's mound in the middle of an empty baseball field. They stood there, huffing and puffing with their hands resting on their knees. Years of smoking and neglect for the care of their bodies had taken its toll on the men's lungs and endurance, all except for Jamal. Jamal stood straight and breathed normally; the benefits of a celebrity life. But Jamal was more thug than celebrity. The tabloids were often full of his antics and arrest stories. Chuck eyed him suspiciously from his bent position with his hands still resting just above his knees. He didn't like celebrities and he didn't like thugs. Jamal was not to be trusted. Of that he was sure, or was it just his bigotry kicking in? He never considered himself to be a racist; he was more of a social bigot. To him it wasn't the same. To a racist, the color of your skin mattered. A social bigot cared more about being with like-minded people, a 'birds of a feather' type of thing and Jamal was not a bird of his particular feather. Their trip to New York and forced fraternization with those like him had convinced him of that.

If they had more time they might stand a better chance of making it out of the city alive. They needed the time to rest, and think, to plan out their escape. But their restful break would be short lived. The ghoulish cries were growing louder and the first of the large crowd of walking corpses were making their way into the park.

Chuck fought to keep his wits about him. They poured in through the gates, and breaks in the shrubbery. A constant thrum of voices filled the air. The playing field was beginning to fill and the three of them were about to be cornered.

"We're not going to make it, guys." Chuck said, and threw his arms up into the air. "The Lincoln tunnel is too far and there are too many of them." Chuck hated the sound of what he said as soon as the words left his lips, but he was ready to give up, to chuck it in and say a prayer for his soul. That's when Jamal said…

"The other tunnel."

"What other tunnel?" Chuck asked, his eyes searching.

"That one," Jamal said, and pointed through the trees.

Chuck's eyes widened. Indeed, there was a tunnel there, and the path was clear. The thought abruptly hit him. What if that tunnel was full of those things too? Then they'd be trapped for sure. He hesitated. The choice wasn't clear. He preferred things easy and this day had become full of tough decisions and dangers.

The sea of swaying flesh continued to crowd into the park. Every second they hesitated lessened their chances of survival.

Chuck said, "Where does it go?"

Jamal calmly pocketed his weapon. Chuck wondered how he could be so cool. Was it an act? The motion was smooth and easy. If only he could be so calm like Jamal, especially after the speech he'd given to them both about keeping their heads. But he was the one on the verge of losing control now, not Jamal and Duane.

"It goes to Queens," Jamal said. Even his voice was controlled and calm.

"Queens is a hell of a lot better than here," Chuck said.

***

There was a six-foot chain-link fence with barbed wire at the other end of the park and Chuck and Jamal cleared it easily. Duane however, got tripped up and dangled by his left sneaker, a maroon low-top Converse, as he crossed over. His head swayed inches above the ground as he reached up to loosen his shoe from the strand of barbed wire. Chuck noticed, and turned to help.

Three of the dead things had already gotten to the fence and tried to reach through the small openings to grab Duane.

With a heave, Chuck lifted him from the fence and he fell to the ground with a thud, his sneaker still hanging from the wire. The nearest dead thing, an old man with a goatee stained red, reached out and snatched up the shoe. "Gimme that!" Duane shouted, and plucked it from the old man's grip. In an instant they were moving again.

***

There were two entrances to the tunnel. Their first choice was the one on the right with dual lanes for traffic leaving Manhattan, and they raced down an embankment and toward the darkness in full stride.

It was difficult to come to a skidding halt as fast as they were running, but nonetheless they did so, and all at once, and just before running into a small group of walking corpses entering the light from the tunnel.

There were six of them and where there were six, there were usually more. Behind them, the crowd they had outrun was getting closer. They could hear them, but not see them, howling and snapping twigs in the small wooded area they had just left.

If they continued on their current path, it would lead them right into the heart of the city, a place they were certain would be even worse than where they were now. Their chance for survival had limited them to one option—the other tunnel, and their followers would only be a few steps behind them the entire way.

The other lanes were lower and they had to hang from a ten-foot retaining wall to drop down to the road. They stood there, staring into the darkness as a chorus of horrible cries gained strength behind and above them. As long as they were moving it seemed they were okay. But as soon as they stopped, it all caught up to them. The trick it seemed was to keep moving and Chuck hoped the wall they had just dropped from would slow down their chase.

"It's too damned dark in there. How are we going to see? Maybe we should try that way." Duane said, and pointed to the other side of the tunnel and toward downtown.

"It's only dark from out here," Chuck said. "There's still power in the city. There will be lights in there. Our eyes will adjust."

At first, Duane refused to move, frozen in place. But as Jamal and Chuck started to walk forward, he hurried to catch up, more afraid to be left alone than of what waited for them in the tunnel.

The tunnel was clear not only of the living dead, but also traffic. It sloped down in the direction of Queens, then it curved to the left. Just as Chuck had promised, their eyes did adjust to the dim lighting. They were unsure where the tunnel was taking them, or what was ahead past the curve, but one thing was certain; their path seemed to be pre-destined, and with a sense of urgency, they moved forward at a loping run.

***

Except for their footsteps, the tunnel was quiet. Only the buzz of flickering fluorescent lights above them made any noise at all. After a while, Chuck paused to light a cigarette. When Jamal held out his hand for one of them, Chuck pulled away. "What do I look like, a cigarette machine? Get your own," he told him.

Jamal grunted. His hand dropped back to his side, and he turned away to quiet his anger. And there it was, just beneath the surface of Jamal's thin, cool veneer, the animal. Always there waiting to strike. It was visible in the flexing of his jaw and narrowing eyes. Chuck noticed, and submissively held a cigarette out for him to take. Jamal placed it between his lips and Chuck lit it. The two exhaled simultaneously before the threesome started moving again, this time with less urgency.

"We ain't gonna make it, are we?" Chuck said, and glanced at Jamal. Chuck had his own opinion about it, but he wanted to get a better feel for Jamal's mindset. Jamal was the one who suggested they take the tunnel and Jamal would be the one to take blame if things went badly.

"We'll make it," he said. "Why wouldn't we? You can't think like that. If you do, you're fucked for sure. Have faith my brother. We will be delivered." Jamal's voice was dark, and raspy.

Chuck said, "Delivered?" A snicker was allowed with the word as he spoke it.

"God will deliver us," Jamal said.

"Last night I watched as you killed without mercy and now you talk about God's mercy to you…to us? What have we done to deserve God's mercy that a million other New Yorkers didn't?"

"Those gang-bangers got what they deserved. It was friends of theirs who came into our hood and brought some bad shit." Jamal said.

"Your hood? How do you get that it's *your* hood? I thought *your* hood was in fucking Hollywood these days. Hollyhood—" Chuck said, and grinned at what he considered an ingenious play on words. "Hollyhood," he repeated, to be certain they had gotten it.

Jamal sneered and gritted his teeth. "That bad shit killed two kids. One of those kids was my twelve-year-old cousin. That's why I was in town. I was here to attend her funeral. They're lucky I didn't see to it that they died a slow and painful death, and if all this shit hadn't happened, I might have done just that. So yeah, I think I can call it my fuckin' hood, Brutha." His anger was obvious now. "Hell, it's bad enough they come on our turf and sell any shit at all, but to come in and sell bad shit? That's a death sentence. I live in Hollywood, but *this* hood is home."

Chuck instinctively took a step away from Jamal and nodded solemnly, "Well, I'm sorry to hear about your cousin. I didn't know. When was her funeral?"

"It was supposed to be today."

"Jesus."

"Yeah, you gotta wonder now, don't you? The last time I saw her, she was pretty as a picture. I just pray to God that this shit ain't touched her precious little soul. She shouldn't be walking around like…those things." His voice cracked as if holding in unshed tears.

"Shhh…" Duane placed his arm in front of them and they stopped walking. "Keep quiet for a second. What's that noise?"

Chuck cocked his head and listened. It was the reverberating rumble of a crowd. The only question was from which direction was it coming? It seemed to be all around them, echoing throughout the tunnel.

The lights overhead still flickered like a slow strobe. They crackled each time with the buzz of electricity, but now he could barely hear them as the crowd drew nearer.

The more he listened, the more he was convinced that the commotion was not coming from behind them. In fact, he was sure of it. It was coming from the Queens side.

And then the lights stopped flickering and the tunnel was pitch black.

Chuck felt the rising swell of panic in his throat and suppressed a scream. If the lights didn't come on soon, they would be forced to move in the darkness. The rumble was getting louder and Chuck fought the urge to explode. Then the lights came on again and the tunnel ahead of them was full of lurching dead.

"I've got enough bullets for us all." Jamal screamed, his voice pitched high, and for the first time Chuck saw fear in him. "I can do both of you and then do myself."

"No." Chuck said. "We passed a security office back around the bend in the tunnel. We'll go there. Maybe there will be someone to help us, or we can lock ourselves in and hide until they pass. If we move fast enough, maybe we can duck inside before they see us—outta sight—outta mind."

***

The office was there, just as Chuck had promised, but there was no one there to help them. It was a small room with a green, steel door and a large window that was reinforced with what looked like chicken wire between two panes of glass. They slipped in ahead of what they now figured to be two approaching mobs, one from each direction and ducked down out of sight. Chuck reached up from his hiding place close to the door and turned the lock.

It wasn't long before the two hordes converged in front of the little office. Chuck expected them to keep going and pass them by like two ships passing in the night and continue on their course. But he was wrong. The window and door became a rhythmic pulse of thrashing limbs. Chuck closed his eyes tightly and beat his head against the wall's cold, subway tile.

"I thought you said they wouldn't follow us Chuck!" Jamal yelled from his hiding place beside Duane, just under the window.

"I said maybe. Now stay down."

Duane cried out above the thrashing and wailing. "We're fucked! And here I am without a good drunk going. There's way too much blood in my alcohol system for this shit. I really hate when that happens because you care about shit too much. Shit like dying—Shit like getting eaten alive!"

Duane jumped up in front of the glass and started screaming at them through the window. "Get out of here you ugly fuckers! Go chew on someone else! What?...YOU WANT A PIECE OF ME?"

To Duane's left, one ghoul had the stump of a human leg crammed into his face and gnawed on it happily as it beat on the glass with its other hand. Duane noticed it and began to laugh.

"Hey you...want fries with that?" he screamed out, his laughter tinged with hysteria.

The cries became louder and the thrashing more intense.

"Get down!" Chuck told him. "You're just making it worse."

"Worse? How can it get worse? We're stuck in this little room with no way out and there's a bunch of rotting cannibals fighting to get in here to eat us, and they will eventually. That glass won't hold them for long. How can it get any worse?"

Jamal stood and pointed his gun at Duane's head. "Sit your white ass down before I drop you like a used rubber, you dumb fuck."

Duane edged closer to Jamal and placed his forehead up against the barrel of the gun.

"Go ahead, ya black, soap opera, hip-hop fuck! I don't care. You'd probably be doing me a favor anyway." Duane pulled away just a bit and reached out for the weapon. "Here, give it to me. I'll fucking do it for you."

Jamal held tight and drew away from Duane. "You're crazy, man. You are one crazy white boy—Fuck you! Let 'em tear you apart. I ain't wasting a bullet on your dumb ass."

Chuck stepped between them, "Knock it off...both of you. I think we've got a way out of here."

"What the hell are you talking about?" Duane asked, still wild eyed as he scanned the room. His hands trembled with adrenaline from his sudden outburst, and he fought to calm himself again.

"The vent," Chuck explained, and pointed to it on the far wall.

Jamal laughed, "Shit man, even if we get the cover off, it doesn't usually work like it does in the movies."

"You got any better ideas? If you do, now's a good time to share them!" Chuck screamed. He noted how loudly he had to speak to be heard over the dead things howling and banging on the other side of the glass. When neither Duane nor Jamal offered an idea of their own, Chuck took it as a signal to continue with his plan.

"We need to pry the cover off first," Chuck told Jamal.

Jamal bent down in front of the dirty, cream colored grate and peered inside.

"No way man, It's not deep enough. We can't fit inside that thing. It's not as big as it looks. It's only about a foot deep."

Chuck sighed, "Just help me get this cover off."

Jamal grunted, then reached out and grabbed behind the corner of the metal cover. There was just enough room for them to get their fingernails hooked in behind and pull.

It creaked and twisted, then with a pop it broke free.

Jamal gave it a toss and peered inside. "You see?" he pointed inward, "Not big enough."

"I thought you said we had to have faith, Brutha," Chuck said mockingly and pushed him aside.

He positioned himself in front of the opening just as the large window shattered. It crashed inward in spider-webbed fractures that clung to the chicken wire between its two panes. Now the crowd was deafening as the glass buffer between them disintegrated. The creatures gripped the wire and shook it furiously. Pebbled glass sprayed the room and peppered the three men at the opposite wall.

"Stand back!" Chuck screamed, and brushed away some of the tiny pebbles. He kicked at the ductwork inside several times until it broke free. Revealed behind it was another, larger space. Chuck stuck his head inside and looked around.

The hidden area resembled a narrow hall. A dim and dirty light flickered overhead. Water dripped from tiny cracks in its moldy ceiling. There was another duct attached to the hall's opposite wall. Chuck was reasonably sure it would lead to another office just like the one they were in now or possibly to another tunnel.

Chuck turned, smiling at their sudden turn of luck "Like you said…you gotta have faith."

16

Roy Burns sat directly in front of his friend.

Daniel hadn't moved in a while. Roy wasn't sure, but as he watched him, it didn't appear that he was breathing either.

The creatures had crowded into the cellblock until not an inch of space remained. The wails were deafening and he clinched his teeth and pulled at his hair in a vain attempt to make it stop. Roy could take no more. He would surely scream any second and place the gun to his own temple. Sheol had come to Earth with the single purpose of finding him. It had, and now reaped as much hopelessness and despair as possible.

As Roy sat there, mentally running through his life's experiences, his current dilemma grew worse. Swiping fingers brushed his back. He was barely out of their reach as they leaned in through the bars. To his left they fought for space close to the cell and to his right more reached for him. Some chewed at the iron bars in a futile attempt to gnaw through, their teeth grinding out and falling onto the hard floor.

Roy called out to his friend. "Daniel?"

He was tired of dealing with this alone. He wanted his friend to answer and give the comfort of companionship at this dire time. But Daniel said nothing, nor did he move, and Roy was sure that he was dead.

Roy held Daniel's gun at arm's length to carry out his friend's wish. He had promised Daniel that he would wait, that he would make sure first. But what did it matter now either way? Dead was dead, and they were both as good as dead at this point.

Roy lowered the weapon.

The room was echoing with the screams and hisses of the creatures as they grew more excited. Roy's hands instinctively moved to cover his ears. He could feel the coolness of the weapon he was holding as it pressed against him there. Maybe it would just be easier if he—

He had momentarily forgotten to watch Daniel. Roy opened his eyes.

If he was indeed dead and the information he had received was correct, he would soon wake. It would not be his friend waking. Rather, it would be something else. It would be something dark and needing. He'd hardly had time to consider that thought when Daniel's eyes fluttered open.

At first, he simply stared down at the floor. He sat still with his arms hanging limply at his side. Roy watched him for a time, silently. Perhaps Daniel wasn't dead after all. Maybe he was still just sick. He didn't seem to be in a mood to attack him.

"Daniel," he called out again.

Daniel looked up, opened his mouth and lunged.

Roy fell backward under the weight of the sudden attack as his gun skidded away. His dead friend clawed at his face and it was all he could do to keep the fresh ghoul at arm's length.

In his effort to repel Danny's attack, Roy had moved too close to the bars and was snatched from behind. He lost his balance and fell against them and was pinned there.

The creatures on the outside reached in through the bars and pulled at him. Roy thrashed against their cold clutches until he broke free. With all his strength, he bulled forward into Daniel. The two men fell against the back wall, but this time Roy was on top and had the advantage. It was something he would never have been able to do if Daniel were alive. Daniel was a born fighter. Under normal circumstances, Roy Burns could never best him.

As he fought to hold his former friend down, Roy searched the cell for his gun. It was on the floor against the bars to his left, but one of the ghouls had found it interesting and reached in curiously to pick it up. Roy dove after it, stealing it from the walking corpse's clammy fingers before he could move away.

Roy turned to his friend who was nearly on top of him again and pulled the trigger.

Daniel's brains splattered in a shower of red and gray against the painted, rear wall of the cell. His body dropped to the floor at Roy's feet and he stepped backward and fell into the iron bars again.

They were on him instantly. For a moment he refused to fight. Life had become burdensome. The will to live was gone. Let them do their thing and end it now, he thought. But those thoughts only invaded his mind for a fleeting moment.

Roy twisted and punched. With a final force of will and strength, he was free and moved to the center of the cell.

He stood there in that neutral space, finally exhausted, his chest heaving. A tiny area less than his arms could span was his world now. He would never venture beyond it. His friend was dead at his feet, hardly recognizable. If he moved in any direction outside that slight space they would tear at him again. The room reeked of blood and spoiled flesh. He wasn't sure, but he thought he also smelled soiled clothing. He had heard that upon death some people loose continence. He had never seen it personally, but now he was sure it was true. The cell reeked of shit. He could imagine Daniel, if he were alive, realizing this and commenting, "Well, I do believe you've shat yourselves ya nasty fuckers." Roy smiled at his musings. The smile quickly faded as he looked down at Daniel's lifeless body.

Roy could no longer see across the room. Not even to the cells directly across from his. The dead were packed in tighter than he thought possible. He rubbed the pistol in his hand and swallowed uneasily. And even though he could not bring himself to commit suicide, his life would eventually end in the tiny cell, dead from starvation, or lack of water.

Roy Burns had found the end of life's journey.

17

Adam opened the door to the lobby and listened.

He could feel the tension swell in his neck as he moved inside and quietly shut the metal door that led to the stairwell behind them.

There was an unnatural quiet. The silence that suddenly enveloped him was in sharp contrast to the horror and ruckus outside. He worried what might be around the next corner, unseen and unheard as he eased down the hall just ahead of Michael

Adam held the tire iron just above his right ear, and at a backward angle. If anything took him by surprise it would get a head full of iron. Dead or alive, now would not be a good time to surprise him. He was not good at this sort of thing. Not like Michael, and he couldn't stop thinking of Meena. Then suddenly his mind focused on his own situation and he flattened himself against the hall's cool, marble wall. There were voices coming from the lounge.

Michael grabbed Adam by the shirt and pulled him back. With a finger in front of his lips he quietly took the weapon from his fixed grip and assumed the lead.

Adam glanced back toward the stairway. If things went badly, a quick retreat was still possible. He brushed away mental images of gray-faced, bloodied ghouls filling the stairwell and blocking their exit. One of those apparitions was Michael's wife, her heart slapping against the scissor clamps. A ghastly sight, one he'd not forget soon.

"Stay behind me," Michael whispered, and peered around the corner until he could see into the lounge.

Two men were seated at the bar. One of them, a pudgy red-faced man in his fifties and balding, chugged the last of his drink. With the rattle of ice cubes, he placed the empty glass on the bar. His gray business suit stuck to him, stained with sweat in large patches under the arms. The other man was younger and wore a tie that was loosened around the collar. He had sharp features and a dark complexion. Middle Eastern, Michael reasoned. An uneasy feeling engulfed him at the sight of the man, his distrust of the foreigner was automatic. "We should leave too," he said to the portly fellow, in straightforward, clear English with only the slightest hint of an accent. "Time is running out."

The fat man said, "Time has already run out. If we were going to leave we should've left when the others did. Besides, we've got a job to do. I'm afraid we are here for the duration now."

Michael stepped into view.

"There's another one!" the Arab shouted, and picked up a wooden baseball bat that had been lying across one of the barstools.

"Oh shit!" the fat man exclaimed, and by reflex sent his empty glass shattering against the wall with a swipe of his arm.

"No!" Michael shouted.

The Middle Easterner stopped, but held tightly to the bat in his right hand, his left arm was outstretched and his finger pointed as if to motion Michael back toward the hall. Michael half expected him to say that the building was theirs and to go find one of their own.

"We're healthy and alive, not like those things outside. We're just trying to find somewhere safe." Michael told them. He noticed Adam still hidden around the corner and pulled him into view beside him.

"Who are you people? This is private property." The older, fat man responded, and pulled a pair of wire-framed glasses from his pocket to see the intruders more clearly.

"I'm Doctor Adam Riker." Adam blurted out and took the lead again. "I live upstairs. You probably know my wife better than you know me…Meena Riker."

"Yes, I know you, and I know your wife. But him…I don't know," he said, and pointed a finger to Michael."

"He's a cop. His name's Michael." Adam snapped his fingers as if commanding an answer to the rest of his sentence.

"Longley," Michael finished on cue, flatly.

"Yes, Longley. He's from Chicago." Adam nodded, and placed his hand on Michael's shoulder as if the two were best of friends.

The Middle Easterner laid the baseball bat on the barstool again and said, "Did you two just come in from out there?"

Adam said, "Yes."

"Is it this bad everywhere?"

"At least in this city it is." Adam told him, "I've not heard that much about other places."

The fat man reached for another bar glass. He filled it with scotch and then dropped a few ice cubes from a silver-serving bucket into the amber liquid. His hands trembled as he did so, spilling a little in the process. He was obviously shaken by their sudden appearance. "Other places are bad too," the fat man answered. "I hear Washington D.C. is the only major city on the East Coast that's functioning at all."

"Well, that's a change from their usual routine," Adam said, and moved to the bar beside the man with the Middle Eastern look about him. "I could sure use a drink."

The fat man nodded, his round face red from the alcohol and heightened blood pressure.

Adam glanced over his shoulder at Michael and pointed toward the bar. Michael understood the gesture, and shaking his head, he declined a drink for himself.

"I know you," Adam said to the Arab, "You're head of maintenance here in the tower, aren't you?"

"Yes—I'm Yusuf Al-Jamil," he said. "Yusuf in English is pronounced Joseph. So please, call me Joseph. It sounds…less threatening to most Americans these days. I've been employed here in this building for several years. New Yorkers can be an unforgiving and suspicious lot."

The fat man handed Adam his drink. "I'm Franklin Baker," he said, more to Michael than to Adam. "I'm the manager of the beautiful Trump World Tower. Seventy-two stories of sheer elegance and over-indulgence," he said, and chuckled. Then holding his arms out, he spun slowly to show off his surroundings. "I doubt there will be much for me to manage after today though. Just don't call me Frank. I hate to be called Frank."

Adam smiled at his comment and the two touched glasses civilly in a toast. He wasn't sure if he was toasting the fact that the future looked bleak for Tower management, or just toasting to Franklin instead of Frank, but he drank all the same.

With one tilt of the glass, Adam finished his drink.

"How many more are still here? I noticed a few cars in the garage when we shut the gate, but not many."

"You shut the gate?" Franklin asked.

"We did." Adam told him. "Well, he did," he said, and nodded to Michael. "I just watched from the sidelines."

Franklin said, "I don't know how many are still in the building. I know there are a few. Maybe we should leave that gate open for a while in case some still want to come home."

"No," Michael stepped in, "From the looks of it you've been in this bar for a while. Obviously you have not looked outside or been to the garage lately, because if you had, you would know how unnecessary that was."

Franklin walked from behind the bar and stood in front of Michael. "Those people own these apartments, Mister Longley. They paid big money for this kind of security and luxury. Am I simply to turn my back on them now? We're safe in here for the time being. I see no reason for rash decisions."

"You do see what's happening outside don't you, Mister Baker?"

"I do indeed, and I'm scared shitless. That doesn't change the fact that I have a responsibility to those people, to ensure their security here in this building."

Michael said, "And what about the safety of those already here?"

Franklin said, "Look, Mister Longley, all the windows on the first floor of this building are tinted. You can't see in from the outside unless we light things up. Even then, it would have to be dark outside for whatever is out there to see inside. They don't even know we're in here."

"The streets are clogged and deadly, Mister Baker," Michael said. "There'll be no one coming home tonight, but if we slip up, even once; it could spell the end for us. I say we lock all the ground floor doors, shut down the elevators and retreat upstairs. It's the only way to be sure. We can wait this thing out up there in relative safety."

"I'll tell you what I'll agree to do, Officer Longley…We'll lock the doors down here just like you want, but we'll stay around for the evening. If someone shows up we can let them inside. There might be a few out there still needing refuge," Franklin said.

Michael sighed, "Fair enough."

18

"They're following us." Duane said nervously. "I can hear them. They've come through the vent hole and are in the hall between offices."

Chuck scanned the small, dingy office they had just crawled into. He could hear them too, but that wasn't what puzzled him. It was the direction in which the tunnel traveled outside this office. If this tunnel went back to the City, it should be directly on the opposite wall from where they entered. It was not. The window facing the new tunnel was on the wall that was to the left of where they entered. This tunnel traveled north, and it was lower.

Jamal kicked at the open vent and a protruding ghoul's head disappeared back into the narrow hall. "We'd better do something fast, or we're as good as dead," he shrieked.

Chuck pushed a metal desk across the floor and slammed it on its side with the top facing the opening. With a pelvic thrust, he pushed it tight to the wall.

"Throw everything up to the hole—everything in the room. We need to barricade it."

Chuck grabbed a chair and tossed it on top. Duane and Jamal heaved a black file cabinet against the desk. Close to the door was a small wire trash can and Duane tossed the flimsy thing on top as Chuck and Jamal watched in dismay.

"Now what good is that gonna do?" Chuck scolded.

"It was a reflex. You said everything, and I was in a zone."

"A zone? You mean zoned, don't you? Now hold that stuff tight to the wall while I check this tunnel out. Something's fucked up."

Duane leaned his body against the desk. "What do you mean, fucked up?"

"I mean this tunnel doesn't go to where we thought it did. It goes north."

"Yeah, yeah," Jamal answered, and moved to the window and stood beside Chuck. Duane's back arched as the desk behind him nudged forward and he applied more pressure to hold it in place.

"This one comes out just up the street from the United Nations building. It puts us square back in the city. It runs beneath First Avenue for a ways and pops up right in the middle of where we don't wanna be."

Chuck shrugged, and glanced back to Duane who bounced against the desk as the horde tried to come through the opening behind it.

"What about the other direction—to the south?" Chuck asked.

"It's no better than the north." Jamal told him. "Either way we're in for a lot of company. But we might get more help if we go north toward the United Nations. There could be military or something up there. You know, they gotta protect the privileged pricks from overseas."

"Then we go north, and we'd better move fast. It's clear to get outta this office right now, but it might not be for long. The way I see it, we don't have much choice but to follow what we have."

"Yeah, I'm with you." Jamal agreed, "and with those things following us the whole way."

"Then we have to slow them down. We can lock the office door behind us. That should help us get a head start."

Jamal smiled, "Wha'chu talkin' about, man? Lotta good that'll do. The door locks and unlocks from the inside. That should slow them down all of about thirty seconds."

"I have a theory," Chuck said, "I don't think those things are too bright. I think if we lock the door, they will fiddle-fuck around in here for a while before they either figure it out, or open it by accident. Either way we have little time to work out our next move. At any time we could become trapped in here. Those things are making a lot of racket. If there are more of them somewhere in that tunnel out there, they could hear it and our only way out of here could be blocked."

"You're the boss on this trip," Jamal said. "I'm just along for the ride, but where do you figure we'll go once we're up top again?"

Chuck said, "If there's no law up there we'll have to be ready for that. We'll have to be ready to run and hole up somewhere. We ain't making it out of this city. We're gonna have to make our stand here and find a place that will keep us safe until help does arrive."

"And when do you think help will arrive?—A day?—A week?"

Chuck motioned for Duane to join them by the door, and said, "Shit, you wish. This ain't hurricane relief. I don't think you can expect to see FEMA moving in any time soon. We'd better be prepared to wait this thing out for a while. It's gonna take the full force of the military to fix this shit."

The desk began to rattle against the wall as the ghouls on the other side fought to gain entry. Chuck reached for his iron pipe-weapon and suddenly realized he'd forgotten it in the first office. With a deep sigh, he opened the door.

"Let's go."

***

The thunderous pounding diminished as Chuck and his two companions left the office behind. He wasn't sure if the monsters were tiring of their effort, or if they were simply fading into the distance. Either way, it was good to hear it less with each step.

They were silent for the better part of their short trip. But now they were nearing the end of the tunnel, and the way out could be seen just ahead.

At first it had been just a small glimmer of light in the distance, but now it was only fifty yards in front of them. The road traveled upward to the surface and the tunnel's entrance was slightly above them. Only blue sky and wisps of white clouds were visible from their standpoint. The smell of smoke and ash blew in through the opening and found its way to their nostrils too. Somewhere above, New York was burning.

Chuck stopped and sat on the curb next to the tunnel's concrete wall. He pulled out his last three cigarettes and passed them around, first to Jamal, then one to Duane who hesitated to take it.

"Go ahead, Dewey. What's it matter now? It'll help calm your nerves."

Duane snatched it from his fingers and stuck it between his lips.

With a flicker of flame, Chuck lit all three and drew in deeply on his own, enjoying what he reckoned might be his last.

The noise from outside could be heard even from where they rested. It was a crying out of sorts that resonated through the tunnel in a tune similar to that of monks at a monastery. It was song, rhythmic and hauntingly harmonic. It was a new and wraithlike sound, one that until today, Chuck was unfamiliar with, but it was unmistakably the song of the dead. There were a lot of them and they were agitated too. The others listened with him quietly as they smoked, taking in tobacco and ghoul song.

After everything they had been through, it soothed them in an odd sort of way.

Then there was an explosion from somewhere outside.

And another.

Duane fidgeted nervously. Chuck sucked in the last of the smoke as the fire met filter. He considered the scorched tip for a moment then flicked it away, satisfied that he had relished every last bit of tobacco it had to offer, and stood. The others followed suit, crushing their own spent butts.

Finally, Chuck said, "I guess it's time to shit or get off the pot fellas. The way I see it, we have little or no chance of getting through what's out there. I can't see them yet, but I can hear them, and it sounds like there's a whole shitload just waiting for us to stick our heads out into the sunlight."

"Did you hear those explosions?" Duane said. "Maybe the military's out there blowing the shit out of them. The United Nations…remember? There's gotta be soldiers there, right?"

They looked at one another, that possibility running through their minds with more hope now. To Chuck, it was an unknown. For all he knew they could walk outside and get the benefit of one of those bombs themselves, if it was indeed the military, and they weren't careful. Be damned if you do, damned if you don't. The irony - shot by one of the good guys.

Jamal drew his weapon and checked its load as if somehow extra bullets might have magically appeared in the chamber. They had not, and the reality that some of the few remaining may have their names attached didn't go unnoticed by anyone.

Chuck stood with his back facing the end of the tunnel. His silhouette glistened with the brightness of day that thinned his dark and wiry frame in contrast to the halo that outlined his lean figure. To Duane and Jamal, his face was featureless, blacked out by the light behind him. But it was stone-like, only his jaw flexed with pause, and dread.

They stood there for a moment, silent, knowing full well that their chances were slim and that death, which had come to so many, was likely just up the street for them as well.

Chuck moved first.

19

The sudden burst of sunlight on their unaccustomed eyes made them squint and momentarily lose focus as they ran out of the tunnel and into the street.

An explosion of unnatural wails filled the city air and echoed between the high-rise towers. The skyscrapers spun overhead as Chuck peered upward, trying to regain his senses. The smell of smoke was strong now and there were blackened rolls billowing into the sky somewhere in the direction of the Empire State Building. Gunshots popped in the distance. Including what sounded like rapid machine gun fire. Rat-a-tat, tat, tat.

They stood bewildered and overwhelmed on an ascending grade just outside the tunnel. To their left was a tall and dark building covered in mirrors. *Trump World Tower* was proclaimed on its façade in brass letters. Behind them, and to the right, the United Nations could be seen through the trees. Thousands of disfigured New Yorkers roamed the streets. They were twisted, awful looking things with missing limbs and deadened eyes. Their purpose had become obvious as they looked on with ill intent.

The circle tightened as the throng began to close in on them, first one and then many. Rank upon rank began to lurch forward. Chuck's lips mouthed the words but made no sound. Again he tried, but still only a whisper slipped past his lips.

Then, finally, he screamed out..."MOVE! MOVE! FOLLOW ME!"

Chuck ran to the left and jumped the wall where it was lowest and hoisted himself up to First Street facing the Tower. "Run fast, run through them." he cried, but the screams around them had risen to a fevered pitch. He was no longer confident they could hear his instructions. The visiting team was about to score a touchdown and the crowd was voicing their displeasure. Only this deafening crowd was closer, deadlier, all around them, now even closer than before, tattered, staggering gimps bent on cannibalism. As Chuck ran, he dared not turn or waste time. He could only hope that Duane and Jamal followed.

Chuck pushed past the first dead thing before climbing the steps in front of the Tower and crashing into the chest of another. With a strong upper cut he sent it reeling backward and pushed through where the crowd was thinnest, punching his way toward the sidewalk in front of the towering, black structure. With a burst of speed he sprinted the remaining distance and fell hard against an unyielding glass door. He had earned himself a little time as he made it there ahead of the pack.

At first he didn't see Duane or Jamal and feared the worst as he searched the swaying crowd for them. Then they emerged from the fray in full stride and dashed to his side, surprisingly unmolested.

Duane was bent forward with his hands on his knees and out of breath. His chest heaved in search of vital oxygen for strength he would surely need again in the coming seconds. He watched anxiously as the crowd moved in on them again. "Now what genius?" he gasped.

Chuck's mind raced. He was out of ideas. He had led them into a trap after all. How could he have known? There were simply too many of them now. They would never escape.

Chuck turned quickly, startled by the sound of tapping on the window behind him.

At first he mistook the person inside for another dead thing trying to get to them, but quickly realized that was not the case. This man was alive and speaking, pressing his face against the window. He was saying something. He pointed too. What was he saying? It was impossible to hear over the noise generated by the eager crowd. Was he saying, *Don't come around?* Yes, he was. No, he wasn't. He was saying, "*Go around.*" That is what he was saying, and he was pointing.

"Go around to the side! Come in through the garage," the fat man screamed, his face still pressed against the other side of the tinted window.

Chuck could feel his blood pressure rise as the crowd drew close and a lump formed in his throat. "No, open the door. Let us in now!" he screamed.

"We can't risk it. There are too many of them. I won't open this door and take the chance of letting them all in here with us. Go now!" With that, the man disappeared.

With no other option, they leaped into action and sprinted around the corner. The ghouls gave chase as they ran close to the building and skirted behind a line of planted shrubs. The shrubs made the running humans hard to reach and the slow-moving reanimates were clumsy. Many fell or lost their balance when attempting to reach them through the waist-high planted hedge. The others were slapped away if they got too close.

Chuck was looking for another door and zeroed in on the underground garage. It was surely the entrance the fat man meant and he made a beeline for it in the open. Duane and Jamal followed, plowing their way through the groping figures.

One of them grabbed Jamal by the shoulder and he spun to meet it face to face.

The attacker was odd, yet familiar to all who called New York City their home. And even though Jamal no longer lived in New York, he remembered this famous face. It was Bob Safire, the weatherman from Channel Twelve. Recognition flashed across Jamal's face as he stared into his glazed eyes. This was not the well-groomed media figure that filled the television screen every weekday at five-twenty. There was no noticeable injury, but he was decidedly pale and poorly dressed with only a pair of dirty, white briefs to hide his nakedness.

Jamal leaned back and punched the phantom in the nose. Unexpectedly, he stayed on his feet and only staggered a few steps backward before covering his face with both hands. Jamal laughed, "I always wanted to do that, you arrogant fuck." With a leap he cleared the gate and fell into the garage with the others. They had room to maneuver now as the crowd collapsed into the barrier between them.

Chuck helped Jamal to his feet and they moved back into the darkness of the garage, putting some distance between themselves and the creatures threatening to break through the gate.

"There's gotta be a door or something in here," Chuck said. "Something that'll get us inside."

The first dead thing climbed the gate and fell across to their side. It squirmed on the concrete as if confused or dazed from the fall before it was able to gain its footing again.

"There." Chuck pointed to the shadows. A door was barely visible. "Run there," he told them, and led the way.

To their relief, the door flew open as they drew near. They ran inside well ahead of the danger. A tall man with a swarthy complexion and a slight accent met them there. "Quickly—this way," he said, and waved them through before locking the metal door behind them.

20

Michael and Yusuf walked behind the three harried refugees.

Street trash, Michael thought, a gangbanger and two rednecks that look like recruiters for a white supremacist group. Theirs was certainly a strange and unlikely alliance. Michael overheard the hyper little hick call the bald redneck Chuck. His head had been shaved, rather than being naturally bald as evidenced by the dark shadow of stubble that had begun to darken his scalp again. He had full sleeves of tattoos that ran the length of both arms. He was lean, and had a cock-sure air about him. The other, in his mid-thirties, was duller, over excitable, and seemed to look to his bald companion for direction, not a leader, but a follower. Michael knew their type. They were wannabes, not the genuine article Neo-Nazis he had encountered back in Chicago, but back woodsy knock-offs. They were out of their element in New York City.

Michael could peg the black one a mile away. He was a gang member, pure and simple. He knew his type too. He recognized the strut and thuggish demeanor. They differed very little from Chicago to New York. Violence and death lurked behind those constantly scanning, bloodshot eyes. This one was almost never out of his element. He could bring death and destruction to any occasion. They were from different camps brought together by unimaginable circumstances. Michael could think of no immediate reason to deny them asylum from the apocalypse outside, but it wasn't as if he hadn't tried. His cop instincts raised an instant distrust of them.

They could stay for the time being, but he would watch them very closely. The black one looked familiar.

Chuck made a beeline for the bar, took a crystal decanter of bourbon from the shelf and a glass. He tossed back six ounces and then filled the glass again. "What the hell is happening?" he choked out in a demanding voice, gasping as the bourbon's heat radiated down his gullet. It instantly eased his taut nerves.

Adam Riker moved close to him, "You tell us. You've been out there more recently than we have."

Chuck emptied the glass for a second time and poured a third. He hesitated before answering and shook his head slowly, as though in a daze, "It's all gone," he whispered hoarsely. "The streets are lost and we're fucked. There are a million people out there eating each other…killing. They're dead, only they're not. They're something else—living-dead. Possessed maybe? I don't know, but there's one thing I do know…" Chuck drank again. "We're in here to stay."

"What about the rest of the City?" Adam asked. "Did you see any evidence that the military had moved in yet?"

"No…nothing. It's all just like this. It's all the same. We're fucked. We need protection. Does anyone have any guns?"

No one answered as they momentarily pondered their bleak situation with its glum alternatives.

"Your friend does," Michael answered finally, nodding at Jamal.

Jamal turned and faced Michael. He pulled the pistol from under his shirt, holding it comfortably in his right hand while caressing the cold barrel with his left.

Jamal said, "Uh-huh. It's mine, and I'll keep it. I only have a few bullets left. If I'm gettin' my ass torn apart by those cannibal motherfuckers outside I'll use one on myself. The others are for any prick who thinks he's gonna take it from me." The threat in his voice was unmistakable as he cast his gaze around to include everyone in the room. "Don't worry though Law-dog, if you don't fuck with me, I'm cool. No problem. But this is mine. Mine. We good?" he raised his eyebrow in a quizzical expression.

"Yeah man, we're good," Michael replied.

You could suddenly cut the tension in the room with a knife.

Michael said, "It's just not much help against the current odds. One gun, a few bullets and about a million crazed, man-eating Deadies. How did you know I'm a cop?"

"Shit man, who the fuck wouldn't? It's *on* you, man. The way you walk, the way you talk. I ain't gotta see no fuckin' badge to know a pig."

"Isn't that quaint?" Michael narrowed his eyes, "It's nice to know you're so good at reading people. I'm pretty good at that too," Michael intoned, as he moved up nose to nose with Jamal. "And I read clearly that you're a piece of shit gangbanger. Too used to living on the streets to know anything about working as a team in a bad situation. You're the kind of guy who doesn't care who dies as long as your ass is safe. You're the guy who gets the other teammates killed." The pitch of Michael's voice dropped lower as he leaned in still closer. "So let me ask you something, *Dog*. How long do you figure you and your few bullets will last when I toss your criminal ass back out that fucking door?" He glared into Jamal's eyes. "If I had to guess I'd say you were wanted somewhere for something. That's why I know your face. And we are not about to endanger the lives of the decent people in this building to help some one-way thug who would just as soon shoot one of us as one of those things outside."

"Shit man, you've got no idea who I am, or where I'm from." The corner of Jamal's mouth raised in a lop-sided grin as he continued. "You don't know me. You look. You judge, but you don't know shit. Teammate, huh? Well, try actin' like I might be a teammate instead of the fuckin' nigga that's tryin' to steal the team's bus. How 'bout that, Coach? As far as guns, you obviously ain't from around here, are ya Coach? Everyone in New York knows the only people who have guns are the criminals, so I guess me being here makes this your lucky fuckin' day, don't it?" Jamal narrowed his eyes at Michael, "And you say you're a cop? You tellin' me you ain't got a gun?"

"You're the one who said I was a cop, not me," Michael took a step back as the tension of the situation began to diffuse. "Besides, I'm from Chicago. It's not my jurisdiction."

"Since when did that make a difference? A cop's a cop, and a cop's always packin'."

Michael turned and walked away from Jamal, keeping an eye on him as he moved toward Franklin Baker. "What about the people who live in this building? Surely there are people here who own firearms."

"Officer Longley, this is the Trump World Tower. You are aware of the sort of people who live in this building, aren't you?" He queried, with an edge of snobbery in his tone. "As a rule, these people pay others to provide their security. They don't carry weapons."

Michael said, "What about the building's security officers?"

"Gone or dead, who knows." Franklin explained, "They're not here anymore. They left hours ago."

"You may be incorrect, sir," Yusuf interjected. "There may indeed be some tenants with weapons in the building."

Michael eyed him suspiciously, having a residual distrust for anyone of Middle Eastern origin. He regarded them all as possible members of some sleeper cell for Al-Qaeda. Maybe he had a stash of enough weapons and explosives to bring down the high-rise? Maybe it was even deeper. Were the towel-head radicals responsible for this? Had they created some biological virus that could turn the dead? But that wasn't their style. They preferred to simply blow things up.

"Sarah Randolph in the Penthouse," Yusuf continued. She may have what we're looking for."

Franklin's eyebrow rose noticeably, "That crazy bitch probably owns an arsenal."

"Crazy bitch—here?" Michael's interest shifted.

"Yes," said Franklin.

Michael nodded, "It's getting dark. Let's make sure we're buttoned down nice and tight. We'll talk to Mrs. Randolph tomorrow if she's still here."

"The doors are locked. What else should we do?" Yusuf asked.

"It'll be dark soon. Turn out the lights." Adam chimed in, "They're not like us. They loose interest easily. We need to make them forget we're in here. The last thing we need is to draw their attention. If we turn out the lights and stay out of sight I believe it'll go a long way toward achieving that. There's no telling how long we're going to be holed up in this building before help arrives. We could be here for weeks, maybe even months. There's just no way to be sure."

"Months?" Jamal yelled. "Do you have enough food for all of us to last that long? How many people are in the building? Shit man, I was hopin' to get back to California soon. All this shit's done put a crimp in my career. Now we got to worry about fucking food and shit for months? I don't think so."

Jamal's ranting about his loss of lifestyle fell on deaf ears, but one thing rang true to Michael, they would need a real game plan, and soon. "How many people are still in the building?" Michael repeated Jamal's question. "It will make a difference in how long we can ride this thing out."

Michael was waiting on Franklin's answer, but he only shook his head noncommittally and said, "I don't know. On any given day you could expect anywhere from a hundred, to four hundred people depending on the hour. And that counts staff. But this isn't any given day, and outside of Mister Al-Jamil, I've seen no staff all morning."

"There didn't appear to be many vehicles in the garage," Michael said, "It looks like a lot of them left this morning, probably trying to get out of the city. Much like your Security men who, at the first sign of trouble, bravely ran away."

"How do you know they ran Officer Longley? Maybe they're out there in the streets somewhere. Maybe they're like those things now because they stayed and fought to the death. Maybe they are lingering in the shadows of the garage waiting to pounce on the next unsuspecting, living person."

Michael snorted, "In any event, we are without adequate armed protection and ammunition. And now you're telling me that we may not have enough food to boot?"

"We have plenty of food in the kitchen; enough to last us a while, if rationed properly," Franklin told him. "Besides, there will be food in the private residences as well. We should be fine. Electricity is what you should worry about. It won't last long with things the way they are. Once we lose power we'll lose some of our food store."

"Michael nodded, "Then we eat the perishables first. Only when that's gone do we eat the canned goods. We'll also need candles. We need to be prepared for the loss of power. I don't think there's any doubt that it's going to happen. We'll lose power for sure."

Michael didn't say it aloud, but what he wanted to say was that his wife was dead and that the world had gone to shit and that he was no longer sure he wanted to live in this '*dead world.*' But he couldn't do that. He couldn't say those things aloud. Jamal was right about one thing, he was a cop, and that fact was written on every part of his being just as blatantly as the tattoos on Chuck's arms. He would hold it together a bit longer.

Michael said, "First thing in the morning we will go door to door and get a good head count on who's here with us."

"We're all exhausted," Franklin said with a huff "It's been a trying day. We need our rest. A few of us can stay down here tonight and make sure the ground level stays secure and let in anyone who might still show up. The rest of us can stay in an open apartment on the fifth floor."

"Whoever stays down here needs to remember to stay out of sight. If those things get in here it's over for us," Michael added.

"I'll do it," Chuck said, "and so will Duane."

Michael pointed to Duane. "Duane? Is that his name?"

"Yeah, that's it, or Dewey."

Michael said, "How about your black friend?"

"His name is Jamal."

"Jamal," Michael said, "You stay upstairs with me and Doctor Riker."

"Why should I have to do that?"

"Because I don't know you and I don't trust you. Until I do, I want the three of you separated at night while we're asleep. Yusuf can stay downstairs with Duane and Chuck."

Jamal said, "Hey, you know what? That's bullshit man and you know it. But okay. I'll play your game. No problem. I don't trust you either. So yeah, I'll play your game, for now, 'cause I'm a nice guy, a team player. I'll play along as long as it suits me, bro."

Michael's eyes narrowed, and he chuckled, "That's mighty white of you—bro."

21

The morning had found Michael less prepared for the task at hand than he had hoped to be. The power was still on and some television stations continued to broadcast. And the phenomenon was everywhere. New York had been hit hardest of all. Every major city in the world had been affected now to some degree, with the safest areas being rural communities and mountainous regions. There was footage being shown of people banding together in armed groups, seek and destroy units, methodically canvassing neighborhoods and pubic areas. One man being interviewed told the reporter he was taking his family to a designated safe-zone that had been set up close to his home.

For the last ten minutes, Michael had been watching from the sixtieth-floor window. A horde of dearly departed forced their way through a makeshift barricade and into the building across the street. Soon after, the crowd dispersed, no longer interested in the compromised building now that its inhabitants were likely dead. Down the street he could see other similar situations unfolding in like fashion, including their own building. Below he could see the gathering throng gaining in numbers. There was an undulating sea of undead pressing against the structure. He wondered how long it would take before they found their way inside the World Tower as well.

They had found a total of fifty-two people in the building, counting themselves, as they systematically moved from apartment to apartment toward the top floor. Only three handguns had been found with precious little ammunition. Less than one hundred rounds were at their disposal. Sarah Randolph owned the Penthouse apartment. She resided alone on the top floor. Michael hoped she would have more to offer in the way of protective weapons. But he doubted they would find enough guns to truly help them with their plight. Perhaps she owned a helicopter. That would be nice, he thought with amusement, an airlift out of hell.

Michael turned suddenly as Franklin Baker reentered the room from his search of the apartment. Unlike yesterday, when he had been dressed in a sweaty three-piece suit, today Franklin wore only a white tank top to complement his gray-striped, dress pants. He wiped sweat from over his brow with a white cloth.

"There's no one here," Franklin told him, "We can move up to the next floor now."

Michael acknowledged him, and watched as another building was compromised. Once more the crowd scattered, finding new purpose with the building next in line.

* * *

The Randolph Penthouse occupied the entire top floor of the Tower. The elevator keypad required a special code to gain access. Before punching in the numbers, Franklin turned to Michael and Adam.

"There were originally two penthouses on this floor," he said, "Sarah Randolph bought them both and combined them into one. She's very wealthy and a bit of an isolationist. I'm not really sure how or where she got her fortune, but it is substantial. With the phones out we are arriving unannounced."

Michael said, "There's no time for formal announcements Mister Baker. Please, enter the goddamned code,"

"Don't say I didn't warn you," Franklin said, and entered the code.

The doors closed and the elevator jolted upward. They listened to a soft, bell-toned, elevator rendition of an REM song. Michael thought it was *Losing My Religion*, and closed his eyes. Somehow, to him, REM music seemed a natural fit for an elevator. *Losing My Religion* also fit the day. At least Michael's interpretation of it, though the songwriter's meaning was different, or so he'd heard.

The door opened and Michael and Adam found a gun barrel pointed at each of their faces.

It took Michael a moment to draw his focus away from the end of the pistol. Once he did, he saw the woman behind the double-fisted weapons.

Sarah Randolph was fifty-six with light brown, shoulder length hair with frosted tips. It was layered in a way that actually accented the frosted highlights in stunning fashion. She wore a black sleeveless top that revealed an athletic body, unmatched by most women her age. Her jeans fit closely to her thighs and legs. Her arms moved not an inch as she held the weapons motionless in front them. Her brown eyes were stern and deep, gleaming with confidence. Sarah Randolph was calm and in control.

Finally, Franklin said, "I'm—sorry to bother you, Mrs. Randolph—but I'm sure you are aware of what is happening. This man is a policeman." Franklin pointed to Michael. "I think you've met Mister Riker. He lives here in the building." Franklin Baker's voice was usually raspy, but now it was shaking nervously as he spoke to Sarah.

It was obvious that Sarah Randolph had heard Franklin and absorbed the information, but her eyes did not move from the two men with him.

Michael slowly moved back and away from the weapon.

"Please, Ms. Randolph, we need your help." Franklin said.

"I'm not here to help you, or anyone else." She explained. "It's not my lot in life. This is private property and you are an intruder. I don't care if you're a policeman or the goddamned President—especially the goddamned President."

Michael had heard enough and spoke. "Fine, if you want to shoot us then go ahead and shoot us. We have over fifty people downstairs that need all the protection we can muster up. Now, if that means you have to be inconvenienced, then that's the way it's gotta be, but protecting this building starts on the ground floor. You have as much stake in that as anyone else and we need your help."

Sarah said, "What you mean is you need more guns."

"Yes, of course we do," Michael answered.

Sarah relaxed her posture and lowered her weapons before turning to walk back into her apartment. "Don't take the elevators anymore unless you want to get stuck between floors, gentlemen. Use the stairs from now on. As you might have surmised, the power won't last forever now that Armageddon's reared its ugly head."

22

Chuck leaned against the wall next to the tinted glass door he had tried to enter earlier. The creatures outside could not see him standing just three feet from them as they moved past.

The crowd was thick, too deep to see its end. It covered every measure of humanity, but Chuck was only interested in one of them.

Standing close to the door, was a woman wearing a silver heart-shaped locket with long dark hair and coal black eyes. She was taller than Chuck who stood only five-nine, flat-footed. Her breasts were full, their nipples easily seen through her thin and wispy nightgown.

She shuffled along sluggishly, leaning to one side. Dried blood caked the left side of her beautiful, ghostly face. Chuck stared, desirous of her in spite of what she had become and motioned for Duane.

"Jesus, take a look at this."

Duane crept closer, "Yeah, I saw her."

"Look at her," Chuck whispered, "She's beautiful."

"Are you outta your mind, Chuck? She's dead…dead and rotting.

"How do you know they're rotting?"

"They smell bad, man. That's how I know.

Chuck said, "I'd do her."

"You're a sick bastard."

"I think she might be the most beautiful woman I've ever seen in my life. You can stand there and tell me you don't think she's hot, Duane?"

"She's room temperature, Chuck…room temperature at best. What's that tell you?"

"She's outside temperature."

"Even worse—Jesus, Chuck."

Chuck moved closer to the glass, and said, "Where have you been all my life, beautiful?"

Duane said, "Get away from the door or they'll see you."

"They can't see me through the tinted glass."

Chuck put his face to the glass and licked a foot-long trail of saliva across the thick pane in front of her.

As if on cue, she lunged forward and crashed into the door. Chuck fell backward into the room and landed on the floor out of her sight once more, laughing hysterically. The woman continued to paw and scratch on the glass as if she still retained an image of Chuck's face in her mind.

"I told you." Duane shook his head, incredulously. "You're going to get us all killed."

"See?" Chuck said, still smiling and ignoring Duane's outburst, "She wants me."

"She wants to eat you, and not in a good way."

Chuck got to his feet and walked back to the lounge. He stood there in the archway between the two rooms staring down balefully into a dwindling pack of cigarettes he had found behind the bar earlier. He had been so busy fighting for his life that he had given little thought to his smoking addiction. Now with time on his hands again, he was forced to scan the ashtrays for smokable butts. Their present situation had forcibly eliminated the luxury option of chain-smoking.

Chuck stuck one of his remaining four cigarettes between his lips, lit it, and inhaled deeply. They always seemed to taste better when their availability was limited. The flavor was better, and the urge to smoke, stronger. He wondered what he would do when the last cigarette was finally gone. There might be some in the building, though he doubted it really. The people who lived there were not low-rent smokers. Their addictions were much more extravagant.

His dead diva had moved away from the door again and others had moved up to take her place. They wandered back and forth in what seemed to be a thoughtless pattern of movement. Chuck watched them and it occurred to him that some of them might have cigarettes in their pockets. How desperate would he need to be to risk it? Certainly, pretty desperate to even think about it.

The outer room was lined with windows, floor to ceiling. They were tinted the same as the door and looked sturdy enough to hold off the crowd outside unless they organized an all out attack. Sheer gauzy curtain panels covered them and allowed the city view to enter the room unobstructed. Small glass tables perfectly accented the meeting area. Comfortable leather square-back chairs accompanied them, two and three to each. It was obvious that the tables had been positioned perfectly to accent the beauty of the room. A balcony hung suspended over half, while the rest opened to a stunning cathedral ceiling. As Chuck crushed his spent cigarette into the plush carpet beneath his boot, he thought about what a shame it was that his free stay at The World Tower could not be more thoroughly enjoyed.

Duane was sitting at the bar with his head leaning into his hands. Under his arms was an untouched shot of brandy. Chuck knew Duane wanted to go home. Even before the plague he had known. He also knew Duane blamed him for their predicament. He blamed him for every wrong turn they had made in New York, but that was just Duane. He never accepted responsibility for anything he might do wrong himself. He fancied the easy approach every time, the path of least resistance. That was fine as long as you were content with where you were at the time, and that was truly Duane's problem. He was content to just be where he was, doing pretty much nothing, without the slightest hint of ambition.

"You shouldn't worry about your family too much. I'm sure there are fewer man-eating zombies in Virginia than here, Duane."

"We have a place in the country. I'm sure they'll be fine." Duane grumbled without moving. Then Duane raised his head, and said, "What did you call them…zombies?

"Yeah, so what?"

"Is that what they are, zombies?"

"Hell, I don't know, Dewey. Why's it matter what I called them? They're deadly. That's all we need to know."

Duane threw down the brandy in one shot, and on reflex winced. The wince was unnecessary. The brandy's quality was high and the drink, smooth. He smacked his lips, savoring the silky flavor. "Where is everyone?" Duane asked.

"They're doing a search for others in the building."

"Have they found anyone?"

"How should I know? I've been down here with you." Chuck said irritably.

"Where's Jamal, with them?"

"That cop doesn't trust us, so he's keeping us separated, but I think so. What is this, twenty questions? Enough already. I don't know any more than you."

Duane considered the bottle of brandy and then decided against another shot. He was not one to grow accustomed to sobriety. But somehow, it didn't seem like the right time to go on a bender.

Chuck said, "What happened to that fucking Arab? He was gone when I woke up this morning."

"I think he went upstairs. I assume to help search the building." Duane said. "If that's what they're doing."

"Why didn't they ask us to help them?"

"Would you have helped?"

"No."

"Then I guess they didn't feel like wasting their breath."

23

Steel…

There would always be a need for it and profits were good; at least until the industry collapsed more than three decades ago. It had a major impact on Pittsburgh's identity. In response to the collapse, Pittsburgh's economy shifted to healthcare, education, technology, and financial services. The city moved past its industrial misfortunes and became a smaller, more desirable place to live. The lesser steel companies soon found themselves out of money and out of business. Sarah's family was more fortunate. They had the foresight to sell before the crash. Her father died soon after, and for the first time in her life, Sarah was alone.

Her father had been a guiding light for her throughout her life. He was a stern, yet loving man, a conservative man, who often dabbled in politics. He brought Sarah up in like-fashion and made sure she was fully equipped to survive in modern society. *"The world is a competitive place,"* he often told her, *"and only the strong survive. The rest die slowly and poor."*

Sarah was determined to not die slowly like her mother, who died of cancer when she was very young. Those days, though distant, were still clear in her mind. The torment her mother had endured, withering away until she finally resembled a paper shell of her former self. In the end, her mother died a quiet death, sedated and unconscious. She breathed heavily, gasping at times until that too, slowed and stopped.

Sarah would have none of that. She would go out kicking and screaming if need be, but not without a fight. No lingering death for her. It would be fast and on her own terms.

Sarah's inheritance had been invested in helping Pittsburgh gain status as an appealing place to live and work by investing in hi-tech companies and cutting edge science. Her father's company once supplied some of the steel to build Pittsburgh's Fort Pitt Bridge. Now she was building bridges to the future; at least that's what she had been doing before the world came apart.

As she watched from her penthouse window, she hoped Pittsburgh, the home she loved, was surviving better than New York. The streets below had been total chaos earlier. They were calm now. The frantic movement of panicked New Yorkers had been replaced by slower, more methodical plodding figures. Abandoned vehicles clogged the arteries of the great city in every direction. Like ants, the figures numbered in the thousands. Maybe even hundreds of thousands as she watched safe within the walls of her sprawling penthouse.

"What will you do with the guns?" she asked Michael who stood just behind her. The others had left and only Michael remained to collect the weapons. She could sense him there without turning, watching her. "The guns will do no good if they get inside. There will simply be too many to shoot."

Michael picked up one of the M16s Sarah had given him and studied it. He was familiar with the weapon. Sometimes he used an AR15 on the firing range. It was more or less the civilian version of the weapon he was holding.

Michael said, "Where did you get these automatic weapons?"

"My father liked guns. He taught me their proper use at an early age. I keep them for security," Sarah said.

"Security? You must have some mean ass enemies. I'm surprised they let you have these in the city."

"They don't."

Michael moved to her side and glanced down at the crowded streets. "The guns are all we have."

Sarah said, "It's a bad plan. You should close off the ground level from the rest of the building. Lock the doors to the stairwells, turn off the elevator, and retreat upward. You can't defend the ground floor. There are too many windows."

"I've already been through this with Baker. He says we can't do that yet. We have to bring supplies up from the ground floor. Besides, we need a way out should that opportunity present itself. If the military shows up there will be no time to waste."

"There will be no cavalry arriving in the nick of time, Officer Longley. Not this time." Sarah told him, "This is only going to get worse. I was listening to the radio earlier. They say it's happening everywhere. Military and civil units have pulled back in many places. Most people are on their own. This is New York City, one of the largest and most populated cities in the world. What makes you think it'll be any better here?"

Michael nodded, "I know. But we can't just give up hope."

Sarah frowned, "I'm not asking you to give up hope. I'm telling you to be prepared. It's only been a day. Look out there. This city is lost. It's overrun. It is, for all intents and purposes, dead. I doubt rescue will even be attempted. People, and that includes soldiers and policemen, are too busy trying to save their own hides."

Michael picked up the weapons and walked to the elevator. "There's a meeting in the lounge in an hour. We want you there," He said the words, and realized that *need* would have been a better choice of words than *want*.

Michael stepped inside the elevator and the doors closed. Sarah listened as the elevator descended from the penthouse floor.

***

Later, when Sarah entered the lobby, she was unprepared for the site that greeted her. Just outside, the menace filled the streets, and for the first time, Sarah had an up close view of the alleged living-dead.

She had seen the reports on the television, but this was reality, and reality called for the suspension of belief in God and Heaven. It relegated Hell to the surface of the Earth, and gave its inhabitants front row seats to the carnage only Hell could bring. Indeed, Hell did exist and mankind had been given a prime example of why they should fear it. Here and now, Sarah could see the ashen skin and sunken faces, the torn limbs and terrible wounds that no person could withstand and still survive. Unlike the constant barrage of violence thrown from the television on a daily basis until it was no longer shocking, this was real, in your face. This *was* shocking.

Sarah moved silently into the room and behind the assemblage where she stood in a darkened corner and watched.

She distrusted people. She was a solitary woman, a loner. She saw people only when she absolutely had to, and she trusted only a select few individuals in her isolated existence, none of which were there in the room with her.

The people who had been found alive in the building's residences were all there. Some she recognized, others she did not. The crowd, which must have numbered fifty or more, mingled and spoke softly to one another; all the while the danger lurked just on the other side of the tinted glass walls.

She thought it careless to tempt fate so blatantly. If the infected dead outside took notice of them, they might converge in an attempt to break through. Certainly, an all out panic would ensue and many in the room now would lose their lives. She had seen on the television the unspeakable horrors inflicted. And then, just as if he'd been reading her mind, Franklin Baker walked to the front of the room and whispered…

"For our own safety we all need to move into the bar area. It'll be a little cramped, I know, but it's separated from all these windows."

The crowd dispersed, shifting quietly into the next room where Michael Longley stood waiting.

The room was indeed smaller, and it took some doing to get everyone comfortably squeezed into it. Sarah found an open area next to the hall. It gave her an open shot to the stairs should something go wrong.

Again Franklin Baker spoke, this time with more volume. "We have some things to tell you. They're important so you must pay attention. We will all depend on each other to survive. And we must follow instructions to the letter." He cleared his throat nervously and continued, "Mister Longley here is a police officer from Chicago. Since he's familiar with proper emergency procedures I'm going to let him explain to you the rules of survival here at the Tower."

Michael stepped forward.

"First and foremost, no one—and I mean no one, may open an exterior door or move close to it. Stay away from the windows. If those things out there see you, it will agitate them. We don't want that." He scanned the room to be sure he had everyone's attention.

"We have the doors locked so it will be difficult to open them without a key but I can't express the importance enough of staying out of sight. That goes for the windows above the ground floor as well. If we don't continue to draw attention to ourselves and our presence here, maybe they'll forget, or lose interest and just go away."

Michael looked from one war-shocked face to another; he seemed to have their undivided attention and he hoped they were listening. He had seen from the windows above what happened when the demons outside decided they wanted inside a particular place.

"No one should be down here at night. The tinted windows keep us hidden in the daytime, but if you come down here at night and turn on a light or bring a candle, the tinted windows are useless. Those outside will see you. Hopefully, we'll have electric for a while, but do not expect it to last forever. It has already flashed more than once since yesterday. It's on now, but we are living on borrowed time. It will likely go out again." Michael looked over at Sarah, recalling their earlier conversation, "And don't expect help to arrive anytime soon," he quirked his head slightly in silent concession of her point. Her expression was unchanged.

"We've done a cursory check of the available food stores in the building. Our early estimates give us a couple months worth of supplies. I would've thought we'd have more, but it seems the wealthy don't really stock up on food. I guess you go out to eat a lot."

There were a few nervous chuckles from the crowd.

"We have men now storing water in as many containers as they can find to fill. I am telling everyone here to do the same from your apartments as soon as this meeting is over. If the electricity goes out we could also lose pressure in the city water lines. Fill anything you have with water, even your bathtubs…especially your bathtubs."

From outside, a great roaring sound erupted that could be heard easily from the bar. It was as if a great wind had kicked up and threatened to tear the building down to its foundation. The room fell silent, listening with un-breathing dread as they envisioned the possibility that their world was finally coming to an end.

Adam Riker and Yusuf Al-Jamil entered the room in a huff. Riker held one of Sarah's M16s at his side. He took three steps forward and stopped. "There are people on the roof of the church next door. I think they're in trouble. The things outside can see them up there and they're all in a tizzy. That's why they're making so much racket."

Michael moved quickly. "Show me."

24

Mary hurried to stack the five gallon buckets of tar against the roof door. It was all she could do to lift the heavy containers three high. And even though she strained mightily to move them, she feared it was too little to stop the fiends as she hoisted the last of nine into place.

Her mind raced as she searched the roof for something more. It would only take the pale-faced monsters a few minutes to climb the steps and force their way through her feeble bucket barricade.

The stained glass windows had been no match for the sheer numbers searching every square inch of the church for entrance. A window shattered and in a matter of minutes, the church was overrun.

Melissa's tiny hands were clenched into fists and she held them tightly in front of her mouth. She was motionless, too afraid to move. Mary could feel the panic rise in her chest as she fought the compulsion to hyperventilate. She scooped her little sister into her arms and raced to the edge of the roof.

Running along its edge, she searched for an escape route. Parts of the church were three stories high, but the area of the roof they now stood on was closer to the ground. The creatures were only several feet below, their up-reaching arms stretched into a grotesque wave of monster tentacles. When they took notice of the girls, who were barely out of their reach, they screamed out in a building crescendo of sound. Ear-splitting waves of chorusing howls seemed to fill Mary's entire world. She became dizzy and lost her balance and fell to the roof surface spilling her sister onto the sticky, hot tar coating. The haunting sounds threatened to follow her into unconsciousness as she fought for clarity.

Then, the sound of breaking glass brought her instantly alert.

Through blurred vision she could see people, living people, on the suspended metal awning covering the rear entrance of the tall building adjacent to the church. They were climbing through a smashed window and calling out. But she couldn't hear what they were trying to tell her. The cries from the dead things in the street made it impossible. Mary leaped up and ran to the roof's edge, cupping her hand next to her ear to better understand their commands.

"We have a ladder in the basement. We're going to extend it and drop it from this roof to yours," a blond-haired man shouted. "When we do, you need to cross it one at a time. Can you hear me? Do you understand?"

Mary nodded, and grabbed Melissa.

***

The end of the ladder came through the window and Michael grabbed it, pulling it onto the roof and out of Yusuf's grip.

Michael and Adam stood on the awning over the Tower's rear entrance. It was the buffer between the two would-be rescuers, a ladder, and the lurking death below.

It was decided that only Michael and Adam would perform the rescue. More people might collapse the awning down into the reaching crowd, no more than ten feet beneath them. Though sturdy, the awning wasn't concrete. Most of the structure was wrought iron and something that resembled canvas but much thicker. If the energized crowd below really wanted, they could send the whole thing tumbling down into their midst.

Unextended, the ladder was only sixteen feet in length. It was their hope that once extended, it would be long enough to reach the two girls and give them a means of escape. It would act as a crawlway of sorts. If it were too short then the girls would be on their own, left to their ghoulish pursuers and likely lost.

With Michael on one side and Adam on the other, they moved the ladder as close to the roof's edge as they dared, raised it to its last wrung, and locked into place.

Just then, the crowd shrieked out in unison with outstretched arms, their eyes locked on the ladder towering above them. It was as if the multitude of disemboweled, ashen faced apparitions were praying to a shining god erected in their midst. Each one seemed prepared to lay down their dead and soulless lives in worship to the polished aluminum Messiah.

Then, the sudden revelation faded and they returned their attention to the people, no longer electrified by the ladder-god.

The discarded deity towered above them ready to be dropped. It swayed precariously as Michael and Adam fought to hold it steady. Michael watched the apparatus jangling loosely where the ladder sections came together in the middle. With the ladder extended so far, there would be little to support where the two parts met, joined by aluminum clamps that seemed far less than adequate for the task at hand. It rattled and clanked with each sway.

"This may not work out well," Michael told Adam. "Ladders that lie flat don't support weight properly. It's extended all the way, and there won't be much overlapping in the track."

Adam spotted the door on the church roof as it slammed into the pyramid of buckets. The top bucket on the stack fell, and rolled across the roof as the door slammed into them. Ghastly faces began to appear in the widening crack.

"We have no choice," Adam called out, and they dropped the ladder.

The other end smashed onto the narrow ledge surrounding the church's roof. As it did so, the end held by Michael and Adam kicked up. The action knocked Adam off his feet and nearly over the side to the waiting crowd below. Michael grabbed the ladder and forced it to stay in place with one hand and grabbed Adam with the other, securing both.

It had barely been long enough. Only inches of the ladder hung over the other side. The crowd below became even more excited by the sudden movement. They reached up to them, flailing their arms, clutching and howling even louder. The great whooshing sound enveloped and swelled in the air again. It effectively sucked the oxygen right out of Michael's lungs as if the crowd had used it all up in that one moment. He knew it was just the shock, and not the ghoulish figures below that had taken his breath. They did not breathe. He had seen no evidence of their chests rising and falling, or their lungs filling with oxygen like the living.

Michael worried that their appearance on the awning would incite the crowd to break into the building. But they seemed to be locked in rapt attention by the actions outside, uninterested in gaining entrance to the Tower. They were unable to grasp the concept of planning or advanced thought. He thought it possible that they would forget about them once they retreated through the window. Logic and reason did not seem to be their strong suit.

Adam held the ladder in place while Michael stood to face the two girls. The awning shook as the crowd moved in tighter, and Michael had to work to hold his balance as he shouted above the din. "We need you to cross the ladder one at a time. Lying flat, and extended so far makes it unsafe. Send the little one first. Lie down to distribute your weight evenly across the length of the ladder. Do you understand?"

The girl nodded and bent down to the little one at her side. It seemed to take a little convincing to get the frightened child to agree to the plan and understand what must be done. This gave the creatures the additional time they needed to force their way through the barricade and spill out onto the roof. As the dead advanced, the small child began her crawl above the waving sea of grasping hands. The older girl watched the dead swarm as they gained access to the rooftop and move toward her. She dashed to the far corner of the roof, a safe distance from the ladder. She was hoping to draw them away from her only means of escape and at the same time give Melissa the time she needed to reach safety. It was a good plan, but the mob split, with one faction following her, while the other continued toward Melissa.

The little girl crawled slowly toward Michael. He bent low and coaxed her in until he could reach out and pull her to safety.

As soon as her sister was clear, Mary ran toward the ladder, pushing aside two ghouls who had closed the distance between her and her goal. She dove onto the rickety makeshift bridge, crawling out onto it just ahead of her pursuers. The ghoulish stalkers followed her example, their extra weight burdening the ladder. Two of them crawled behind her. Another tried to cross standing, and fell into the crowd below.

"You've got to hurry now." Michael's voice shook with dread. His worst fears were realized almost as soon as the plea left his lips.

Halfway across, the two sections of the ladder began to bow, dropping her precariously closer to the pit of death below. Mary froze, afraid that her movement would cause her to sink further, but her inaction could not prevent the ladder's certain failure.

Michael and Adam watched from the other side as the ladder creased in the middle and slowly bent into a V-shape. It finally gave way from the combined weight of the girl and the ghouls that followed her. It fell soundlessly into the throng of inhumanity waiting below.

A wave of reaching arms softened Mary's descent into hell. Then with eyes wide, they tore into her, hungry sharks ravaging a bucket of human chum thrown into their midst. The tiny, helpless wisp of a child watched in utter horror as her screams froze, unreleased, in her clutching chest. She could only stand, unmoving, silent and devastated.

Michael moved quickly and pulled the girl away from the unfolding horror and carried her to the window. Franklin Baker pulled her inside to the safety of his waiting arms.

Adam felt the tug as Michael grabbed him from behind and pulled him to the window too. Like the tiny child, they had a good view to the vicious attack below. The consequences of their actions became clear with a terrible thud; the reality that the Devil's minions were devouring the Earth hit home all too clearly, and in vivid Technicolor.

The sun was setting as Michael crawled through the window. He looked back just in time to see the city lights blink out. Seconds later their building went dark as well.

This time it did not return.

25

"Where? Where? Where is that volume?" Doctor Willem Diogenes Ainsworth-Taylor, III muttered determinedly. Talking aloud to himself was just one of the illustrious scholar's many and varied eccentricities.

He absently laid one leather bound tome aside while reaching for another. "Time is short. She'll not last another hour." The book in his tenuous grasp fell to the floor, adding to the growing chaos in his usually well-ordered library. He had taken great pains to design each and every facet of this room and had seen each detail meticulously carried out by the workmen and artisans who were required for the task. The walls were lined from floor to ceiling with hand-hewn, planed bookshelves crafted from American chestnut beams. They had cost more than two years equivalent of his comparatively meager salary at NYU. But cost was no deterrent to the Ainsworth-Taylor's, they were "old money", his wife Jane in particular, which was the reason she always got her way. It was simply what she was accustomed to. So before agreeing to take the tenure that was offered him at University, this room had been his one indulgence.

At Jane's urging, and urging was a mild word for what Jane did when she was determined to have her way, Willem had agreed to move into this bustling and ever vivid community within the city of Manhattan. In spite of the fact that he was dreadfully uncomfortable in the confines of the Trump World Tower luxury apartment, in this room he was at home. If he were going to take the position, he needed a place to write his highly sought after musings on ancient cultures and religious practices. In essence, the library was his personal cocoon.

Jane was sick now, terribly sick. Before barricading themselves in the apartment, Jane had scuffled with, and been seriously injured by her personal assistant, Walter. Walter was a flamboyant, wide-eyed, exaggeratedly effeminate young man with androgynous good looks. And according to Jane, exquisitely refined taste. Walter was dead now, lying in state in the guest room at the end of the expansive hallway outside his library door. His hands and feet were bound, his lips sewn shut to conceal the contents of a large container of course sea salt that Jane had always insisted be kept on hand for her favorite libation, a blue Agave Margarita. Salt, no rocks, and certainly not frozen. Jane was a purist and ever so particular when it came to her Margarita.

Jane was an elegant brunette. At forty-five, she still managed to retain that ageless beauty reserved for aristocrats and those with no real worries beyond which charity functions she would attend and which she would ultimately have to decline. She was an elitist in the purest sense of the word, but not so with Willem. How he had ever managed to capture and hold her affections, he still did not know. He loved her madly—desperately. And that desperation translated itself in his every move now. It was up to him to save her and time was running out.

"Here—at last," he exclaimed. He clutched a worn, ancient manuscript to his heaving chest as he dropped back into his leather reading chair.

He flipped open the pages of the book, which were dog-earred at intervals throughout. His eyes were quickly scanning up and down the pages as he thumbed through. "Ah, here—here it is," Willem said.

Willem continued to read aloud from the tattered, handwritten letter that he had carefully preserved between the pages of the book.

"Though I feel sure you will find what I am about to tell you incredulous, I assure you, I am still in full command of my faculties. When our party staggered into the native village after being three days lost in the jungle,

dehydrated and suffering from maladies whose hideous description I will spare you, for expediencies sake…"

His words fell off as he scanned down the document, replaced by a low hum.

"…afflicted by a…"

The hum increased in tempo.

"…the dead, and they were well and truly dead, I swear it on my very soul, were reanimated with an uncontrollable instinct to consume living, human flesh…"

The humming pitched up and down as his eyes continued down the page and then on to the next page of the letter.

"…the witch-doctor employed this gruesome, but effective remedy and was successful in stopping the progress of the reanimation."

"Arthur!" Willem shouted to their chauffer and friend who was watching over Jane while Willem searched for the letter. "Arthur, come help me. We need to gather some items from the storage unit. Quickly. Leave Margaret to watch Jane and come with me now. Hurry." the letter fluttered to the floor as he dashed from the safe confines of his library. He grabbed a small ring with several keys on it from the antique ceramic basin atop the washstand by the door as he went. His mind was racing ahead, mentally sifting through the contents of the locked storage room in the sublevel of the building. There would be little time to get what he needed and get back. If Jane passed before he could do what must be done then it would be too late. She would be lost to him forever. All that would be left would be to stop her from becoming one of them. But no, that was not an option. He had to save her. Without her, he would be lost, as good as dead himself.

The two men raced pell-mell down the stairs, grabbing the metal railing to swing themselves around each turn as they descended. They had slipped quietly out the door of the apartment, instructing Margaret to lock the door behind them.

There had been virtually no activity on the fifteenth floor of the building since yesterday. Then the apartment Superintendent, Franklin Baker, and a tall blonde man, Michael-something or other, had asked them if they wanted to move down to one of the lower levels. Doctor Ainsworth-Taylor had politely but firmly declined. The television news had been reporting the "epidemic" around the clock with their usual flare for sensationalism. He believed them to be safer, separate, on the fifteenth floor. The apartment was well stocked and at least marginally equipped for emergencies.

He and Jane had discussed their options at the outset of the ensuing pandemonium. They had agreed to wait it out until things had calmed down a bit. Then, Arthur could drive them to their little house out on Long Island. "No sense in getting caught in the stampede," he'd told her. "Getting caught on the bridge for hours in traffic that's not moving, in a world that is moving toward madness is simply not prudent." And so, they had stayed in the apartment. Jane had called Walter and told him to come to wait out the proverbial storm with them. Arthur and Margaret, his wife, who had been in their employ for several years now were already there watching the events unfold on the news.

Walter had arrived at the apartment, disheveled and bleeding from a bite wound on his arm. He had gotten it as he shoved a crazed woman away from the closing elevator doors in the lobby.

Franklin Baker and the blonde policeman had knocked on the door and asked them if they wanted to move downstairs when they were in the throes of fighting Walter's rapid descent into feverish oblivion. "No thank you," Willem had told them "the last thing we need at this point is to add our number to the teeming masses below." The unspoken truth of the matter was that he would not risk trusting others. He needed a better handle on what, exactly, was really unfolding, and how best he could deal with it.

It was only a very short time later that the power blinked out and Walter expired. Jane had fallen ill from her injuries, and Willem had used his knowledge of ancient cultures and voodoo to ensure that Walter would not rise. It was too late for poor Walter but not for Jane. Not yet.

***

The two sweating, heaving, middle-aged men pounded down the final flight of stairs to the building's storage level. Willem felt as though his heart might explode and Arthur's beet-red face made it appear that he was not faring much better.

The ceilings in the sublevel were only eight feet high and the hallway was a narrow three feet wide. The battery powered emergency lights gave off an eerie glow in the confined space. Willem felt his claustrophobia clawing uncomfortably at his clutching stomach and his vision was growing dark around the edges. He fumbled with the key ring as he reached the door of their personal storage unit.

Willem worked quickly with an efficiency born of dire need. Fortunately the storage space was meticulously ordered and catalogued, a side effect of Willem's mild Obsessive Compulsive Disorder. He pulled first one, then two labeled crates from the metal utility shelf, holding the tiny flashlight in his teeth so he could use both hands to rummage through the contents of the box.

Arthur peered nervously over Doctor Ainsworth-Taylor's shoulder, watching him toss several items into an empty cardboard box whose contents the doctor had dumped onto the floor. He would need something to carry his booty in.

The Doctor glanced back toward the door of the storage room wondering what the source of the steady tick-thump, tick-thump, tick-thump could be.

This whole situation had Arthur completely out of sorts, but he trusted the doctor's judgment and determined early on to do whatever must be done. He heard the tick-thump again, louder this time as Doctor Ainsworth-Taylor rose and turned toward him. He was wrapping a dark nylon string around a riveted, plastic button on the end of a box to secure it.

"I have it, Arthur" Willem announced "Let's go. We've got fifteen flights of stairs to climb and it will take me at least twenty minutes to prepare for what must be done."

Arthur turned, and moved through the door, adding the beam of his little silver flashlight to the flickering shadows. As he moved forward he came face to face with the source of the mysterious tick-thump. It was Joe Jenkins, one of the building maintenance workers.

Before Arthur's surprised croak could be fully uttered, Joe's chubby fingers closed on his throat and the two men fell back through the doorway. Willem fell headlong into the wall of metal shelves, sending the cardboard box sailing over the two struggling men. It tumbled out into the dimly lit hallway.

Willem scrambled to his feet looking from the struggle at his feet to the box in the hall and back again. Joe's short, compact body seemed to completely cover Arthur's spare form. He watched in horror as the flesh and tendons were torn free of his chauffeur's neck just above his bony clavicle. Arthur's strangled cry snapped Willem out of his trance and he dove over them.

He skidded to a stop against the far wall of the hallway beside the box. He snatched it up and looked back at his friend, hesitating instinctively, though he already knew Arthur was beyond helping.

Arthur screamed at him "Go!" and before he could repeat it, Joe's bloody maw closed on his gushing throat and tore another mass of artery and flesh. Arthur was gone and his hot, sweaty corpse was being torn apart.

Willem turned and ran as fast as legs would carry him, the box firmly in his grasp. Back to Jane he ran. He did not look back.

Part 3
Broadway Is Dark Tonight

If the inhabitants of the Trump World Tower were reduced to cannibalism, then indeed, all things might be as they say, equal.

—Sarah

26

Sarah placed a white vinyl and metal folding chaise on the wide stone ledge that bordered the roof, and then used a plastic storage crate as a makeshift step to more easily reach it. Someone had stashed the chair neatly folded into a narrow crevice behind one of the huge air conditioning units. The units no longer droned on with their endless white noise since the power grid fell, their whirring fans were silent now, replaced by a slight breeze that seemed to whisper to her. It murmured indiscernible secrets in hushed and fearful tones and she strained to understand the barely audible warnings. Normally, Sarah would have dismissed such foolish meanderings as childish nightmares running rampant in her adult mind, but not tonight. Tonight she listened intently until the whispers wafted away on the gentle wind.

Sarah reclined in the chair, relaxing as the terrible whispers faded from her thoughts, and held the half-full brandy snifter close to her nose. With a swirl of her wrist, she gently encouraged its sweet bouquet to float above the narrow rim of the glass and fill her senses. Once the delicate scent faded, she sipped the savory warmth and gently swirled the liquid again, repeating the technique. Sarah was partial to this libation; she enjoyed the myriad of sensory stimulus that could be had from a snifter of good brandy. With each sip the shock of reality washed away, like fading blue pools of ink running gently off a page in the cleansing rain, and she felt the tension in her neck begin to ease.

The residents of First and Forty-Seventh were scouring the floors below for any available source of light. They would wait out the sudden phenomenon in the building until help could arrive. Sarah did not share their optimism. She had seen the writing on the proverbial wall and it was written in blood and viscera. The scruffy lunatics, who drifted up and down the city streets with signs draped across their chests and backs, were ultimately correct. The end *was* nigh. She wondered if those same lunatics still roamed the streets below, their apocalyptic messages still draped across their chests. Now they had a new passion to drive them. With glazed eyes and cooled blood they would now seek to spread the apocalypse they had once prophesied.

Sarah found the solitude on the roof comforting, a respite from those thoughts as she stared off to the West. Here, eighty-six stories above the carnage in the streets, it was quiet and dark. The cries of millions of walking dead were reduced to a gentle thrum that softly drifted up to her. Yes, from that height it was even soothing, like the distant sounds of a string quartet steadily playing the same note.

As night set in, the silhouette of New York's skyline was dark and ominous. Still noticeably absent were the Twin Towers of the World Trade center, long since lost in the terrorist attack of 2001. A single Freedom Tower that touched the heavens now marked that spot. Three other buildings were part of the new complex, but the Freedom Tower overwhelmed everything around it. Sarah longed for the nostalgic days before September the eleventh and the Freedom Tower, before flesh eating ghouls, before the end of that world. She liked the city view much better before Broadway went dark. She could still see Broadway with its shadowy and looming silhouettes, even on this darkened night. Sinister things were surely happening there now. No living person dared move about in the streets. Not this September. Like before, September had witnessed the arrival of Hell to New York City. Only this time it had opened up wide and spilled its contents out across the land. Yes, it was September in New York and once again the City was laid bare.

It came as no surprise to Sarah that New York had fallen into chaos so quickly, and without a struggle. Its citizens were, for the most part, so pre-occupied with their own lives that the situation had overwhelmed them before their morning shower. They were not prepared. They panicked, and their lack of control had cost untold numbers their lives. A frenzied evacuation had made matters worse. Most streets were impassable before the morning rush hour. For those stuck in the city, fortification was their only real option. In Sarah's mind, this was a no-win scenario. As they searched for light below, the same could probably be said for many other buildings on the same street and across the city. Most would fail, not for lack of effort, but because they refused to accept the bare minimum. In times like these you must be willing to rough it. In their desire for light they were in essence creating beacons, invitations to dinner to the willing and able crowds. When they saved the little girl from the church next door they let every ghoul in the area know where they were hiding. In response, a hundred thousand dead things swarmed the plaza surrounding the Tower. It was only a matter of time before the ground level was compromised. There would be no escape, and no rescue would be forthcoming. The only question in Sarah's mind was, 'How long?' How long could they survive? Even if they could hole up in the building and wait it out, how long would they need to wait? Did the cannibalistic ghouls have a life span? If they didn't consume something, would they simply wither away? Sarah pondered that question for a moment. They were supposedly dead already. Could they die a second time? Certainly living beings were dependant on nourishment, but these things could not be considered living. That being opposed to the residents of First and Forty-Seventh who were alive, and whose food supplies would eventually run out. What then? Would they too be forced into cannibalism? "*All things being equal.*" It was an old saying, one whose meaning Sarah had a clear grasp of. Nothing is really equal in life. The scales are always tipped. In this case they were tipped in favor of the dead things shambling about in the streets below. If the inhabitants of the Trump World Tower were reduced to cannibalism, then indeed, all things might be as they say, "equal".

There were many factors working against them. Even as Sarah reclined in the chair sipping her brandy, the slightest, sickly sweet hint of rot was rising up to her on the gentle breeze. Several days in the late-summer sun had begun to take its toll on the bodies of the deceased. If the residents of First and Forty-Seventh did not succumb to starvation, they certainly would as a result of disease from so many rotting corpses. On their feet or not, they were beginning to rot and smell. Of course, they would avoid starvation or cannibalism if the dead things got to them first, which seemed the more likely outcome.

Finally having enough of her view to the West and of a darkened Broadway, Sarah rose from her seat and walked the ledge to the other side of the building. It faced the East River. In the distance, the horizon was aglow with the twinkling lights of a powered suburb. Somewhere beyond Queens there was still electricity. For a moment it gave Sarah hope. Maybe she had been mistaken in her belief. Maybe the authorities were getting the situation under control after all. Then the smile of hope that had suddenly creased her face vanished as those lights unexpectedly blinked out. Like a mirage in the desert, the lights were gone and so was her momentary glimmer of hope.

The absence of city lights made her realize that in the sky above her, the stars were shining brightly. Sarah couldn't remember the last time she could see the stars from inside the City. Their beauty was almost lost to the desperate situation at hand. Yet, she directed her eyes upward and tried to enjoy their magnificence, if only for a fleeting moment.

It was then she noticed the lone light moving between them. It was an airplane, military probably. Certainly it was not a commercial jet. All commercial air traffic had been grounded. She had heard it on the radio before the station went into total chaos, and finally silent.

The plane streaked on toward the West. As Sarah watched it move away she surmised that it might be a good idea to keep a lookout on the roof. If they were going to be rescued, that rescue would not come from the streets, but from the air. She was about to go back to her penthouse when something else caught her eye.

The area surrounding the East River was dark except for one small, glowing light. In the middle of the river directly across from her, and barely visible, was the outline of a small boat. The light was coming from inside the boat's cabin, below deck.

Sarah watched for the steady light to flicker. It would indicate movement inside the boat. She pondered the possibility that the occupants were safe there, secure in the middle of the river. Maybe the reanimates couldn't swim, or maybe they just didn't like water. Perhaps it was safe there.

The light in the boat remained steady.

Sarah studied it for a moment. It could be important. In the light of day she could get a better look.

27

The child was thin and waifish, with slightly translucent skin and a fairy-like, otherworldly quality. Adam Riker shined a beam of light in her eyes and moved it swiftly from left to right. Her pale blue pupils remained motionless. Her breathing was shallow, her face pallid. The child's lower lip trembled and moved forming silent words, but uttering no sound.

"She's still in shock," Adam explained, and clicked off the thin, black flashlight. "I have no way to treat her…everything I need is at the hospital."

Franklin wrapped a small, green blanket around her, one he had been holding in his hands. "If she's in shock, we'll want to keep her warm, right?" he looked at the doctor for confirmation.

"Yeah, that's right," Adam told him. "Just let her rest. Hopefully, she'll be better tomorrow."

Franklin smiled thinly. "She might as well just stay here with us. My wife Clara will look after her."

Adam eyed the fragile, gray-haired woman standing to Franklin's left and nodded his approval. She was tiny, barely over five feet tall and probably no more than ninety pounds soaking wet. She had brown eyes that reflected the same uncertainty he saw now in everyone's eyes. It was Adam's first acquaintance with her, but thought she would be good for the little girl, a grandmotherly figure to nurture her body and help sooth her tortured mind. She had survived a terrible ordeal, making her total recovery unlikely, at least anytime in the near future.

"Still no idea of who the other one was? Was she this girl's mother?" Franklin asked with concern, nodding toward the little one.

"No, we don't know. She was obviously someone close, but she has been too traumatized to talk about it."

Franklin removed his glasses and cleaned the lenses of the greasy fingerprints impairing his vision. "Did this little tyke see what happened to her?"

"She had a perfect view of the carnage, Mister Baker, in all its mind rending horror," Adam said.

Franklin nodded, and moved to the window.

The Bakers lived on the seventh floor. The larger apartments were near the top. The Baker's apartment was considered luxurious, but one of the smallest available in the Tower. Theirs had only two bedrooms and the city view left a lot to be desired, being straight into the building next door.

As Franklin looked intently at the landscape below, Adam watched a scene unfold in the distance. Another building was falling to the walking corpses. He had no desire to watch this one to its inevitable conclusion. He had watched this same scene unfold over and over again. He knew the hideous hordes would soon move away, their purpose fulfilled.

"We have to close down the ground floor soon, Mister Baker. Procrastination will cost us dearly," Adam said, and moved to the middle of the room. The child was sleeping soundly now, nestled beneath the green blanket.

Baker huffed, "Like I already told Officer Longley and Sarah Randolph, we have so many supplies down there. We have to bring them upstairs before we can do that. We're working on it."

"Then we'd better work faster. If those things get a hankering to come in, there won't be any way to stop them. If we close off the first floor, we'll be safe. The doors to the stairwell are made of steel. We can lock them and those things will be sealed off from the rest of the building."

"You call them 'things'," Baker intoned scornfully. "They're people."

"They're not. They're something else."

"You're a man of science, Doctor. Are you telling me you believe what the media reports are saying?"

"As hard as it may be to believe, I know what I've seen with my own eyes; patients who had sustained injuries they couldn't possibly have survived and yet, they did. They got up and walked. They attacked us, Mister Baker. They attacked everyone in sight. Maybe they're not dead as we know dead, but instead, a kind of *living* dead."

"You're making no sense. That sounds absurd. If that's true let me ask you this—why?"

A voice interjected, "Because Allah is punishing us."

Franklin turned to meet Yusuf's gaze. "Allah?" he asked, incredulously.

Adam glanced over at the child; concerned that Franklin's sudden outburst would wake her. She shifted slightly, but continued to sleep.

"Allah does not exist. Besides, it's not his style. His style is to strap a bomb to some poor, impressionable youth and have him stand in the middle of a crowded marketplace and blow himself up," Baker said, in a lowered tone. "Allah is nothing more than a means to achieve a goal set up by radical militants. Allah does not exist, and he never did."

Yusuf bristled at the fat man's assertions. He was noticeably upset by Baker's comments and moved closer until they were only inches apart. "You lump us all together. Place us all in the same group as a few extremists. What if I placed all Christians in the same group with those who carried out the Inquisitions? How would that make you feel? You claim to have faith? And yet your god has no name. How can you feel close to a god you do not know? A god with no name is a god with no heart, with no wisdom. That is a god that does not exist."

"Let me say this—"

"Stop it!" Adam interjected sternly. "This is neither the time nor the place for debating theology. It doesn't matter how it happened, or why. What's the difference if God did it, or if it was some kind of weird space radiation brought down by a meteorite, or whatever? Our dilemma's the same. We have to figure out a way to survive, at least until help arrives."

Adam's words had the effect of diffusing the two combatants. They each realized the futility of their quarrel and took on a less aggressive posture.

Adam watched Sarah as she quietly entered the room

unnoticed by the others. She was dressed in military fatigues and boots that could effectively kick the toughest mule into action. There was a shiny revolver strapped to each hip. Adam likened her appearance to some kind of comic book heroine, an uncommon analogy for any woman, much less one in her fifties. But she was somehow sexy in that getup. She was attractive, self-assured and in great shape to boot. Only her eyes defined her age, reflecting a wisdom that only comes from a life fully realized.

Sarah rested her hand firmly on the pistol on her right hip. "Put someone on the roof at all times," she blurted out.

The remark caught Franklin off guard and he turned. "What?"

Sarah said, "Rescue from the street is out of the question. There will be no rescue from the ground. But there could be one from the air. If we don't have someone on the roof, would be rescuers might never know we're here."

Adam nodded, "Can't we just put up a sign or something? You know, saying we're here and alive, or something like that?"

"That's not good enough," she explained, "no one would see it at night. We need someone up there at all times. We need movement and visibility. I'm sure we have flares in the building somewhere. If a plane flies over, even at night, they need to know we're here."

"Alright," Franklin told her, "There may be some old traffic flares in the basement. So who gets the task?"

"I want someone I trust and someone who won't fall asleep at the wheel. Whoever we choose should stay in the Penthouse with me. It will be too tough to make the trip up the steps every day with the elevators down."

Sarah hesitated, and scanned the room. Her eyes rested on each one of them before making her decision. "I want Yusuf."

"Me?" Yusuf asked, surprised by her choice.

"Him?" Baker laughed, "I didn't figure you for someone who would trust the likes of Yusuf. Not that I don't trust him myself," Franklin said. He was still slightly embarrassed for his earlier display of religious bigotry. "It's just I pegged you for a hardcore right winger who didn't trust anybody, especially an Arab."

"I am Iranian," Yusuf corrected him.

"Yes him, Mister Baker. I trust him because he's been in the building for years. If he were going to do something diabolical he would've done it long ago. The good doctor here needs to stay with the majority, and the few other responsible ones will be needed to keep everyone organized. Besides, just because he's an Arab, as you put it, doesn't make him a bad person. It sounds to me like you left wingers are just as suspicious as the right, Frankie."

"Indeed, we all are, Miss Randolph. And please, call me Franklin." There was a hint of malice in his voice.

Sarah ignored his comment and turned to Yusuf. "You'll stay in my apartment from now on," She told him. "I'll give you breaks from your post." Begrudgingly, Sarah addressed Franklin again. "Get those people out of the lounge and off the ground floor. You're risking all our lives now, mine included. I won't allow it any longer. Do it quickly or I will."

"We were just talking about that," Adam chimed in. "We know our predicament and were just about to initiate a plan, do you have any suggestions?"

Sarah motioned Yusuf to go ahead of her and moved to the door. "With the power out we need everyone together." She told Adam. "I suggest we house everyone from the fourth or fifth floor and up. There's no need in everyone climbing more stairs than necessary. That still keeps most of us near the ground should the need arise to be there."

"Does that mean you'll be moving down with the rest of us too, Sarah?" Franklin asked.

Sarah smiled, "I don't mind the stairs."

28

It was just before noon and Duane sipped his cheap bourbon and cringed at the harshness of its flavor. "We're never going to see home again." He said it solemnly and glanced up at the windows for what seemed like the hundredth time. He had quickly become accustomed to the fine, rich bourbon of the elitists at the Tower. But suddenly the quality of the booze had taken a nosedive. There was an open bar policy and many of the building's occupants were open to the idea of drinking their fears away. Under the circumstances, he didn't blame them. It seemed like a good idea to him too.

Duane watched the undulating mass of mutilated bodies roam aimlessly outside the lounge windows. It was a constant waltz of lumbering death, the end of which could not be seen. It brought to mind an old Star Trek episode. A planet had become so overpopulated that its inhabitants would have given anything to have their own personal space, no matter how small. They'd die for it—kill for it. But killing, like death, was not a part of their genetic makeup. Thus, paradise had become an overpopulated living Hell.

In that story the teeming masses moved to and fro, much the same way they were doing now on the opposite side of the Tower's tinted glass. They existed in a world without an inch of personal freedom. Yes, it was very similar. No disease and no death. But that was where the worlds differed. In the real world, death was real; death was everywhere, delivered by the dead themselves.

In the end, Captain Kirk came to the rescue and saved the day in his usual fashion. Sleep with the pretty alien, slip on his boots and move on to his next sexual conquest.

Chuck had obviously ignored his comment, pretending not to hear it. He was of course trying to avoid another argument. If they'd left for home when he had suggested, they wouldn't be in this fix. There were now more than one hundred thousand walking corpses just outside the building. They searched to find a crack or a seam to pry open, stick in their fingers and pluck out the clam. Tomorrow there would be even more. That's assuming any of them made it through the night to see another day. Judging by the speed in which the buildings around them were falling victim to the swarming ghouls, it seemed unlikely.

Chuck reclined in the chair next to Duane. A magazine covered his face. But Duane knew Chuck was only pretending to be asleep. How could he simply block out what was all around them and just nod off? What could he have found so interesting in that People magazine? Had he really been reading it, or simply looking at the pictures before using it as a blindfold to block out the light? Didn't he know the world was dying? Who cared what Jennifer Aniston was doing? She was probably dead by now anyway. Hollywood pukes. They could all be devoured as far as Duane was concerned. They didn't live in the real world, not their type. They were too concerned with throwing red paint on fur coats or being photographed in just the right outfit to know anything about life in the real world. Well, how's this for the real world, Mister Pitt? Oh, you're missing an arm? Sorry to see that. Bang—well placed shot to the head. Angelina, you're next. X-wifey is already dead. Oops, not really, let's get inventive with this one and stick a grenade in her mouth. When all else fails, Hollywood puts a grenade in your mouth. It's a good substitute for storyline. Sorry Charlie and buh-bye. "Who's next?"

Duane realized he had been grinding his teeth. The rich and famous always had that effect on him. He never considered that it might be because he was jealous of their success and fame. Rather, it was because they were less than real, less than human, like the things outside.

Chuck's dead beauty made her hourly rounds outside the glass barrier. That's how long it took her to make her way back to the window from her trip around the lurching crowd. He had been sitting there drinking for two hours and had seen her twice.

Today, her skin was a different, deeper shade of blue, less gray now, less alive. Her waning beauty was still evident though. In Duane's mind it was best that Chuck stay asleep, if he really was. Seeing her would only get him keyed up again.

As the walking corpses moved past the window, it was as if they knew they needed to be there but couldn't remember why. If they were to suddenly remember, the windows would not prevent their entry. Soon, they would lose their front row seat to Hades. The ground floor would be evacuated once vital supplies were gathered and it would be officially off-limits to anyone in the building. The windows would pose no further danger. At least, that was the general consensus, and the people inside would be safe to rot in a more traditional manner, one story above the clear and present danger.

Home seemed light years away. A lengthy trip made further by millions of flesh eating monsters. Duane hoped things were better there in the foothills of the Blue Ridge Mountains. His town was a small community and he was sure its people would hold things together longer. The television had hinted that smaller towns and less populated areas were doing okay. Maybe only the cities were trouble spots. There was certainly something to be said for small town common sense. They weren't as prone to the silliness of being politically correct. Given time, Duane was sure that the big cities would eventually come up with laws and bylaws and regulations and everything under the sun to protect these new, 'sub-humans'.

'Dead Rights.'

He could see it now; people on trial for killing the dead bastards. Wasn't it always the way? No such stupidity in Virginia though. Beat 'em down and shoot the things in the head. End of problem. Yes sir, Duane imagined Warren, Virginia was faring quite well.

Duane eyed the dwindling bourbon in his glass dubiously. The supply of ice cubes had long since melted in the absence of electricity. The top-shelf bottles were suddenly empty or missing. Still, he'd had much worse. The real shame was that soon it would *all* be gone, even the cheap stuff. Duane was certain that if he searched hard enough, he could find more liquor in the apartments above. If there was one thing the rich saw to, it was a fully stocked bar. Maybe one of them had a guitar too. Now might be a good time to pluck out a Beatles tune, or maybe a little Tom Petty. Now that the world was ending, what better to do? Screw and play music. It seemed he'd devoted his life to both…and to drinking more than his share. He could never forget the therapeutic value of alcohol on the troubled mind.

Duane absently swirled the fiery liquid in the glass thinking of better times. It was never a good thing to have too much blood in the ole alcohol system. Sobriety had never suited him. With all the problems in the world, it served to shut them out. Numb his senses and accept no responsibility for the way things were. Play a song and be the ruler in his Feudal kingdom. And none should be the wiser…his lonely kingdom.

Duane placed the glass on the arm of the chair. It clinked out a C note when he did so.

Chuck stirred, and at first Duane thought that maybe the C note had awakened him. But after thinking it over, he knew that wasn't the case. Chuck was not a light sleeper.

Duane glanced anxiously back toward the windows. Chuck's dead beauty was gone and he relaxed.

"We're never going to make it home," Duane repeated making sure Chuck had heard him this time.

Chuck threw the magazine to the floor and stood up abruptly. He stretched for a moment with his arms raised and yawned, turning slightly from left to right as he did so. His T-shirt with the rebel flag was smudged with dried blood and sweat and he paid no mind to his own foul, unwashed odor. It was as if he were waking to nothing more than another day as an unemployed union worker. As usual, Chuck was greeting the new day at noon, still wearing the clothes from the day before, or the day before that. Yesterday the end of the world had overwhelmed him. Today, the Apocalypse was merely a distraction. No big deal. Duane couldn't quite figure him out, and he wasn't sure if he should try.

"We are home Dewey, get used to it," he finally answered.

Duane said, "I don't want to get used to it, Chuck. Later today they're going to close off this floor and for all intents and purposes turn this place into our coffin. I for one don't want to be stuck here."

Chuck smiled.

"What's to fret about, Dewey? We're in a luxury high-rise. The world outside is history. We're still alive, longer than any of those poor bastards out there. Coffin?—Damn, I could only hope for such a fine box in which to face eternity. I'll take it."

Duane irritably tossed back the remaining liquid from his glass and walked into the darkened lounge toward the stairwell. His voice echoed back to Chuck.

"We don't know that the whole world is history, Chuck, just this fucking, goddamned city. It's your fault we're here. It's your fault we'll die here...Fuck you, Chuck!"

29

Michael Longley pressed his ear against the door to Doctor Willem Diogenes Ainsworth-Taylor the Third's residence. And even though his ear was pressed tightly, it seemed the harder he pressed, the less he heard for his effort. The cut on his forehead still bled from time to time but the lightheaded feeling he had been experiencing was gone.

Jamal Owens stood just behind him. Michael could sense his distrust and anger simmering just below the surface, just as he could see it in the narrowing of his eyes and the flexing of his jaw.

Franklin Baker studied each key as he flipped through a large copper ring. He squinted to make out the small, faded numbers embedded on their heads. His eyes were failing. Even the black-framed reading glasses he was wearing now did little to help him see the small detail on the keys with only an oil lantern to light the darkened hall. He often complained about his worsening eyesight to anyone who cared to listen and was always cleaning their smudged lenses in a vain attempt to better see his surroundings.

"I think this one's it," Franklin said, and moved to the door, holding the chosen key separate from the others. "I've not heard from anyone who lives here since we went door to door. But they keep private. Doctor Taylor is a bit of a hermit, always busy with his studies."

Michael drew a pistol from his belt. It was one of the weapons Sarah had given him earlier. It felt good in his hand, and with the street gangster standing just behind him, it made him feel safe.

Michael leaned away from the door to give Franklin the room he needed to unlock it and the inner mechanism clicked with the turn of the key. Michael stopped him before he had the chance to open it and with a nudge, the fat man was pushed away.

Inside, the curtains were drawn and the room was eerily dim. It took a moment for Michael's eyes to adjust, and he waited uneasily until he could see more clearly before making the move inside.

Michael leaned against the wall just inside the door and motioned for Jamal to enter and stand on the opposite side. The tactic offered them time to get adjusted to their surroundings, and at the same time kept their backs safely against the wall.

From the apartment's foyer, Michael watched for signs of danger as he peered through the darkness to a larger room. What little light the room offered came from around heavy floor to ceiling curtains that covered the windows.

Michael glanced back at Jamal, hoping to see a hint of support or an 'I give a shit' expression on his face. Something that would say, "I've got your back." But Jamal only watched with what could only be perceived as indifference.

Sarah was better suited for the job, but she still refused to be an active participant in securing the building or gathering resources. The good doctor had his hands full with the medical needs of the survivors, and the other two, Duane and Chuck, offered little promise to be of any usefulness at all. So here he was, stuck with Jamal as his wingman.

Michael cocked his ear toward the silent darkness of the residence. But the silence was misleading. He felt it in his gut. Danger lurked there. The sweet stench of rotting flesh tickled his senses and he pulled the neck of his t-shirt up, covering his nose like a bank robber. Jamal followed his lead by imitating the move. Michael watched him, thinking that he looked comfortable, even natural that way. The bandit look suited him.

Michael moved forward and with each step he braced for the assault he knew must surely be coming. Though the smell of decay was slight, it was there.

Across the room, Michael reached over a sofa to the window behind it. He threw open the curtains and the room was suddenly flooded with light. It was all he could do to catch his balance as he instinctively reeled back, and away from the corpse lying on the couch just in front of him. It was more than he could do to stay on his feet as flash after flash of Rebecca's dead face filled his inner eye. The scissor clamps rattled and swung from her open chest. He heard the clamps now ringing loudly in his ears as he went down. It was only after his ass unceremoniously hit the floor that he realized the rattling metal was the umbrella rack behind him, now tipped over on its side and spilling its contents. Jamal cried out, and fired his weapon into the couch before realizing what he had done. He had been foolish and wasted a bullet. Bullets were gold.

Michael scrambled to a crouched position and leveled his weapon. He stopped short of pulling the trigger himself as he studied the body of the woman lying on the couch.

She was middle-aged with short hair that curled around the sides of her sleek face. Her eyes were shut and she seemed to simply be asleep, except for two very strange details. Her lips were sewn shut. Black thread was laced between them, now more blue than red. Her hands and feet were bound with yellow nylon rope. She did not move, nor did she struggle to break free from her bindings. Unlike the ghouls outside, she was motionless, dead in the traditional sense and without any evidence of head trauma.

Michael got to his feet and holstered his weapon. "What do you make of that?" he asked, pointing. "Someone sewed her mouth shut. Do you think it was to keep her from biting?"

Jamal found a pen on the table beside the sofa and stuck the tip of it between the woman's lips, pulling them apart as far as the thread allowed. It was enough to expose the white crystals inside. "Heh," he chuckled softly, "nah man, not exactly. I've heard of this before. It was to keep her from coming back."

"What?"

Jamal removed the pen and her lips slowly fell shut again. He held the pen up so Michael could see the salt on its tip. "You fill the mouth with salt and then sew the lips shut. It keeps you from becoming a zombie, or something like that."

"A zombie? Are you saying those things outside are zombies? What are you telling me, that this is one big voodoo spell cast on the entire world?" he asked incredulously.

"I didn't say that. All I'm saying is what these white folk did here is from old voodoo legend. It doesn't mean that someone cast a spell on the world, but you know as well as I, in most legends there's some truth. Maybe this disease or whatever it is has been around for a very long time. Maybe it's reared its ugly head before in localized outbreaks. Maybe it's where voodoo legend comes from."

Michael studied the woman. "Do you think it worked?"

"She ain't movin' is she? And I'll bet she's been dead since this whole thing started the other day. It's a bit warm in here with the power out. She's already begun to smell."

Michael found himself suddenly impressed with the young man and his knowledge on the subject. He was beginning to think that Jamal could be of some use after all. And then he was knocked from his feet by a shadowy figure. But instead of continuing its assault on Michael as he expected, the apparition whizzed past him and on to Franklin Baker who still stood just inside the door.

The specter moved quickly and took the fat man off his feet. Both went skidding across the slick floor to the other side of the room until they rested against the far wall. Baker lost his grip on the ring of keys and thrust his hand up to meet the biting face of his assailant. The little man was ferocious and his jaws snapped repeatedly at Franklin's darting fingers. Michael had no more than gotten to his feet when another walking corpse dived onto him from the shadows. And as Jamal stood stunned and unable to make a decision, Michael's attacker screamed out and lunged.

Michael reached for his weapon and in one fluid motion pulled it free from its holster and placed it precisely into the dead thing's descending, gapping maw. He focused just in time to see Jamal standing just above and in the direct line of fire of an exiting headshot. "MOVE!" he shouted, and Jamal dove to the left.

Michael pulled the trigger.

The rear of the dead thing's skull exploded as the bullet did its job before lodging in the wall near the ceiling. The air became even more putrid as the creature's skull contents spilled.

Franklin Baker screamed out as the little man bit down on two of his fingers, ripping the flesh from them with a twist of his head. Blood squirted out and covered the exposed bone with red. Still unfulfilled, the ghoul dived into the fat man's throat. With the ferocity of a lion he tore the flesh and jugular vein from the left side of his neck. Life-giving blood jetted across the room is a steady stream and Franklin Baker fell still.

Michael fired.

The ghoul's head whipped back. Then, and as if in slow motion, fell forward onto Baker's chest.

Michael swung the gun in several directions; prepared for the next attack should it come, but found only Jamal. He glared at the rapper, fighting the urge to punch him in the face. Instead, he shoved him backward with a hard-thrust palm to the shoulder. "What the hell's wrong with you? You could've pulled that thing off Franklin, or shot it. What the hell were you waiting for?"

Jamal said nothing as he stared back, blankly.

"He's dead now. He's dead because you froze up."

Then in a flash, Jamal's gun was in front of Michael's face. He held it there sideways in his right hand. Michael stared down the barrel, and like that rainy night in Chicago, he could smell the gunpowder.

"I'm tired of your shit, Officer Longley. How 'bout we take care of this issue right now? Caught in the crossfire. Who'd know? Now wouldn't that be too bad for you?"

Michael Longley wasn't sure if Jamal would actually fire, but he knew he had to act fast, and unlike Chicago, this time there was no hesitation. Michael reached out and just as quickly as Jamal had pulled the gun, Michael snatched it from his grasp and pointed it back at him.

Jamal stood there for a moment, his teeth sawing across one another as his angular jaw flexed. Then he stormed from the room, leaving Michael alone with a dead Franklin Baker who had just opened his eyes.

Michael pointed Jamal's weapon at Franklin's face and used one of the remaining bullets.

PART 4
Candlelight Dinner and Drinks

No bastard ever won a war by dying for his country. He won it by making the other poor dumb bastard die for his country.

—General George S. Patton

30

Michael's accusation still echoed in Jamal's mind as the evening wore on. It slowly gnawed away at the cool indifference he had tried to display at the time, the sharp edges of truth flaying his conscience like a whip until he thought he would surely go insane. "*He's dead because of you,*" Michael had said. Indeed he was, but where was it written that he must react? When the dead walk, all words of wisdom fall on deaf ears, and all works of courage vanish, twisted into one's own need to survive. Pure motorized instinct.

Then why did he feel guilty? Why did he feel to blame? He was not accustomed to these emotions. He'd be damned if he'd let it suddenly get a foothold in his psyche. Survival instinct indeed...it was kicking in now with all cylinders firing.

Jamal stood in the stairwell on the sixth floor. The steps descended, first to one landing, then another, all the while using right-angled turns between the landings to reach the bottom.

The lounge was now off limits as was the entire ground floor. Once again he'd become an outcast, shunned by the others. Even Duane and Chuck were keeping their distance, more interested in fitting in than sticking up for him. Or was it that survival instinct again? There was safety in numbers. Even *they* had lent themselves to the collective group. "Stay clear of the black thug." Those were the whispers behind his back. He was sure he'd heard them, faint mumblings, barely audible. He was accustomed to being a hated man. The absence of others of his race in the building had not escaped his notice either. No black man would ever get a fair shake here, especially one like him who didn't have the common decency to mind his place. He would bet his last Grammy that the only blacks who had ever darkened the doorstep of the World Tower were in service uniforms. It was strangely unsettling to be the only black man in the building, and as far as he could see, the only one alive in the entire world. Who knew what was outside New York City.

The door opened and Jamal turned with a jerk.

A girl with long golden hair smiled coyly at him. He had taken notice of her during the lounge meeting and they had passed once in the stairwell. On each occasion she had watched him intently with a look he had come to recognize and welcome.

Jamal's eyes swept over her lithe frame. He wanted to get acquainted more intimately, but with things unfolding as they were that opportunity had not yet presented itself.

Jamal returned the smile.

"Fancy meeting you here," she said, and moved casually to his side. "It's getting stuffy in these apartments with no air conditioning," she said, and removed a pack of menthol cigarettes from her pocket. She removed one of them with the tips of her long fingernails and offered it to Jamal. He stuck it between his full lips and waited for a light. She quickly obliged him with a red BIC lighter and then took one for herself.

She pursed her lips and exhaled the smoke to the left of Jamal's face. "I'm Karen," she told him softly with a flip of her hair that caused some of it to cover her forehead with golden bangs.

"I'm Jamal."

"Yeah, I know…Jamal Owens. I used to watch your soap." Karen took another drag and licked her lips. "So why'd you quit the show?"

"I didn't quit," he told her.

"Well, it's not the same without you. You were the only reason I watched. I like your music."

Jamal sighed, "Yeah, well, I guess that's all been said and done. At least for a while," he said, and laughed.

"Yeah, I guess so." Karen said.

Karen flipped her hair away from her face and crushed the half smoked cigarette beneath her brown, leather boot, exhaling smoke as she did it. "So, you wanna go up to the roof and get some fresh air? I could sure use some and it looks like you could too. Besides, the exercise will do us good."

"The roof?" Jamal asked, and chuckled.

"Why are you laughing?" Karen asked.

"Because there's some Nazi bitch that lives in the penthouse. If we go anywhere close to that roof she's liable to blow our brains out first and ask questions later. Besides, there are people on the roof. They're waiting for the military to come save us in an air lift."

"That seems like a stretch," Karen said.

"Yeah, that's what I was thinkin' too. How bout if we just slide on down to the bar and make ourselves a drink? Now that sounds like a better plan."

"I thought the downstairs was closed off?"

"Yeah, it is, but I know where Michael hid the key and I stashed a bottle of good bourbon."

Karen smiled again, this time wide. She seemed anxious to have a drink with him. Jamal knew ready and willing when he saw it.

For Jamal, things were looking up.

31

The tiny child was sweating. Wringing wet, as if she'd walked uncovered through a pouring rain. Her eyes were wide and her mouth was gaped open in horror as she sat bolt upright on the sofa in Clara Baker's seventh floor apartment. Clara sat in a wing chair with a blue floral pattern staring silently into a corner of the room. The news of her husband's death had sent her into her own trance-like state of shock. She was oblivious to her surroundings.

Doctor Adam Riker moved from his place watching the old woman to the tiny waif's side. He wiped her glistening forehead with a white cloth and tried to calm her. He glanced over his shoulder toward Sarah who stood watching his efforts. He had hoped she would take more interest in the little girl and lend a woman's touch to the situation. Instead, she crossed her arms and walked to the window with her back to them. It was obvious to Adam that Sarah had no woman's touch. Emotion was something that evidently wasn't a prominent part of her make up.

The little girl trembled as she pointed to the door of the apartment. Her breathing was heavy and quick, and her face was pale white.

"It was just a bad dream." Adam told her, softly.

The little girl looked at him and seemed to settle. Her breathing slowed and Adam laid her head back down on the pillow.

"She's still in shock." Adam said to Sarah who still had her back to him. "We need someone who can care for her all the time. This has all been too much for her young mind."

"She has someone," Sarah said. "Clara will see to her."

"Clara's in no shape to watch over the child. Hell, she's in no shape right now to watch over herself." She needs someone too."

Sarah turned quickly.

"If you think I'm going to become some kind of live-in nurse and clean up after a crying child or wipe the ass of an invalid you've got another thing coming, Doctor Riker. My home is upstairs and that's just where I'm headed. The only reason I came down here today was to help you seal off the ground floor of this building. Once I go back upstairs I won't be returning. I'm going to lock my door and ride this thing out alone. I have no plans to hang out down here in the sanitarium with the crazies or with the unwashed on the fifth and sixth floor. Thank you Doctor, but *no* thank you."

Adam said, "Fine, go back to your penthouse where you're queen of the tower. Go ahead and pretend that no one needs your help and that you're better off alone. We'll make do…all us, unwashed."

Sarah said, "The unwashed rich stink just as much as the unwashed poor, Doctor, and I *am* better off alone. There are too many people down here. It will end up getting you all killed. At least up there I have a chance. Besides, I'm needed up there too. If rescue is going to come, it will come from the air. We need people on the roof at all times. We can't afford to miss anything. Even a distant plane could see a flare on the roof. There are others who can see to the old woman and that child."

Adam sighed. There was no use arguing with Sarah. He had not known her long, but she wasn't someone that required extended contact or intimate time together to get a handle on. Sarah was not a complex woman. She was black and white. To her things were either right or wrong. There were no shades of gray or situations unique. Straying too far from the old ways meant certain disaster in her book. Once her mind was made up, discussion closed. At least, that was Adam's opinion.

Adam said, "Who's up there now?"

"I think they're *all* on the roof right now. They were supposed to change shifts tonight at nine o'clock, but I told Yusuf to stay for a while with Duane and Chuck before he went back to my penthouse to sleep," Sarah said.

"Why do you need both Duane and Chuck on the roof for the night shift?"

"Because, I don't trust either of them by themselves to stay awake all night. It takes the two of them to do the job of one, good man. I asked Yusuf to stay a bit so he could assess their ability to do this simple task before leaving them on their own."

***

Yusuf's slight accent made it difficult for Duane and Chuck to understand him clearly at times. But they nonetheless enjoyed his company. Chuck considered Yusuf a sturdy enough fellow and strangely, he liked him. It was strange because he didn't usually like foreigners; he had not been exposed to them much growing up. He had been born and raised in Virginia, an honest to goodness red, white and blue country boy. There were times as a child when food was scarce and the house cold. Still, his father trucked on and did what he could, doing without himself to feed the family. He was a strong and proud man. Handouts were out of the question. That mentality had rubbed off on Chuck, but not exactly in the same, god-fearing way. It was true that Chuck had never taken a handout, but he had on more than on one occasion slipped his hand in someone else's pocket to take what wasn't his. His mind was at conflict with its two sides. What he knew to be appropriate, and what his laziness afforded him. He was unpredictable and unreliable, and he was fully aware of it.

"There is a light in the boat anchored in the East River," Yusuf told Chuck, and pointed across the roof. "Sarah wants us to keep an eye on it." He gave the pair of binoculars he'd been holding to Chuck who walked to the East side of the roof where he could see the river more clearly and raised them to his eyes.

Chuck searched the darkness until he found the little light shining from the middle of the river. It was indeed a boat and there was indeed a light shining inside that boat. It could plainly be seen through the small window facing them.

Chuck lowered the eyeglasses.

"It's kerosene, you know?"

"Ker-o-sene." Yusuf said slowly pronouncing each syllable.

"Yeah, like gas. It's not electric."

Yusuf nodded, "I know what it is."

"It's not running off the boat's batteries. That means there must be someone on board. Someone had to refill it. It would never burn this long without being refilled."

"You could tell that from here," Yusuf asked.

Chuck smiled, "I have good eyes. Besides, there's a flicker. It's oil—or kerosene alright."

Yusuf nodded and walked away. "I will tell Sarah the light is kerosene."

32

Jamal replaced the shade on the oil lamp and lowered the flame. Karen filled two rocks glasses with some of the bourbon that Jamal had stashed behind a mirror over the bar and then handed one of them to Jamal. Her eyes never left his as she did so.

"Don't you feel naughty for being down here where we're not supposed to be?" Karen said, and took a sip from her glass. Her blue eyes watched him from above the rim as she drank. Jamal returned the obvious eye contact with an undressing of his own. He approved of what he was seeing. Karen was tall and curvy. She had nice hips and her skintight jeans defined them nicely. Her breasts were full, but not too large. That was good too. He was never into those cow jugs that quivered and quaked when the girl moved. These were large, but firm. Just the way he liked them.

"I go where I want to go. Michael Longley is not the boss of me," he said, and killed the first glass of bourbon. Jamal placed the empty glass on the bar and Karen filled it again. The rhythmic song of ghoul cries was background noise to their conversation and Jamal gave it little notice as he drank his bourbon. The oil lamp danced and flickered against the far wall of the bar area. Only a short wall separated the bar from the rest of the lounge and the windowed portion of the ground floor. While the direct flame of the lamp was not visible through the windows, its light flickered and cast shadows against the tinted glass to tantalize the crowd outside.

***

Jason Watsby was a fireman. Somewhere, sometime he had been, but not now. Now he was unsure of exactly what he was. He studied his gray and lacerated fingers as they rested upon the glass in front of him. He had just noticed them, and now he moved them close to his face for a better look in the dim moonlight.

He turned them around so that he could see the palms. There were lines there on the skin. He cocked his head in fascination as he studied them. But no matter how hard he tried to focus his fractured thoughts, their meaning remained a mystery. However, he had come to understand the importance of the hand itself. It was useful—useful to do things.

Jason Watsby's eyes looked up from his cold gray hands to the flickering light on the other side of the glass. He was not sure why, but he wanted to follow the light. He wanted to be close to it. There was color in the light. Not like the grayness of the world around him. The light meant warmth, but not the kind that warmed the body. That kind of sensation was alien to him now; a nearly forgotten sense from a life now equally forgotten. This light somehow meant warmth of the soul. Something he unquestionably lacked. And even though he didn't quite understand, the light also meant life. Life was the opposite of what he had become. And what he had become was alone. In a sea of walking death he was alone. He was in a dream world not quite aware of his surroundings. Neither did he understand that those around him lived in that same state of mind, a kind of sleep walk with ill intent. Yet, ill intent implied a motive. There was no motive in Jason's new world, only instinct.

And instinct was inescapable.

Instinct was Jason's destiny and his only option.

Jason raised the fireman's hammer resting beside him and swung it at the glass.

The crash of the glass sent Jamal reeling backward with one leg in his pants and hopping on the other. He fell into the table behind him and crashed to the floor where he frantically tried to pull his tangled jeans up. Karen pulled her blouse over her head and searched for her own jeans in the flickering light. A sudden breeze tainted with the scent of rot filled the room. Karen did not have to see around the corner to know what that meant. She snatched her jeans from the floor behind the bar and wrestled with them.

Karen said, "The key! Where's the key? We have to lock the door behind us on the way up."

Jamal searched his pockets for the key that he had used to open the door to the ground floor.

"It must've fallen out when I was getting undressed," he screamed.

"Find it you idiot!"

Jamal noticed how much they had to raise their voices to be heard. The rhythmic pulse of wails had gotten much louder, almost deafening. He was searching the floor around him when the undead mob rounded both ends of the short wall between the bar and lounge area.

Karen was caught in between and tried to run through. She was snagged by the faltering grip of cold fingers in the back of her collar. It was enough to send her to the floor where her head impacted squarely with the hard tile. Her eyes stared blankly at the ceiling, and to her benefit, she wasn't cognizant as the flesh was ripped from her stomach. And as the crowd fought for their share, she never once screamed as she was eviscerated. Karen's head lolled slowly to the left. Her eyes closed and she died quickly.

Still unable to find the keys, Jamal regained his footing and raced down the hall toward the stairwell door where he stopped and turned.

The crowd had swelled to fill the room. He could no longer see Karen. She had been there a moment ago. Had she gotten by him unseen? It was unlikely. And just as he was ready to turn and leave, she reappeared, rising from within the throng. She staggered toward the table where they had sat earlier. Only now could he could see the full extent of her terrible injuries.

As he watched her, the crowd rushed forward and walking-dead Karen was pushed head first into the table. The lamp, still burning, crashed to the floor and the wall was an instant curtain of flame. Jamal considered for a moment that the sprinkler system would extinguish the fire. Yes, it would snuff it out and they would be safe above. But then, it suddenly occurred to him that he still lacked the key to lock the door, and the sprinklers would not work.

The city's water had failed. There was no longer pressure in the lines. The fire would not be doused.

Some of the dead things shied away from the fire as it spread up the wall and licked out across the ceiling. The rest of them moved in unison toward Jamal. They would follow him. They would climb the stairs to the floors above and fill the high rise. Soon the growing fire would also follow.

Jamal raced upward, away from the smoke, rising flames, and death incarnate.

33

No one had seen the little girl wake, or leave the apartment and go to the stairwell. She was standing there when Jamal rounded the platform to ascend another rise of stairs. Their eyes met as he brushed past her and continued upward. She peered through the railings to the empty stairwell below, and as if given some kind of advanced warning to the unseen danger, her eyes widened and she raced back to the apartment.

Adam slept, slumped uncomfortably in the blue floral wing chair. The child stared at him hesitantly as if contemplating whether she should wake him or not. The sudden clarity of their peril spurred the ethereal waif to action and she began shaking him with all her might.

Adam woke with a start, finding himself immediately confronted by the wide, frightened eyes of the distraught child. "What's wrong?" he asked, and sat upright in the chair.

Without answering, the child ran from the room and into the hall. Adam leaped from the chair and followed.

She made it all the way into the stairwell before he could catch her. That's where Adam snatched her up into his arms, turned, and stopped.

He smelled smoke, and there was a racket that echoed from the stairwell below them. Adam leaned over the rails, fully expecting to see Michael and some of the others on their way up. Instead, his blood ran cold, and the air was sucked out of his lungs like a kick to the chest.

The stairwell below was filling rapidly, inch by inch, foot by foot, with the walking, devouring dead. The mob that filled the streets was now inside the building and had somehow gained access to the stairwell.

"Oh my God." he said, and gasped for breath as the awful truth instantly hit home.

It was too late for the people below. The dead were already up to the fifth floor. Most of the tower's inhabitants were on the fifth and sixth. Michael was on the forth. He was unsure of how bad the situation was, but there was smoke and where there was smoke, there was usually fire. If a fire were out of control, then no place in the building was safe. Below, they could lock themselves inside their apartments, but the fire would eventually accomplish what the walking dead could not.

Adam raced back to the Bakers' apartment and scooped a sleeping Clara up from her bed and tossed the disoriented, old woman unceremoniously over his shoulder. With his free hand he grabbed the child and raced back to the stairway.

A thickening haze of smoke hung in the air of the stairwell like a gauze curtain as the monsters passed the landing one floor below them. Many were bloated and swollen, more grotesque now than he remembered. Adam pulled the child along as he moved up the stairs with the old woman slung across his shoulder. The people below were likely lost to the swarming crowd and fire.

***

At the forty-first floor, Adam stopped to rest and leaned Clara against the wall. His eyes closed involuntarily. The old woman's small, frail body had become suddenly heavy and there were still fifty floors to climb. His body ached and the extra weight had worn him down.

He could easily submit to the exhaustion and sleep. There had been little time for rest and now it was catching up to him.

Adam willed his eyes open.

The little girl sat cross-legged in front of Clara Baker. She cocked her head inquisitively from side to side. Adam watched until the child's expression transformed from curiosity to alarm.

Clara's head jerked forward and a gurgling sound erupted from her lungs as her eyes flew open. The glaze of death was there. Maybe it had been heart failure, or a sudden stroke. Maybe she had simply grieved herself to death, but Adam Riker was suddenly aware that he had climbed nearly forty floors with a dead woman draped across his shoulder.

Adam leapt to his feet and pulled the child safely behind him. With a staggering kick he sent Clara's living corpse back down the stairs. She fell in a heap on the landing one floor below, where at first she remained still. Then, she began to stir, dragging herself up by the limited strength in her frail, dead arms one step, then another, dragging her broken body toward them. It was no longer a helpless old woman; it was one of them now, no bite, and no contact with the living dead. Just as Michael had thought, the dead, for whatever reason, came back.

Without another thought for the old woman, he grabbed the child and began climbing again.

34

Adam and the child finally arrived at the Penthouse floor where he stared at two doors. One was to the roof. The other, he assumed opened to Sarah's penthouse apartment. He had never been there by way of the stairs, but he knew it was the only apartment on the top floor. He had just reached out to turn the knob when it opened suddenly. Sarah stood there, still dressed in her army vest and green camouflaged pants with the two shiny pistols still strapped to her waist.

She brushed past Adam and the girl and moved to the stairs where she peered over the edge.

"How far behind are they?"

Adam said, "I don't know. Twenty floors? Maybe less. I came up ahead of them as fast as I could."

"How many others are coming up with you?"

Adam was unable to catch his breath long enough to speak clearly. "There's *no* more coming. Not live ones anyway. Those things—somehow they got inside. They were to the fifth floor before I knew it. I grabbed the girl and Clara and headed up."

Sarah said, "Clara? Where's Clara?"

Adam exhaled heavily.

"She died on the way up. I carried a dead woman halfway up this skyscraper. I really wish I had known that. She was dead for a while anyway. She woke up hungry so I kicked her dead ass down the steps. Oh, and I almost forgot…" Adam chortled, and the edge of hysteria in his laughter made Sarah wonder if the Doctor was having a breakdown. "There's a fire too. I think it's out of control on the ground floor. We won't have to worry about those damned cannibals for too long. The fire will be coming along directly."

Sarah pulled them both into her apartment and locked the door behind them, then scurried out of the room leaving the two of them standing there alone. Adam pulled the girl along in his wake until he found a chair and fell into it. He had almost slipped into a state of exhausted unconsciousness when a thump to his chest brought him sharply back to reality.

"Well, at least we won't have fifty people fighting over these." Adam opened his eyes to see Sarah standing in front of him and an orange canvas bundle that looked like a backpack on his chest. "What's this?" he asked. Sarah held three more.

"What do you think it is?"

"Oh shit," he mumbled.

Sarah said, "It's easy to use. You just secure a static line and jump. It opens automatically."

Adam said, "Jump? Where? Down?—Down is bad. And why do you have parachutes in your apartment for God's sake?"

Sarah said, "They're called 911 chutes. After terrorists took down those two towers in 2001, some people kept these on hand just in case. It seemed logical to have a few on hand myself since I live a thousand feet above the ground. And as it turns out, I guess I was right."

Adam asked, "Where's Yusuf?"

"He's still on the roof. Evidently, he didn't feel those two clowns from the south were quite ready to handle the job themselves."

Sarah dropped the other parachutes and flung open the door. She stepped out into the stairwell to encounter a horde of reanimates nearly to the top of the stairs.

"Twenty floors behind, like hell," she yelled, and in a flash pulled her rifle from its sleeve on her back and held it crossways in front of her.

Sarah screamed out and charged into them with such force and momentum that the ones standing at the top of the steps tumbled back into the ones behind them. The maneuver sent them all falling down into a twisted pile of writhing limbs. At that moment she saw

Michael Longley turn the corner at the landing below and attempt to maneuver through the pileup in the stairwell.

"Doctor, isn't that...?" the unfinished question hung in the air as they both stared in horror.

Michael's left arm was missing from the elbow down. His ears had been bitten off, and his nasal cavity could be seen where his nose should have been. His lips and the flesh of one cheek were gone as well. It made him difficult to recognize. What remained of his face was contorted into a grotesque bloody grin as he stared up at them.

"Jesus, yes," Adam choked out; his stomach heaved and churned at the ghastly sight.

Without another second of hesitation Sarah raised her gun and shot him in the forehead. The wall behind him was painted with splattered gore and Michael's body dropped. She flipped the rifle over her left shoulder and into the hunter's pouch again, and then returned to the penthouse doorway. She tossed the other orange canvas parachutes to Adam and snatched up a large green satchel.

Leaning in with her right shoulder, Sarah stormed through the other door and onto the roof of the World Tower with Adam and the fair-haired child following in her wake. She used a key to lock the door behind them and then stormed across the roof to the side facing the East River.

Chuck, Yusuf, and Duane stood by the roof's ledge as they watched her deliberate approach. Jamal paced atop the roof's four-foot high ledge, wringing his hands in an obvious state of extreme agitation.

Without a word, Sarah climbed onto the ledge and looked over to the scene below.

"We've got trouble," Chuck told her. "There's a fire."

Sarah looked up toward the red glow in the eastern sky. "The sun will be up soon." She said, "We need it to see where we're going."

Sarah jumped down from the ledge. "The fire seems to be fully engaged on the ground floor and probably well into several floors above from what I can see from here. It's only a matter of time before it moves up to us. We'll die from heat or smoke inhalation before the fire reaches us. You can already smell it. We can't wait too long. The fire will create a wind that could blow us off course."

"Off course to what?" Adam asked.

Sarah counted heads. There was one unexpected addition. Jamal had not been invited to roof duty. She turned to Adam.

"Did he come up here with you?" She asked, and tilted her head toward the street thug-turned-rapper-turned-soap-star.

"No," Adam replied curtly.

"What I wanna know is how that fire started," Sarah said, loud enough to be heard by everyone. She glanced at the frightened, wide-eyed child. "I'm fairly certain that the baby didn't go down to the first floor and start a fire. And I know it wasn't Duane, Chuck, or Yusuf. They were up here with me." Sarah walked to where Adam stood.

"Was it you, Adam?"

Adam stood silent, shocked by her implied allegation.

Sarah repeated the question, and drew one of her pistols, holding it at her side.

"Was it you, Adam?"

"NO…Of course not. Are you crazy?"

Without moving the weapon, Sarah continued.

"No, of course it wasn't you. But, it had to be someone. The fire didn't start by itself, and those things gained access to a bolted, secure stairwell, which means that someone was down there where they weren't supposed to be. And in the process let those monsters inside the building. Someone who was running scared and didn't think to secure the locks behind them."

Sarah swung around to where Jamal stood on the ledge and pointed the gun at him. "It was you, Meadowlark. You were the only other person with notification enough to get ahead of that horde and make it to the roof. You knew about the fire, and the goddamned neo-zombies. This is your doing."

"It wasn't my fault. They broke inside before I knew it. They started the fire, not me." Jamal's eyes darted furtively, looking for backup in the faces of the remaining survivors.

"You went down there at night and into an area that was strictly off limits for this very reason. By doing so you effectively signed the death warrant of virtually every survivor holed up in this building." Sarah narrowed her cold, hard gaze at Jamal, "Including your own. You've made it easy to decide who we won't be wasting a parachute on."

"What?" Jamal cast about furiously, groping for a leg to stand on, for any excuse that could redeem him in their eyes.

"Chuck…Dewey…it was an accident. I just wanted to spend some QT with a fine, little piece of—man, you understand how it is, right? It was an accident. I'm sorry."

Chuck took two quick strides toward Jamal and pulled him down onto the rooftop, taking a broad swing at the same time. The punch connected squarely with Jamal's jaw as Chuck fell on him in a flurry of violent punches, screaming, "YOU STUPID FUCK! I'LL KILL YOU!"

Jamal tried in vain to fend off the fast series of blows to his head and shoulders. As Chuck began to wear down, Duane stepped up, and with Adam's help they pulled Chuck away from Jamal. "Let it go, Chuck. We've gotta get this thing figured out and get outta here. You're wasting time."

Chuck stood up. He shook with anger.

Sarah had been watching the scene unfold with her own brand of cold, calculating anger. "Meadowlark, you are going to be our distraction when we try to escape…the bait—the slight of hand. You will be the diversion we need."

Sarah moved toward Jamal, keeping her gun aimed steadily at his chest.

"Someone else will have to stay behind as well," she said. "So don't feel privileged, Meadowlark. You're not the only one who will have to die on this roof. You'll have company."

Jamal backed away from Sarah's pointing gun. "Oh sure, let the fucking nigger take the fall, right? Ain't it always the way? What happened to drawing straws?" he lashed out.

"It's not because you're black. It's because you're an asshole. These are my parachutes and my plan. I don't intend to be the person who stays behind…and fuck drawing straws. The rest of you can do whatever you need to decide who goes and who stays, but do it quickly. One of you can carry the girl, so she can go. Though I don't see why. She'll never survive the trip away from the city. She'll only serve to slow the rest of us down."

"I'll take her," Adam offered.

"No Adam, I think it's best that Duane take her. He's the lightest. The chute should handle them both, but the rest of you have a decision to make. Who stays and who goes."

Duane said, "Yeah, I'll take her. That means I get to go, right? No straw for me?"

For a time there was silence except for the creatures pounding on the door at the far end of the roof.

"I'll stay." Yusuf volunteered.

"No," Adam interjected. "I'll take Yusuf with me."

"For God's sake. Get it through your thick skulls," Sarah screamed. "The parachute won't carry two people out of the danger zone. You'll drop right into the crowd below. Hell, we might not make it anyway. It's a long way to the riverbank from this building. I don't care who stays, but one of you must, to ensure the survival of the rest."

"It's alright, Adam," Yusuf explained. "I don't want to go. From the looks of things, there's nothing left out there anyway. I am okay with this."

"Survival of the fittest?" Adam shot Sarah an angry look.

"Not hardly," Sarah replied, looking pointedly toward the little girl. "I just know the odds, and I don't like taking unnecessary chances. If we are going to make it, we need to work as a team. Jamal is not a team player. He sealed his own fate. We're better off without him." Sarah tossed a parachute to Chuck and Duane, and then showed them how to put their arms through the straps and join the buckles across their chests. She checked each one for snugness and to ensure it was secured properly before equipping herself for the jump.

Jamal took the opportunity while Sarah was distracted to climb to his feet. He searched frantically for anything he could use as a weapon to defend himself, or better yet, attack. Sarah quickly turned her attention back to him and landed a jarring blow to the side of his head with the barrel of her handgun. "Step over to the north wall, Jamal,"

"What?" Jamal shook off the blow, and coiled his body to spring at her if the opportunity presented itself.

"What are you doing, Sarah?" Adam asked.

"DO IT! God damn you, do it now. There's no time," she said, and pushed Jamal back with a palm thrust, all the while her gun pointing at his chest.

"What are you doing, Sarah?" Adam asked her again.

"You see? It doesn't really matter." She explained. "But I needed to make a decision. We only have four parachutes. They won't carry two people. One of the lighter men can take the little girl. Two of us must stay behind. Those two will certainly die. It would be of great help to us if there were a distraction of some kind to draw the crowd below away from the east side of the building. Even a little might make the difference."

Jamal's eyes widened as Sarah's intentions became clear to him. "You can take your Sigourney Weaver bitch attitude and go fuck yourself. I ain't gonna do it."

"There's no other way. Your body might draw them away and give us the extra room we need close to the river. But I'll give you a choice. You can make the fall from the ledge already dead, or you can jump alive, and experience the fall before you die."

"WHAT? NEITHER!" he screamed. Jamal was shaking his head as he watched his chances dwindle away like sand through an hour glass "No…Please, don't do this. It was an accident. I didn't let them in on purpose." He was wringing his hands now, imploring her, "I don't wanna die. I'll do whatever you say."

Sarah was losing her strength to carry out the pending death sentence, a moral luxury they could not afford and she squeezed the trigger.

Jamal grunted as the bullet hit his well-muscled abdomen, his eyes wide with disbelief as he slumped against the ledge wall.

His hands were covered with his own hot red blood and he held them out for all to see as if to hold off another shot, and at the same time, show Sarah the awful consequences of her action. "Oh-no," he whimpered, and collapsed to the surface of the roof.

Jamal was breathing unevenly. "Man. You are a cold bitch," he said with a slight chuckle, and his head tilted back to rest against the ledge. What he said next was unintelligible to those standing by, but Sarah heard him clearly…

"God will forgive me because I will ask him to do so. But will he forgive you? Will you forgive yourself?" Then he fell silent and closed his eyes.

Sarah spun on her heel to face the others. When she was only met with shock and silence, she lowered the weapon and returned it to its holster.

The smoke was beginning to swirl around the roof in the morning wind. To their good fortune it blew in an easterly direction, but Sarah knew the fire below could quickly change that and she took that factor into account as she formulated the plan in her head and climbed up onto the ledge behind Jamal.

There was enough pre-dawn light to see clearly now. A massive crowd filled the area around the Trump World Tower in all directions. Across the city it was more of the same and her present view confirmed this. Indeed, the crowds congregated around other buildings in much the same way they did around their own.

The chutes were not designed to carry a person a great horizontal distance. They were intended to save a desperate person from a burning structure, a vertical descent with limited control. They were clearly about to make a move born of desperation.

"There's a hook at each corner of the roof, but we'll all be using the same one." Sarah walked over to it. "Here, near the eastern corner. It gives us our best chance to make the river. Attach your line to it. It's simple. You run and you jump. Jump out as far as you can. Once you are in the air, steer to the river. Get as far as you can before hitting the ground. We want to get past the crowds below. Use the two straps with handles to steer. The left one will guide you to the left. The right one will take you right. It's just that easy." Sarah looked at their rapt faces, "I'll push Jamal over the ledge to hopefully draw the crowd away from this side of the building. Whatever time it buys us will be fleeting, so you all have to be ready to do this. Cowboy up, gentlemen."

If any of them felt remorse for Jamal's impending fate, it was overridden by their desire to survive and so no one mouthed further objection. But Sarah's heart was pounding, and her chest was tight with building anxiety. Not for the jump, but for the cold-hearted act she had just carried out. She had been the judge, jury, and executioner for a man she barely knew, a man who might have simply made a terrible mistake. But the situation had called for extreme measures and she would be the one to carry the terrible burden of her actions.

"Duane, are you wearing a belt?" Sarah asked.

He pulled up his shirt to show her that he wasn't, then dropped it again.

Sarah sighed, and unfastened the strap on her green army satchel and grabbed the girl. She placed her in Duane's arms, facing him. Her tiny, thin legs wrapped around his wiry frame. Sarah pulled the strap tight, first around the child and then around Duane until she was confident it would hold. Then she leaned in to the girl and spoke softly and reassuringly to her. "When you both jump, you must hold your arms around his neck as tightly as you can.

Understand?" The child said nothing. Maybe she understood. Sarah couldn't be sure. "She'll never make it," Sarah said, and gave Duane a yellow utility knife. "She has to hold on for herself. If you try to do it, you'll go off course. You don't want that. As soon as you're down, and if she doesn't fly loose, pull this release line. The chute should auto-release. Use this knife to cut yourselves free from the rigging I just made to hold her to you."

Sarah turned to Adam and Chuck. "Both of you…all of you…do it quickly. Get out of the chute and run for the river. Swim to the boat. She pointed to it so everyone would understand where to go.

For a moment, she stared at Yusuf. She admired his sacrifice and found herself unexpectedly emotional about his decision to stay behind, or was it what she had done to Jamal still plaguing her conscience?

Sarah reached into the green satchel and tossed him a pistol. "In case you'd rather take an easy way out," she said.

Yusuf tossed it back. "That is not an option for me."

Sarah gave the weapon to Duane and then pulled two more from the satchel and gave one to Chuck and the other to Adam along with some ammunition for each.

"Everyone get on the ledge. It's time to go."

35

"What is the difference?" Adam asked Yusuf. "You're refusing the gun because you believe God will turn away from you if you use it, even if it's only used to choose the less gruesome of two certain deaths?"

"Yes, that is true. I will spend eternity in Hell, without God." He continued, trying to clarify for Adam. "It is written that He who commits suicide by throttling shall keep on throttling himself in the Hell-fire, and he who commits suicide by stabbing himself, he shall keep stabbing himself in the Hell-fire. I do not wish to spend eternity commiting this act of cowardice."

"It is no different if you stay on this roof. If you stay here, if you refuse to try to help yourself, you are committing suicide." Adam paused as his words penetrated Yusuf's thinking, "I am offering you a way down, God is offering you a way down. To deny it is to deny God. Am I not right?"

Yusuf wanted to answer and he stammered for something to say. He wanted to counter Adam's logic, but in the end he only sighed and dropped his head.

"I have a belt and so do you," Adam stated matter-of-factly, "We can use them to tie ourselves together too."

Sarah's head was pounding. Time was ticking by and she wanted to scream at the folly of his idea, but she kept quiet, finally weary of her efforts to make them understand. Their life, she thought resignedly, and live or die, it was their choice.

"I'll do it," Chuck intervened. "I'm smaller than Adam. If anyone does it, it should be me."

Sarah said, "Jesus, do what you want. It's your lives. Do with it as you will, but for God's sake let's get it done," Sarah climbed onto the ledge. "You're first Duane, you and the girl."

Sarah connected Duane's line to the hook as Chuck and Yusuf tied themselves together with the belts. Once they were finished, they connected their lines to the hook as well, first Chuck and then Adam.

"Everybody set?" Sarah asked. "I'm going to buy us whatever time I can by throwing our friend over there off that side of the building. As soon as they start to move in his direction you have to go." She looked from one to the next.

Sarah jumped down from the ledge and sprinted across the rooftop to where Jamal lay in a state of semi-consciousness. His breath rattled and rasped jaggedly, his head lolled to one side as his life was slipping quickly away from him. Four men and a frightened child watched silently from their perch as Sarah struggled to push Jamal up onto the ledge. Jamal's head suddenly raised and in a last moment of lucidity he looked directly into her eyes and said, "Bitch, I got this. My terms," and with that and the last of his waning strength he pulled himself up onto the ledge, rolled over and disappeared.

Sarah paused for a moment before she ran back to the stunned group at full speed, not waiting to see what effect Jamal's fall had on the crowd below. Either it worked, or it didn't. It made no difference in what they had to do next.

"Get ready!" she shouted, "We can't wait too long between jumps. Once we start we have to all go as fast as we can. After the first person jumps, they will take notice and come after us. We can't give them time to cut us off from the river. What I'm saying is if you freeze I will leave you behind. Is that understood?"

Sarah pushed Duane and the child to the spot on the ledge that would give them the required momentum they needed, "Start here. Hold the little one's feet up and run to the edge. Jump out as far as you can. Remember, the chute will deploy automatically."

Duane was trembling noticeably. "GO!," she screamed, and he took off like a shot before his fear could completely immobilize him.

He leaped out into open air with his tiny passenger clinging tightly to his neck. Just as Sarah had promised, the chute deployed. The hot orange rectangle whooshed out above them as it filled with air. Duane dangled beneath it, doing his best to steer and maneuver it toward the East River. The little girl hugged him tightly, and buried her face in his shoulder.

"They're gonna make it," Adam whispered, hoarsely.

"We don't have time to wait and see," Sarah warned. "You're next Chuck—you and Yusuf."

Chuck and Yusuf were entwined in an embrace. Belted together, they were face to face, like a doomed couple in their final embrace before they hurled themselves from Lover's Leap.

They tiptoed their way to the starting spot. "We can't run tied together like this."

"I told you this was a bad idea," she scolded, "Yusuf, turn around. Put your back to Chuck's chest, hurry."

Sarah loosened the belts enough for him to place his back to Chuck then tightened it again. "You're taller, so bend forward a little so that Chuck's feet are off the ground. You do the running to the edge and jump. It will be easier that way. Chuck, you pull the ripcord and then hold onto Yusuf until after the parachute extends and inflates. There will be a jerk. After that, you can let go to steer the chute. It'll be up to him to hold on then any way he can."

Chuck nodded, and Yusuf ran, bent and staggering under the weight of his burden, to the roof's edge and leaped.

The chute opened with a jerk, and Yusuf almost slipped head over heels out of the belt straps. Chuck grabbed him and held tightly until he could pull himself upright again. The two of them glided toward the river above and behind Duane's descending chute.

"It's going to be close," Sarah told Adam. "If they make it, it won't be by much."

Adam sighed, "Then that means you probably killed Jamal for nothing."

"I killed the son of a bitch because he was a thug, Doctor Riker. He was a bad guy. He would've sacrificed each and every one of us to save his own ass and I won't apologize for that, nor will I feel guilty about it." But she did feel the rising guilt and she fought to hold it where it had been, in her chest and not in her throat where it would surely make her scream.

"Isn't that what we're doing? Whatever we must to survive?"

"I didn't see you offering up your chute for him, now did I, Doctor? It's your turn." Sarah nudged him toward the mark. "Jump."

Adam fumed. His nostrils flared and his breathing was noticeably heavy. He glared at Sarah for a moment then ran to the edge and disappeared over the side. Sarah ran out behind him and looked over. His chute had failed to open properly. He dropped a hundred feet before it deployed and caught the wind. Just then, a series of windows in the lower floors exploded in a spray of glass, and a burst of heat from the raging fire caught the chute as it rose. The force of the blast sent Adam to the left and off course. He tried to adjust by steering to the right, but his efforts had little effect on the direction the chute was going. Unless something extraordinary happened it would not make the clearing close to the river. It would not even clear the throngs of walking dead that peppered the streets and sidewalks directly below. Adam Riker was descending into the bowels of hell and there was nothing Sarah could do to stop it.

Sarah clipped her line to the hook, secured her green satchel of weapons and ammunition, and sprinted into empty space. Her chute opened just as she had expected and she steered it to the river behind the other two.

***

Adam Riker watched helplessly as the crowds below grew larger. He kicked his legs and pulled with all his might on the right handle to steer the chute away from the waiting crowd. It finally did respond, and moved to the right, but he was already too low and dropping too fast.

In his mind, his descent to the ground slowed as his thoughts raced. Where was Meena? Was she alive? He had not thought about her much since returning home, but now on his journey to certain death she was all he could think about.

"Meena, I'm sorry," he whispered, and kicked his feet and pulled hard to the right to reach a small clearing that had seemed to magically open below him.

Several feet above the crowd he pulled the quick release and dropped to the asphalt. The opening was about twenty feet wide and thirty feet long. Instantly Adam was on his feet, survival instincts kicking in, and with newfound hope he was running through the crowd.

He bulled forward and thrashed through them with as much strength and speed as he could muster. Their faces were pale, devoid of humanity, hideous apparitions with their cold, lifeless hands reaching out for him, touching him. Adam slapped them aside as he ran, willing himself through the thickening horde. But now his efforts were becoming more difficult as the crowd closed in on him and his progress was slowing. The mob had condensed until he could no longer move forward. He was motionless in a sea of walking death so tight that he was unable to even drop to the ground beneath them. Then the piercing pain of sinking teeth on his left arm, a gray face on his throat—more pain. Where were the others? Did they make it?

The gray face twisted and pulled.

36

Duane pulled the quick release as soon as his feet hit the ground. The impact was much harder than he had expected and it sent him rolling head over heels, scraping across the concrete sidewalk on the other side of the road. The belt holding the little girl snapped, and the two of them separated. She dropped beside Duane, catching herself with her hands as she hit the high grass of the uncut lawn.

The girl was shaken and dazed from the impact. She knelt as if in prayer with her hands on her knees and head bowed. But Duane's attention was drawn to the crowd behind them. They had landed forty yards past the massive crowd, but the chute floating toward him now would not be so lucky. It was Chuck and Yusuf. From his vantage point it looked doubtful that they would make it past them at all. Duane grabbed the girl and carried her to the river's edge. Once there, he turned again.

Only two chutes were in flight. The third was nowhere to be seen. The higher, further one, was Sarah's. Either Adam had not jumped, or he had fallen into the crowd. There was also the possibility that Sarah had shot him dead before the jump. She was lethal and unpredictable. Duane waited and watched as the two chutes drifted down.

Chuck released the chute and Yusuf's feet hit first as the two men rolled head over heals across the asphalt.

"Undo the belts!" Chuck screamed.

Yusuf reached down and unbuckled the two belts, then tossed them aside and crawled crablike away from Chuck before leaping to his feet.

Sarah watched as the mob followed the fleeing survivors in the direction of the East River, potentially cutting off her own route of escape. She had jumped last, and in doing so, had greatly lessened her own chances of survival. She had acted against her nature, against everything she believed in. Not only was she allowing others to come with her, but one of them was a child. Survival was priority number one. And priority number two was to allow nothing to come between herself and priority number one. Not only had she failed at that, she had failed at rule number three; keep your head down. In allowing the others to go first, she had allowed the crowd to become aware before it was her turn to jump. She was exposed.

Sarah glided to the ground, holding her legs out in front of her as she leaned back like a child on a swing, touching down just in front of the advancing crowd. She released the chute just then as if parachuting from the roof of a high-rise was part of her everyday routine and without missing a step Sarah took off running, leaving the orange chute to drop and cover several of her pursuers as it floated down behind her.

***

The East river was dirty. It had an odd smell, like motor oil and rotting vegetables. Trash floated by as the survivors swam toward the boat. A plastic bottle half full of red liquid, two jagged pieces of wood, and a bloated body drifted past. The body was face down in the water and motionless. Its arms were extended out on both sides. They bobbed slightly, like floatation devices, as it moved past them. The swimmers watched it suspiciously, trying to swim in a wide berth as it floated silently onward.

It seemed as if they would never get to the boat. Exhaustion was stripping them of their strength, and they had to rest twice before reaching its side.

Sarah held her finger in front of her mouth to quiet them. The boat was salvation. The boat was a way out of New York. The boat was also danger. Its protective occupants could spell doom.

Sarah moved to a ladder on the port side and boarded first.

The deck was strewn with rotten fish heads and beer cans, and a dog was barking viciously from the cabin below. Sarah assumed a defensive posture and took aim at the cabin door from behind a large barrel of rainwater. Yusuf leaped onto the boat behind her and scurried to her side.

"It's just a dog," he whispered.

"A pissed off dog," she snapped, "I didn't run from those things on land to get bitten by a dog now. Besides, there's someone on this boat. I know it. That lamp didn't light itself. They may not appreciate our coming over here. I know I wouldn't."

Yusuf said, "Not everyone has your remarkable social skills."

Sarah ignored his remark and moved from her place behind the barrel to a crouched position behind a rail where the steps descended to the cabin below. The dog growled ferociously, provoked into an all out rabid frenzy by her sudden move.

The boat's occupants were surely aware of their presence. Even without the dog's agitation their arrival had not been stealthy. She would have to take a risk and once again expose herself. Her predicament brought to mind something General George S. Patton had once said...*Don't you die for your country. Let that other poor son of a bitch die for his.* Her country was the country of the living. The enemy's homeland was the land of the dead. It was a growing power and one that was going to be increasingly hard to defeat. Only the dead could ignore their arrival to the boat.

Sarah stood, and dropped down the steps to face the door to the cabin below.

A large German Shepherd bared his teeth and snarled. From the shadows behind, a lone figure emerged. The Shepherd moved around behind the figure and then along side it and took position there. Its snarls and barks subsided somewhat, but its teeth were still exposed. The dog obviously felt more secure beside its owner, a standing corpse wearing a green army coat and Bermuda shorts. The dead man patted the dog's head slowly, almost lovingly. Sarah half expected him to say, *Good dog—good dog,* but instead he only moaned.

"It's alright, come on out," Sarah called to the others, and lowered her gun. With that, the dead man became irate and moved swiftly to the door, crashing into its glass with bloody hands. The dog exploded in a frenzy of snarls and snaps. Sarah fell back and moved to the top of the short stairs.

"What in God's name?" Chuck joined Yusuf at Sarah's side. Duane climbed aboard the boat with the child clinging to his back.

"The dog is protecting its owner," Sarah said. "It won't let us into the cabin. If I can't get in there I can't start the boat."

Chuck bent low for a better look. "Is the dog dead too? It looks pretty mad."

Sarah gave him a withering glance. "No, the dog is not dead."

"How do you know?"

With a straight face, she replied, "Because it seems to be acting quite lively."

"Why hasn't the dead thing eaten the dog?" Duane said. "I've seen this before. A dead blind man was being led around by his seeing-eye dog. It was a Shepherd, just like that one. He wasn't trying to eat his dog either. Neither were any of the others."

"Well, he's not Chinese. Maybe he doesn't like dog meat," Chuck said with a laugh.

"No," Yusuf interrupted. "I saw on the television before the emergency networks took over. They will eat any living thing—man—dog—cat…anything. I think it's something else…something deeper, the connection a man has with his dog. Maybe a part of who they once were is still there somewhere, buried deep inside. That dog is all that lone creature has left."

"Who cares," Sarah said. "I certainly do not."

Sarah raised her weapon and shot the dead man in the forehead, shattering the glass in the cabin door as the bullet passed through. The dog exploded with rage and leaped into the open window of the door.

Sarah fired again.

The dog dropped in mid-flight, into the area in front of the door at the bottom of the steps. It whined weakly and then died, its chest no longer heaving.

"Oh man," was all Duane could get out of his choked throat.

Sarah holstered the gun and glanced over her shoulder to Manhattan, "Rule number one folks, just survive. Rule number two..." Her words trailed off as she watched.

The Tower was engulfed in flames and smoke. The great crowd had moved to the river's edge but seemed too afraid to venture further. In the distance, a larger fire burned somewhere to the north. From their place in the middle of the river the chorusing cries of the dead dominated the moment, floating out to them as one massive effort in harmony. There was but one purpose for the multitude, one desire for the starved, and one craving to be satisfied. Sarah watched, and she knew that New York was lost.

"Get those things off the boat," Sarah pointed to the man and dog. "We need to get away from this city before they decide to nuke it."

Yusuf's eyes followed Sarah's to the skyline. "Where will we go?"

"I don't know," she said, and stepped over the dog and man to walk into the cabin. "Maybe an island."

Yusuf sighed, shaking his head at the irony, "Didn't we just come from an island?"

Sarah allowed a small grin to crease the corner of her mouth. "Yes, I guess we did."

—End.

ICE STATION ZOMBIE
JE GURLEY

For most of the long, cold winter, Antarctica is a frozen wasteland. Now, the ice is melting and the zombies are thawing. Arctic explorers Val Marino and Elliot Anson race against time and death to reach Australia, but the Demise has preceded them and zombies stalk the streets of Adelaide and Coober Pedy.

The Coalition

When the dead rose to destroy the living, Ron Cutter learned to survive. While so many others died, he thrived. His life is a constant battle against the living dead. As he casts his own bullets and packs his shotgun shells, his humanity slowly melts away.

Then he encounters a lost boy and a woman searching for a place of refuge. Can they help him recover the emotions he set aside to live? And if he does recover them, will those feelings be an asset in his struggles, or a danger to him?

THE STATE OF EXTINCTION: the first installment in the **COALITON OF THE LIVING** trilogy of Mankind's battle against the plague of the Living Dead. As recounted by author **Robert Mathis Kurtz.**

MACHINES OF THE DEAD

The dead are rising. The island of Manhattan is quarantined. Helicopters guard the airways while gunships patrol the waters. Bridges and tunnels are closed off. Anyone trying to leave is shot on sight.

For Jack Warren, survival is out of his hands when a group of armed military men kidnap him and his infected wife from their apartment and bring them to a bunker five stories below the city.

There, Jack learns a terrible truth and the reason why the dead have risen. With the help of a few others, he must find a way to escape the bunker and make it out of the city alive.

JUDGMENT DAY

Dr. Jebediah Stone never believed in zombies until he had to shoot one. Now they're mutating into a new species, capable of reproducing, and the only defence is 'Blue Juice', a vaccine distilled from the blood of rare individuals immune to the zombie plague. Dr. Stone's missing wife is one of these unwilling 'munies', snatched by the military under the Judgment Day Protocol.It's a new, dangerous world filled with zombies, street gangs, and merciless Hunters desperate for a shot of blue juice. Has the world turned on mankind? Is Mortuus Venator the new ruler of earth?

TIMOTHY

MARK TUFO

Timothy was not a good man in life and being undead did little to improve his disposition. Find out what a man trapped in his own mind will do to survive when he wakes up to find himself a zombie controlled by a self-aware virus.

NECROPHOBIA

An ordinary summer's day.
The grass is green, the flowers are blooming. All is right with the world. Then the dead start rising. From cemetery and mortuary, funeral home and morgue, they flood into the streets until every town and city is infested with walking corpses, blank-eyed eating machines that exist to take down the living.
The world is a graveyard.
And when you have a family to protect, it's more than survival.
It's war.

Made in the USA
Lexington, KY
10 February 2013